ABOUT THE AUTHOR

A.S. Balfour has been writing plays since the 1960s. He won a prize in a National Play Competition for his play *Pastoral*. He won an Arts Council grant for his play, *Marcus Rex*, performed in Birmingham in 1977. *The Hokey Cokey Man*, his last play, was produced at the New End Theatre in Hampstead in 2009, based on the life and times of his grandfather, Al Tabor, a society bandleader who wrote *The Hokey Cokey* during the war. To see photos and hear Al's music visit www.thehokeycokeyman.com.

Waiting for Walter is his first novel.

FOREWORD

In the spring of 2011, while on holiday in Prague with friends, I visited Franz Kafka's house. There I bought a book. In it, I came across a short story by Dora Diamont, Kafka's lover, about a walk in a Berlin park where Kafka saw a little girl sobbing. When she told Kafka that she had lost her doll, he told her not to worry as he knew where her doll was and said he had a letter for her from the doll. He promised to bring it the next day. The following morning he ran to the park with the letter and read it to her. The doll said even though she loved her very much, she was tired of living in the same family and needed a change, but she promised to write every day and share her adventures.

Over the next three weeks Kafka told the little girl all about the doll's new family, her new school friends and her new-found obligations.

Having to bring the story to an end and fearful of upsetting the little girl, Kafka told her, sadly, this was to be the last letter, but the good news was the doll had met a handsome young man and was going to get married. Kafka described all the wedding preparations and their beautiful new house far away in the country in great detail. The doll said she hoped her friend would understand. She did – and the little girl skipped away happily.

Kafka died of TB one year later.

Three months after I read this affecting tale, I began writing *Waiting for Walter*, a love story about learning to say goodbye..

A. S. Balfour

ACKNOWLEDGEMENTS

I thank my family for their unquantifiable support during the five years it took to write this novel.

Thanks to my dear, late friend, Ted Dickson, with whom, for so many years, we shared a writer's spade.

Thanks to Sundra for allowing me to quote from her poem *Jetty*, one of a collection called *Starchild*.

In the great divide between Germans and Jews in the run up to and during WW2, it is with special thanks I remember three remarkable men: Pastor Dietrich Bonnhoefer, Pastor Martin Niemöller and Pastor Hermann Maas.

Thanks must go to the poet Nelly Sachs, the first German jew, post war, to receive the Nobel Prize for Literature.

I have quoted from Rainer Maria Rilke's magical *Letters to a Young Poet*.

I say a 'hello' also to Goethe for his poem on the gingko biloba leaf.

And finally thanks to the unknown little girl in a Berlin park who lost her precious doll and to her saviour, Franz Kafka, who helped her say goodbye to it.

CHAPTER 1

She was walking towards Bond Street Station on the other side of the street when he saw her. A girl above average height, head of long blonde hair held high, clothed in a tight green sweater. The same swing of the hips inside a tight white cotton skirt. It was uncanny! She even wore the same white stilettos and the same white handbag swung by her side. Dodging the traffic he rushed across the road and called out, "Leni!" She couldn't have heard because she turned into the Tube station and made her way down the steps of the Underground. He ran after her but lost sight when she melted into the rush-hour throng.

That night he dreamt she ran towards him across a vast graveyard under a moonlit sky calling his name. He reached out to her but as fast as she ran she couldn't close the distance. Then as if out of nowhere, she grasped his hand. Martin sat bolt upright in a sweat. He rubbed his hand and turned towards his wife. Her breathing, unlike his, was regular and deep. He rested his head back on the pillow. He hadn't stopped thinking of Leni all day. What were the chances of seeing a girl the image of Leni dressed in the same 1950s fashion walking down Oxford Street in 2002? Of course he hadn't seen her face-on and logic said even if he had she would've had to be a youthful doppelgänger or else a figment of his imagination. None of these obvious probabilities reduced the impact of this mysterious sighting.

Then there was the dream. He wasn't a believer in matters mystic, but that was twice now in the last twenty-four hours he'd had a strange sense of an invisible force bending him towards her.

At breakfast as Esther spoke of their son Ben's up and coming wedding to Lara the beautiful Hindu girl, Martin tapped lightly on the shell of his soft boiled egg without making an impression.

"For goodness' sake! What on earth are you dreaming about?!" Esther exclaimed. Then, not receiving an answer she continued, "Arul thinks it's wonderful our two great cultures are coming together. Don't you agree?"

Martin finally broke into the egg. "Absolutely!"

"Did you know that in a Hindu wedding the bride and groom are supposed to circle a fire seven times? I'm glad they've decided to stick with the *Sheva B'rachot!*"

He couldnt wait for Esther to leave for her office so he could go upstairs, pull down the loft hatch and climb the rickety wooden ladder into the unheavenly void where all the clutter of their long, agreeable marriage was stored.

Once inside the loft he sat down on an upturned orange crate and surveyed the dusty boxes of goodness-knows-what-was-inside. The sun's rays pierced the roof window and he was blinded by a dazzle of light reflecting off the buckle on an old grey canvas bag. He shaded his eyes with his hand. Crouching to avoid the rafters he walked over and unzipped the bag. Among the many envelopes inside, a photo caught his eye. He took it out. He couldn't take his eyes off the beautiful nineteen-year-old girl in the picture. She was posing next to an old tree, one white stiletto pointing slightly forward in front of the other. She wore a dark jumper over a straight white skirt and carried a small white handbag over her right arm. Her full flowing fair hair fell to her shoulders. Her eyes were laughing and the tip of her tongue poked out in mock anger. Heidelberg Castle was in the background. He smiled and wished she were still cross with him. He took his wallet out of his back pocket and put the photo inside. Then looking down at the heap of envelopes he picked up an early letter to him after she'd returned home to Germany. It was in the old green ink and the familiar pressed flower was pasted on the top right-hand corner. He held it up and inhaled deeply. Even after all these years there was still the faint scent of Chanel No. 5. His heart leapt as he recalled his personal introduction to German-Jewish relations and the start of their passionate love affair in London.

Kehl. Tuesday, 20 Jan 1959, 10pm

My wonderful darling,

Five minutes ago I have been talking to you on the telephone. I hardly can believe it. My heart is still beating so fast, I feel as if I have a fever. When I put the receiver down, I sank into the armchair and everything swam round and round. I thought I would faint. I cannot stop thinking of you whatever I do. Why cannot I be with you? It is all so terribly depressing. One minute I dream I am dancing with you at the Moulin Rouge. Then I open my eyes and you are not here. Many boys ask me out but I see only you, darling. My mother says it is hopeless our love. There is a big wall between us. But I am determined to climb it. Even if I can't I still will love you all my life. Sometimes I feel we are like two lovers tied to two ships' masts breaking in half in a storm. It is all so sad. But then the sea is calm – the sun shines and I remember Walter and your promise on our first night together. Do you remember this? I hope so. One photo of you is by my bed. You are looking at me so sweet. Be good, darling. Know that I love you always. Didn't you just kiss me through your photo?

Good night, darling. Kissing you.

Leni

P.S. I am reading a second time the Sholem Aleichem book you gave me for Christmas. I love it so much.

December forty years ago – Victoria Station – an exchange of books! *Tevye the Milkman* for *The Sorrows of Young Werther,* Goethe's famous novella. Martin knew the book was in the bag somewhere. He rummaged around under the letters and found it. He picked it up and read the inscription on the inside cover:

> *To my best friend, Walter*
> *With love from Leni.*

From the moment he saw the name *Walter* the die was cast! He'd introduced him to her at the club when they'd first met. It could've been a minute ago – the memory was sharp.

CHAPTER 2

It was 1958 and the Americans had a new satellite in space. The Moulin Rouge in London's Finchley Road was dimly lit, smokey with a small dance floor, a few round tables and chairs and a bar at the back. Six days a week a five-piece band played a mixture of Continental and Latin American music. It was a popular place for North West London's au pairs looking for a little romance in the big city on their night off. It was also the pulling ground for any would-be Romeos anxious to be the one to help them find it.

It was Tuesday at the club and Nick and Martin stood at the bar, drinking cokes. Nick was tall with a swarthy complexion and wavy black hair; a young Walter Matthau with world-weary eyes perpetually half-closed scanning the terrain for prey like a trapper. Martin was a couple of inches shorter, slim with fair hair neatly parted to one side. He appeared relaxed and easy but this was deceptive for his intense and edgy nature rarely allowed him to feel that for long.

"Thinking about the Americans getting their satellite into orbit, are you?" he joked trying to catch Nick's attention.

"Do you want to know what I think?" said Nick, still looking around.

"Well?"

"How many fellers do you reckon are here tonight?"

"Not very many. Seventeen or eighteen."

"And shall I tell you something? Not one of them, not one, is thinking about that satellite."

"Is that a fact?"

"There's only one satellite everyone here is considering, Martin, and it's not up there in the stars; it's going round down here on the dance floor."

Martin knew exactly which one Nick was talking about. She was the girl in the green tartan suit with the Bardot looks.

"I reckon that's the best piece of German engineering since they came out with Mercedes," Nick said.

"I wouldn't mind taking her for a spin," Martin said.

As the band played 'La Paloma' Martin watched intently as she danced by with a tall, smart-looking guy with a moustache.

"I tried to chat her up when you weren't here last week. For a German she wasn't arrogant at all. In fact she was very friendly and I thought I was on to a good thing, but she'd only dance with me once, same as everyone else."

Martin stroked his chin and watched as she danced by again. He wasn't sure if she'd glanced at him or not, but he was mesmerised by her. Her dance steps were not exaggerated and she herself seemed unaware of the effect her slightest movement was having on all the men watching. As the music came to a stop, he saw the young man ask her for another dance, but she declined with a smile and went over to sit down next to another girl at a table.

"What's her name?"

"Leni."

"Well, at least I know she'll go round once," and with that Martin walked over to where she was sitting and asked her to dance. She smiled and accepted. They stood together on the dance floor waiting for the band to strike up.

"You're Leni, aren't you?"

"Yes."

"I'm Martin. I've just been hearing all about you."

"I hope it is not so terrible," she teased. Her voice was deep and sexy like Marlene Dietrich, but more playful. The band started to play 'J'attendrai'. She danced with poise but was not haughty in any way and her blue eyes sparkled with the playfulness of a kitten.

"What makes you think it would be terrible?"

"I saw you talking to your friend Nick."

"Did you?"

"I know it is something bad because he is looking so *miserable*."

There was something about the way her voice leapt when she said the word *miserable* that totally enchanted him. He slid his hand further round her waist.

"He said you only dance with everybody once."

"And this is why he is *miserable*?"

"He's not used to this."

"You are joking."

"He's afraid to ask anyone to dance tonight," he said in mock earnestness.

"No!" There was a tiny sadness in her voice.

He realised she thought he was serious, and the quick look of concern on her face touched him.

"Don't worry, it won't last. He likes to act as if he's drowning, so some pretty girl might jump in and save him."

"Ah, so this is a game," she smiled, catching on. "And what do you do?"

"Me, oh, I just pretend to be brave and try hard not to ask the same silly questions that everybody else does."

"Why do you try so hard not to ask something if you want to know it? I will tell you. I am from Kehl in the Black Forest. I like London very much, and I am staying here nine months with a family and going to school to make better my English, then I will go home and get a job as a hotel… receptionist?" she said, questioning whether she had the right word. "The one, how do you say… stands behind the desk and… welcomes the visitors!"

"Receptionist," he confirmed. Then speaking above the music, "Your English is very good."

"But I would like to speak *better!*" There was a sharp positive inflection on the *better*. "I have always loved languages."

"Then perhaps I can help you. I always wanted to be an English teacher," he lied, trying to find common ground.

"*To be or not to be? That is the question.* No?" she recited grandly.

"Shakespeare is England."

"And Goethe is German," she countered.

Goethe was clearly someone she thought of highly, and if he wanted to improve international relations it would do no harm to act interested.

"So what's his latest?" he enquired.

"Latest?"

"Book?"

"Well, I am still on the first." She laughed. "He wrote it nearly two hundred years ago. It is called *The Sorrows of Young Werther*."

"As recent as that," he smiled back, covering up his ignorance. "You must tell me about it sometime," he added, thinking the last book he'd read must've been *Biggles Delivers the Goods.*

He was pleased that she was amused and it seemed to him they were really getting along quite well. Then she flashed a smile at Georgiou, the singer, who had started to sing directly to her. He sensed too many greedy hands ready to snatch her from him as soon as the music stopped. She was friendly enough, but what if he was a one-spin-only? He might not see her for another week. Suddenly he stopped dancing and held her.

"Leni!"

"What is the matter? You look so *miserable*," she said.

"When the band stops playing, what do I have to do to persuade you to dance with me again?"

He had managed to sound relaxed but his heart was pounding. This could be a bad move. But she just laughed.

8

"Naughty one! Why shall I tell you this?"

"Because I never heard anyone say *miserable* like you," he said, imitating her playful inflection, and again she laughed.

"Are you crazy?" She started to dance, but he wouldn't let her go.

"I mean it. I promise I will never tell anyone else."

"That is because you are a selfish one."

"Then you won't tell me?" he said sadly.

She smiled and whispered, "*You* don't need to know this."

"I don't?" He was mystified.

"Of course not." She took his hand. "Now come on, let's dance, Martin!"

It was hearing his name on her lips, her decisiveness, her familiarity and her reassurance; they overwhelmed him. He was The One. He couldn't believe his luck. Six dances followed!! It'd all happened so easily. He felt he should take a bow. He guided her off the dance floor to one of the free tables. He was intoxicated by her Chanel No. 5. He bought two cokes and joined her at the table. Though he wasn't particularly interested in literature, he thought a little more enthusiasm might go a long way.

"So tell me more about this Walter."

"His name is Werther," she corrected him, "and he is a poet who falls crazy in love with a beautiful girl, Lotte. When he finds out that she is promised to another man and that she cannot give him up, he shoots himself. It is all very tragic."

"Well," he said thoughtfully. "If I were Walter…"

"Werther!"

"I think I should've liked Goethe to give this ending a bit more thought."

"Thinking is for mathematics and philosophy. Love answers to feelings." She frowned.

"But don't you see," he persisted, "he didn't need to kill himself."

9

"So how would you end it?"

"Well, for a start if Walter was so crazy in love he'd never give her up. He wouldn't let anyone stand in his way. He'd do whatever needed to be done. Despair wouldn't come into it. To keep her he'd sacrifice everything. That I promise you."

She seemed to think this over for a while, and he thought he was about to be reprimanded for challenging the mighty Goethe; but instead she suddenly smiled and said:

"I think I like this Walter. Maybe you are right. Napoleon read the book seven times and he does not like this ending either," she laughed. "But at this time this story is very popular in Germany; many young men dress like Werther and wear yellow trousers and a bright blue jacket. It is very fashionable."

"Can you see me in yellow trousers and blue jacket?"

"Why not? Maybe one day I will!" she said playfully. She took his hand and studied his palm and told him she saw lots more dances together.

"How can you see that?" he asked in all seriousness.

Her eyebrows arched as she laughed. "Because I know it before I met you."

"You're joking."

"No, I saw you looking at me with Nick. You were stroking your chin and I thought what a sweet little chin you have."

"That was it?"

"And an honest face."

Leni and Martin talked and danced the evening away together. He told her he worked for his father who was a ladies' hat manufacturer: that his mother was American and he'd lived in the States for a while, and that his grandfather had been a concert violinist who'd once had his own band. She seemed to enjoy the family-cocktail.

"My grandfather is a violinist too, in the Berlin Philharmonic Orchestra."

"No kidding!"

10

"My mother is a dressmaker. She made this suit."

"Really!" he said, admiring the cut.

"When is your birthday?" she asked.

"September."

"Mine too."

"Sport?"

"Tennis and swimming and dancing." She laughed.

"I don't believe this! What's your favourite fruit?" He was enjoying the game.

"Tomatoes and pickled cucumbers."

"My God! Are you Jewish?" He laughed.

"Jewish, no, but I like chicken soup. I am staying with a nice Jewish family with lovely children. Are you Jewish?"

"The last time I looked," he said with a cheeky grin.

He wasn't sure if she'd got the joke but she didn't seem put off. She went on to say that her greatest love was music, especially Beethoven. He confessed he'd never been to a concert, and that he'd never heard a Beethoven symphony. All he knew about Beethoven was that he was deaf.

"But your grandfather is a musician!" she exclaimed, horrified.

"I know the beginning of Beethoven's *Fifth*."

"Only the first movement?"

"Well, perhaps not all of it. But I know the *da da da – da* bit," he said.

"Are you crazy? You must hear the whole symphony. It is fan-tas-tic."

"What is so special about Beethoven?"

"Because his music is so dramatic of course, because he has spirit, and because he is German," she announced proudly.

They danced on until Georgiou's final song 'Moulin Rouge'. Then when she went to collect her coat from the cloakroom Nick drifted over unnoticed and said:

"You're in a trance, Martin."

11

"She's so innocent."

"Is she? You're not going soft on Germans, are you?" A lascivious grin crept over Nick's face. "Well, just in case you've any doubts I wouldn't mind collecting the reparations."

"Thanks, you had your chance, Nick," he said as he saw her making her way towards him, her grey wool coat buttoned up to her neck. "I'll call you tomorrow."

A few minutes later as Martin was driving her home he promised, a little half-heartedly, that one day they'd hear Beethoven's *Fifth* together in its entirety. He kissed her goodnight on the cheek and they arranged to meet again that Saturday.

The evening had been a triumph. As he drove off he thought how fortunate he was to have won her over. He smiled and touched his *sweet chin* with his thumb – or was it a *miserable* chin? Then the doubts started to set in. Why did she have to sound quite so proud when she spoke of Goethe and Beethoven being German? There were six million reasons she shouldn't be so proud. It was just thirteen years since Hitler had shot himself. He couldn't help wondering what her father had done during the war. His father wouldn't even touch a German toaster never mind cross a German border! Nick was right – he was going soft. Growing up with unquestioning schoolboy vengeance against the Krauts they'd agreed that whereas it wasn't considered sporting to go the whole way with a nice Jewish girl, German girls were fair game. Just as Jews had been numbers on a German scorecard now they would be numbers on a Jewish one. When someone pokes you in the eye for being a bit Jewish you poke them back, and after that you poke their children back. No sooner had Martin finished applying the old simple tit-for-tat logic to the case when his judgement ran into a problem. Something was wrong. Her smile and raised eyebrows when questioning something he'd said stuck in his mind and he just couldn't think of Leni as a number. The sound of her voice skipping over the syllables when she said Beethoven's *Fifth* was fan-tas-tic would stay in his mind forever. She wasn't a number, she was a personality! She'd existed as a personality from the moment he'd first heard her utter the word mis-er-able!

CHAPTER 3

Martin's grandfather, Nathan, was a Russian immigrant who had escaped religious persecution during a terrifying pogrom at the turn of the century. He disembarked in London a penniless refugee his only possessions a wife to support and a will to work. Three years later he opened a small hat factory in London's East End and Solomon and Sons was born.

Now, carrying his box of millinery samples, Martin took the train from St Pancras back to Luton; where the factory had had to move after the original premises had taken a direct hit during the Blitz. Monty, his uncle, ran the office while his father handled production and was in the thick of it on the factory floor. Monty loved to argue. He'd argue over anything, particularly football or politics and Albert always gave way, except if there was a problem at work then if Monty was at fault he couldn't contain himself. Albert never joked about work and without his brother's sarcasm would find a few choice words that left everybody silent. There was nothing Albert couldn't do. When it came to making a hat: cut, machine, block, polish, trim, he could do it all as well as anyone in the trade. There were a thousand old and new blocks and assorted patterns. If a customer called up who had lost the number of a shape from twenty years ago, with the barest description Albert would know it instantly. That February the retail trade was quiet but if there were any work to be had the Solomons would be sure to receive their share; such was their name in the trade. It had certainly served Martin well that morning!

At the station Martin phoned the office with a huge order – 250 dozen felts from their largest customer – urgent delivery for two weeks. Now, as he settled down in the carriage, he thought how lucky it was that the buyer had chosen all small shapes, which meant the blockers would be able to make good use of the large stock of small, cheap, Polish, felt hoods. He could imagine his father, right now, sorting the hoods out for the blockers. By the time he arrived Trixy and George would be hard at it.

He opened the *Daily Telegraph* to find out what concerts might be coming on at the Royal Festival Hall the following week. To his amazement, there it was: Beethoven's *Fifth Symphony*, conducted by someone called Otto Klemperer. *Must be a German*, Martin thought.

Back at the factory, two cutters and forty machinists were all working flat out finishing yesterday's work. He bumped into his father who instructed him to go down straightaway to the basement to make sure the blockers were making good progress. Martin hesitated.

"What are you waiting for?" his father demanded.

Downstairs in the basement, the walls were lined with shelves supporting hundreds of hat blocks, heroes of previous fashions. The blocking plant comprised six four-foot-long steel benches, each one supporting two metal blocks bolted into place. Under each one a gas ring supplied the heat. A second ring fed heat to the mould above. Piles of Polish hoods were stacked up ready, but that morning things were not going well. Martin stood watching as George, the larger of the two men, unleashed a blast of hot steam from one of the vents behind the blocks, forcing the bell-shaped hood to bow and give up its rigidity. He quickly whisked it away before it had a chance to cool and revert to its original stiffness. Then he turned back, and he and Trixy, who was standing on the other side of the bench, used all their combined strength to try to pull it down over the piping-hot metal shape, but the hood would not give.

George was growing more and more frustrated, because the work was hard and slow, and any pieces over 150 dozen were on commission. It was clear at this rate there wouldn't be much of that! Suddenly, in a fit of rage, George ripped the hood off the block and flung it aside, bellowing:

"These Polish 'oods are too small for the fuckin' blocks! Or perhaps you think they're all right!" he said, addressing Martin.

"Are you sure?" Martin asked, hoping he'd cool down.

"Perhaps you want to try one yourself?" he suggested, lowering his voice in a well-meant threat.

Martin looked at his soft hands. He couldn't even pick a steaming hood off the steam vent let alone pull it over the hot block the heat was so intense.

"With my hands? I'll take your word for it, George," he said.

"Don't know why 'e buys 'em," Trixy said, siding with his workmate.

Trixy always agreed with George, unless they were discussing which horse to back. Then, as George always said, 'Trix knows 'is 'orses!' This was odd, because he so rarely won.

"Don't be daft, Trix, 'e buys Polish 'cos they're cheap, don' 'e?" George cried, with a note of triumph as if he'd seen through some devious trick.

He complained bitterly that there were another 220 dozen of the little blighters to get through by Friday. This was worrying because, according to his father, the big man was an excellent blocker with twenty years' experience in the trade and Friday was the deadline. Martin was just wondering how this would all pan out when George, struggling with yet another hood, violently flung it on the floor and came up with the solution.

16

"If you want to be helpful, Martin," he said, "why don't you just count out 220 dozen of them nice, large English hoods in the stockroom?"

This was not what Martin wanted to hear. He reasoned with George that he knew very well there was a large stock of English hoods, but he also knew that they were held back for the larger shapes. He also knew that to win this order, they had to be keen on price, and that meant using the small Polish hoods.

"Look," George bristled, "don't start gettin' all reasonable with me. If your father thinks 'e can find a blocker to do a better job with this lot let 'im bring 'im 'ere!"

The more Martin tried to reason with George, the more exasperated the big man became. He told him, "As far as I'm concerned, 'e can send the whole fuckin' lot back to fuckin' Poland. Do me a fava' n' call the Guv down," he ordered.

Martin rushed up to the machine floor, wondering how on earth his father would sort it out. The Singer Cap machines were all whirring away and he found Albert busy on a machine, making up a sample. He leaned over his shoulder, and whispered:

"Dad, it's the Polish hoods. They're all too small."

"Tell George I'll be down in a minute," Albert said, finishing the sample he was working on, quite unperturbed.

Martin ran down the stairs to give George the news, wondering if he was about to walk out and what would happen with the orders if he did. Albert was a man of medium height with broad shoulders but he was a good two stone lighter than George.

A few minutes later he stepped down into the basement, his shirtsleeves rolled up, revealing his strong forearms and thick wrists. His hands were almost as hard and rough as George's from working on the baking-hot metal blocks. He approached the blocking bench calmly.

"What's the trouble, George?"

He might as well have been asking George what he'd had for breakfast. It was a casual approach, and Martin was doubtful it would go down well.

"It's these Polish 'oods, Guv. They're all too small. Can't do a fuckin' thing wiv 'em. We've tried everyfink."

Trixy nodded in agreement.

Albert didn't speak. He licked a couple of fingers and smacked the block lightly, checking the temperature. The spit sizzled and disappeared. He picked up one of the hoods and put it on the steam vent, then turned the steam up full blast and waited till the hood began to yield. Then he took the felt and positioned it over the hot block. He did this without asking either blocker for help. Martin watched, amazed, as his father's strong hands gripped both sides of the blistering hot hood. His shoulders set, his forearms bore down. There was no huff or puff as his knuckles rolled into the blistering hot felt. He then quickly reached for the string, wrapped it around the groove in the block, stamped it up into the mould above and locked it in place. A few moments later he released it and Martin watched in wonder as he held a perfect shape up to the light, checking for stress fractures.

"No signs of any holes in that," he said. He picked up a second and a third, all with the same result. "Give them a bit more steam, George. There's a lot of guts in these hoods!"

That was all he said. There was no reproach in his voice. He put the last blocked hood down and Martin watched dumbfounded as he disappeared upstairs. George was silent, then suddenly bellowed to Trixy:

"Well, get 'old of a fuckin' 'ood, Trix!"

Martin watched them for a bit, as first one, then another hood passed successfully through the process without a word being said, and after a while he asked George if he thought they would be all right now.

"They've got to be, 'aven't they," George said.

"So how do you know when they really are too small?" Martin asked.

"When your father can't pull the fuckin' 'ood over the fuckin' block!" he bellowed.

Martin went upstairs again to his father, who was back working on a machine, and told him that George seemed to be managing all right now. Without altering his position or momentum as he worked over the sample, Albert said calmly:

"There's nothing wrong with the size of those hoods, Martin. The only problem was George's effort."

Martin thought he detected a wisp of a smile, but Albert was soon entirely focused on making his new sample. Martin made a mental note: if ever he had a showdown with his father, he'd better make sure he had his story straight. He was about to ask him what he would have done if George and Trixy had threatened to walk out, but he already knew the answer to that one.

Leaving his father up on the machine floor, Martin now rushed down to the office, picked up the phone and dialled the Royal Festival Hall Box Office. He was glad to find two tickets available for a performance of Beethoven's *Fifth Symphony* for the following Sunday.

CHAPTER 4

Saturday arrived and Martin was sitting in his father's grey Ford Zephyr, outside an imposing house in North West London waiting for Leni. In the few days apart he'd revised his history syllabus and was back on the old track. He glanced impatiently at his watch. Soon his beautiful, innocent new German number with the sexy voice would learn that when a nice Jewish boy takes out a nice German girl in his nice Jewish car he might just be taking her for a nice Jewish ride! His mind was set until she suddenly appeared at the front door wearing the same green tartan suit carrying that same white handbag over her arm. The moment she turned and smiled at him his revision went down the drain.

Up until that moment he hadn't really wanted to go to this concert at all, even though he'd bought the tickets. Two and a half hours of classical music was not his ideal way to spend an evening. And it wasn't just Beethoven's *Fifth* on the programme; there was to be an overture and something else that he couldn't remember. That was a lot to sit through and that was the reason he hadn't phoned and told Leni that he'd bought the tickets. But when she sat down beside him in the car and the scent of Chanel hit his nostrils his very first words were:

"I've got tickets for the Beethoven."

"Darling!" she cried. "I did not think you are so interested."

"It's Sunday week, eight o'clock. I hope that's all right. I took a chance. They were the last two!"

"Don't worry, darling. I am glad you took a chance. You see, we are meant to go to this concert together."

"You believe that… meant to?"

"Of course I believe it – because I wished it," she said quite unabashed. "And you have the two last tickets, don't you?"

Martin patted his breast pocket. "Right here." He put the car into first gear and they moved off.

"I can play the first movement of Beethoven's *Moonlight Sonata* you know," he said.

He told her he'd heard it once on the radio and fallen in love with the piece and made up his mind to learn it. He'd found this Russian teacher, Mrs Rabinowitz, who'd insisted he learn other stuff first, so he'd studied it on his own. It'd taken him three months, but as soon as he'd learnt it he'd given up the lessons.

"Why did you stop?"

"Girls."

"Naughty one!"

She enjoyed teasing him and laughed.

"I can play the whole of the *Waldstein Sonata*! I was not so int-er-es-ted in boys."

Her tuneful reprimand beguiled him.

He tuned into Radio Luxemburg. The Platters sang 'Smoke Gets in Your Eyes'. He took her hand and held it on his knee between gear changes all the way to the club.

At The Moulin Rouge they danced close as Georgiou sang: 'Yellow Bird.'

His mournful rendition of the song was clearly directed at Leni, and he continued eyeing her right till the end. He waved a sad farewell to the imaginary bird then opened his arms with a winsome appeal to Leni. She responded by teasingly beckoning him over to her. Georgiou laughed, blew her a kiss, she shrugged her shoulders as he started singing his next song; while Martin pretended to enjoy the fun. This might have all passed uneventfully, but shortly after they'd sat down to enjoy a cigarette together, a tall, suave young man approached them, introduced himself to Martin as Peter, and politely asked if he could ask Leni to dance.

"Go ahead," Martin replied, concealing his discomfort as Leni rose and was escorted to the dance floor.

Leni clearly knew this Peter and had seemed pleased to be asked, and if Martin had been hoping for the slightest sign of reluctance from her there was none. Georgiou now put his saxophone to his lips and started to blast out 'Tequila', the latest Latin American hit that was top of the charts. Peter was a flashy dancer full of dramatic gestures, engaging in too many dramatic clinches when none was called for. But Leni was unperturbed. The little movements of her hips and shoulders, or even her eyebrows, contrasted seductively with Peter's exaggerated kicks and arm jerks. She was the main draw. First Georgiou and now she was flashing smiles and pouts to Peter. He felt undermined. Then the band stopped playing and he watched the pair talking together. Peter took a small notebook from his pocket and wrote down what Martin presumed was her telephone number. Martin now began to worry like Othello on speed. This usurper wanted more than a dance. He wanted regime change, his regime. True, Martin hadn't lost her yet, but the warning signs were there.

The question was: should he ask her about this notebook incident when she returned to their table or not? Martin took a deep breath and wisely did not.

"He's a good dancer," he said, dead cool.

"He is a show-off," Leni laughed.

Martin and Leni danced on for an hour or so, and she was warm and friendly, but he couldn't get that Peter out of his mind and he was put out by her encouraging smiles to others. She'd made him feel special, but now everybody seemed special. She would pay for her little games. He was good at games. He suggested they go for a coffee.

The waitress in the coffee bar on the ground floor below the club cleared the used plates and cups and gave the table a cursory wipe then asked if they wanted to see a menu. Martin ordered two cappuccinos and two pieces of lemon cake. Then he offered her a cigarette and they both lit up.

"My mother makes wonderful *zwetchgenkuchen*."

"Does that taste as good as it sounds?"

"It is plum cake! I think you would like it. She makes it for my father once every week ever since they are married."

"Even during the war?"

"He is more than forty when it started. He is a teacher," she said innocently.

"Was he terribly strict?" he asked her, imagining a stereotypical Nazi saying 'Good morning, boys,' and giving the Heil Hitler salute.

"No, he is not strict at all. But my mother – she is strict. I will tell you something about my mother. When I am seven years old I liked to collect these pencils with the rubber on the top. Do you know these pencils?"

He nodded that he did.

"One day, when I am with my mother in a shop, I saw a beautiful green one and I wanted it. So I asked her if she will buy it for me. It is not very expensive, but she said: 'No, I think you have enough of these pencils.' So when she is not looking, and the shopkeeper is serving another customer, I took it!" she exclaimed.

"You took it?"

"Very quickly!" she said, the last word springing from her lips as quickly as he imagined her taking it. "When we arrived home I took it upstairs to my room, and put it in my little desk with my other pencils. The next day, when I arrive home, my mother is waiting at the door with the green pencil in her hand. 'Where did you get this pencil?' I told her one of the girls in my class gave it to me. She is furious. She said she could tell from my face that I am lying and would come with me to school the next day and talk to this girl. So then I told her the truth and I thought that would be the end of it; but the next day she did come to school with me and took me to the headmistress and told her the whole story. Well, I was so ashamed I cried." She laughed. "After this I never tried to deceive my mother again."

"What about anybody else?" he asked.

"What are you thinking, naughty one?"

"You gave that guy Peter your telephone number, didn't you?" He'd tried to sound nonchalant but there was no disguising the jealousy.

"Are you crazy? I gave him my friend Margot's number. Do you think I am going to leave you and go with him?"

She looked outraged.

"I am sorry," he said, climbing down. "I've got a suspicious mind." The waitress arrived with the coffees and cake, and as Leni tried it he was fascinated by the natural elegance with which she undid the small gold clasp of her handbag, withdrew a lace-trimmed handkerchief and neatly wiped a few crumbs from her mouth. "How do you like it?"

"It is good. But my mother's is better!" she said, announcing it like an award. "But I would like to know who is this girl who makes you so suspicious," she frowned.

He hesitated.

"Now *I* am jealous," she teased.

"It wasn't actually a girl," he said. "It was my mother."

"Your mother!"

"You see one day in the middle of the war she walked out and never came back."

"No!"

He'd grabbed her attention all right. By opening up he was drawing her in. "I had this nanny who told me she'd gone

24

because she'd done a bad thing, and that she was a bad penny, whatever *that* was!"

So Martin brought his mother to the table and introduced Leni to the striking gypsy princess with the raven black hair, black eyes and gypsy spirit; who could as soon give you a gypsy curse as a gypsy kiss; and he put her on trial in front of a relative stranger. He told Leni that, since he was a young child, her tempestuous nature had unsettled him. She was clearly engrossed.

"I did see her a few times after she left. She took me to see cartoons in town with this American pilot who flew B17s. He was good fun, and I laughed at Donald Duck, but felt guilty and disloyal to my father."

"This must have been very difficult for a little boy."

"The hardest time was when she left for America. My father never spoke of it. Nothing at all! Not a bad word; not a good one, ever. Nobody in the family did. There wasn't a photo of her in the house. The trouble is silence can open a door to some pretty destructive voices. One day I asked him why she had to leave. He took a long time to answer. 'I don't know what Mummy was thinking, but I know what I am thinking. It's time you had a bath.' Then he took me upstairs piggyback, singing this song, 'Sonny Boy'." Leni seemed genuinely upset and he felt encouraged to rumble on. "I'll never forget the look on his face. I felt terrible. I thought somehow I was to blame."

"But how could it be your fault?" she cried, rushing to his defence.

"I promised myself that I would never let him down. I was six years old. After she left he packed me off to boarding school. In the beginning she sent me comics from the States. My favourite was about this radio reporter who whenever he shouted 'Shazam!' a bolt of lightening struck and he turned into this amazing superhero: Captain Marvel. I wanted to be like him!"

Martin became increasingly animated as he relived his hero's daring-dos. "Our dormitories were on the third floor in the old building. Below us was a flat roof. If you lowered yourself out the window you could run all the way round and get into the bathroom on the other side. One of the boys dared me to do it. It'd been snowing that December. At lights out I yelled 'Shazam!' and was off. But when I reached the other side they wouldn't pull me up. They shut the window. So I raced back round to the dorm. Unfortunately for me the headmaster was talking to a teacher in the garden below. I had to lie flat on the roof so they wouldn't see me. By the time the boys finally pulled me back up through the dorm window I had snow all over me and I was frozen. In the morning Matron couldn't understand why I was sick."

"You could've died," Leni gasped.

How had they become close so quickly? By now they were the only ones left in the cafe. The waitress came over and put down the bill in a saucer with a clatter. She was ready to clear up and go home; but they didn't notice her impatience.

"Listen, I hope I'm not boring you with all my stuff."

"No, I want to know what happened with your mother."

"Well, next time I heard from her was ten years later. My father had remarried. One day – the phone rang – I was about sixteen, and this husky voice at the end of the line says, 'Hello, honey, this is your mother speaking'."

"My God, it is like a movie!"

"We met up at my grandparents who I also hadn't seen for ten years. When she found out I knew nothing of what had happened except what the nanny had told me she launched straight into her own account. She told me it was my father's fault that he'd never paid her enough attention. So she went to a tea dance in the West End – got picked up by a GI and had this one-night fling at the seaside. She didnt even particularly like him! "

"No!" Leni exclaimed, shocked. "But why didn't your father ever tell you this?"

"I don't know. He just couldn't. I guess it was the shame of it. He wanted to protect me. Saying nothing was the best he could do."

"How sad."

"She just wanted to teach my father how to treat the daughter of a society bandleader – but it backfired. She told me they had a big divorce. It was all over the press: The Scarlet Woman. She said losing me in the custody battle had been the worst moment of her life. She tried to kill herself – took sixty aspirins. She would've succeeded had her mother not found her in time. When it was all over she just wanted to get away so she married the American pilot and ended up living in a one-room tenement in Brooklyn. She said she'd been young and stupid and all the while she'd been away there wasn't one minute when she hadn't thought about me. When the war was over she told me she only stopped sending the comics because she couldn't afford to send them any more. They were constantly moving from one state to another because he couldn't hold down a job. It was only now that he had a super job with great prospects she could afford to return to England, and she'd phoned my father, the first day she'd arrived back, and told him she wanted to see me." Martin leaned forward. "She was the most passionate, warm, committed mother and best friend you ever had. Not how I'd remembered her at all. Now I thought she was amazing and I fell in love with her like everyone else who met her for the first time. She just wanted me to know the truth."

"My God. She must have been so ashamed."

"Ashamed? My mother's never been ashamed of anything her whole life."

"But it must've been so difficult for her – to tell you the truth."

"You think that's what it was, the truth? That's her big story: *Never be afraid of the truth, honey. I've never told a lie in my life!* That's why she told me she phoned my father from the hotel to tell him what she'd done. Meanwhile, the facts are, after a month the comics dried up and there wasn't so much as a letter or a card from her for ten years. You don't have to rob a bank to buy a stamp," he said, bitterly.

"No, of course not, " she said trying to soothe him.

"I didn't really get to know her until I went to live with her in the States. I was there several months. I had a job in a roofing factory. A lot of the time she was all sweetness and charm but cross her once and she's as charming as a cobra. When they had to move again I came home."

He'd never talked so openly about his mother before and now felt naked and vulnerable and a little guilty as he continued to blame her. "I've always been a bit suspicious of girls."

Leni leant forward and took his hand. "You don't have to be suspicious of me," she said.

He paid the bill and suggested they go for a drive. She agreed immediately. He felt he'd won her over. How honest she thought he was. But that was all part of the game, wasn't it? Now he could take her – but why should he want to take anything from her? She'd been so reassuring and so sweet. How well she'd listened. How understanding she'd been. How patient over the Peter-moment.

Martin turned left into the Heath car park on West Heath Drive and swung into one of the empty spaces. There were about a dozen other cars there, spread about and the only light came from the street lamps behind them. The sky was cloudy and there was a slight drizzle outside. He knew it wouldn't be long before the windows started to steam up and they would be in their own foggy little den. He lit two cigarettes.

"Do you know Keats? Right behind us, just back there,"

he pointed, "is the house where he lived. And down that hill there's an old pub where a woman shot her racing-driver boyfriend for carrying on with another woman. She was hanged for it. Romantic spot, isn't it?"

"I have been somewhere like this before," she said. "We have our own Hampstead in Kehl. We don't have any murders and there are no famous people. It is only five minutes from where I live, near the river. You cross a little bridge and there is a field with trees, and an old farmer's hut, where the witch from *Hansel and Gretel* lived. That is what we pretended when we are growing up." She laughed. "It is also very romantic."

How could a girl as beautiful as Leni manage to look so sexy and sound so innocent at the same time? What a wonderful combination, he thought. He was sure she was a virgin. Meanwhile, it was 11 pm and soon he would have to take her back home. For all he knew she might be thinking that right now.

"I would like to have gone there with you. That little house in the woods."

"I think you have been there with enough girls," she smiled.

"Not true," he said, defensively. "Besides, this is different."

"You are a naughty one!" She laughed again.

He was embarrassed. Then he noticed her white handbag nestling in her lap.

"No, I mean it. Remember at the coffee bar when we were having our cappuccinos and cakes? You opened your handbag and took out a handkerchief to wipe some crumbs from the side of your mouth. I... I know this sounds crazy, but all I was thinking was if only there was a way I could somehow climb into your handbag and hide there until you went home. Then when you put it down on your dressing table we... we could carry on... our conversation."

"I don't usually talk to a man in my handbag."

29

"And I've never wanted to climb into one before."

"You are crazy."

"No, I mean it," he said again seriously. "Look, I've never imagined anything like that before in my life. I don't even know what made me think of it, except I noticed the bag again just now, there on your lap, and it reminded me. I know it might sound a bit strange, but I've got to tell you I have never really noticed a handbag until now – not anybody's. Yes, I've seen them in shop windows, and women walk down the street showing them off, but I don't ever remember seeing an ordinary white handbag like yours, one that actually stuck in my mind; not one I thought of travelling in."

Leni squeezed his arm gently. "Darling, you don't have to do this."

He knew at that moment he didn't need magic and he didn't need tricks, and he didn't need to say anything. Her voice so rich and warm buoyed him up on a current of warm air. It was crazy. She was an eighteen-year-old German girl who knew so little of life yet it was as if she'd looked into his soul and seen a light through the cracks. Then he knew it wasn't a game at all, at least not like one he'd ever played before. He ran his Jewish fingers through her silken fair German hair. But she did not seem so German now, nor he so Jewish. He did not think of what separated them, only what united them and that didn't need words. Her searchlight-blue eyes now showed him the way. They kissed, their fingers arguing and interlocking frantically. His free hand strayed to her thigh, rubbing gently up and down, and he felt her shape shift beneath the green tartan fabric. Slowly, she began to give way as his hand slipped under her skirt. At the feel of her naked flesh his little charger now soared upright, huge, throbbing madly in the intense heat of the moment. "Hold me!" he pleaded. "Hold me," as though his life depended on it. At first she seemed unsure, then she gripped him tight as his fingers thrust into her soft, wet furnace. Immediately, violently, he died too soon. Slowly, she freed herself and slid gracefully away to the other side of the seat. He told himself next time he would die a slower death.

Later, after he dropped her off and they kissed goodnight, she said, "Thank you for telling me your feelings."

It was extraordinary – as if he'd given her an honour. *Most unusual*, he thought. He watched her graceful, cat-like walk up the drive to the front door, and was fascinated by the way her hand seemed to hang in the air after she blew him a last kiss. The confusion he'd felt when he'd picked her up earlier had completely disappeared. Now it was clear – they were children of the world. He felt like a snake that had sloughed off an old skin. In his bright new skin the world would forever be different; every experience would be touched by it, every memory a reflection of it. He smiled to himself as he drove off and thought back to that seemingly insignificant, but fortuitous, moment when Leni withdrew her handkerchief from her handbag at the cafe. Then he started to drool over the way she held a cup of coffee. He liked the way she took his arm as they crossed a road. For someone who didn't usually do these drooling sums; all these little drooling observations were beginning to add up.

He turned left out of her road instead of right. It was several minutes before he realised, but he could have taken any turn that night, and it would have been right. He could have driven on the wrong side of the road and that would also have been right. Nick was right. She really was the very best of German engineering.

CHAPTER 5

It was a beautiful spring Sunday in Regent's Park, cherry blossom swayed in the breeze as Leni and Martin strolled hand in hand to the boat station. Once there, Martin hired a rowing boat and helped her into the gently rolling vessel. Restricted by her tight white cotton skirt and her high heels she sat down knees locked together to one side. Martin pulled on the oars taking them further into the lake. She looked as free and untroubled as the gulls perched on the row of wooden posts overlooking the shallow waters. A young girl peddled by on her small blue bicycle.

"I had a bicycle like this. It is a birthday present from my father but just when I learned to ride it I lost it."

When he asked her about the incident she explained without bitterness that at the end of the war their town was under French occupation, and the army had not only commandeered their house but everything in it. They'd had to live in a farmhouse for several weeks up in the mountains, and then had stayed with an aunt in the suburbs for seven years until the army left and they could come home.

"Everything in the house is smashed, and our lovely piano is gone, and my beautiful bike. It is terrible." Then her face lit up victoriously. "But we had our house back!"

"You must love the French."

"Why not? Today I can love anybody."

She seemed incapable of bearing a grudge. He couldn't decide if that was a strength or weakness as he had always found it an irresistible motivator.

Martin rowed over to the little island in the middle of the lake. A family of ducks quickly paddled away as they approached. They both chuckled at the sight of the six ducklings trying to keep up with their parents.

"We used to swim in a lake near our house," she said.

"You won't see many people swim here. In the 1860s a lot of people fell through the ice and drowned. Now they've made it too shallow for drowning."

"I should like to be here in 1850," she said, with an uptick on the date.

"Next time I must take you somewhere more dangerous, perhaps the Limpopo, where they have crocodiles, and waterfalls, and maybe a hippopotamus under the boat. I think you'll like that better."

"There is always a hippopotamus under the boat... or in the bed," she added.

He downed oars. "In the bed?"

"This morning at one o'clock Mr Goldberg came into my bedroom when I am sleeping. He climbed into my bed and told me he loved me!"

"He what? He told you he loved you! You're joking! What about his wife and children? I thought he loved them. I thought you said he was a nice family man."

"Do not worry, darling. He did not stay very long."

"Not very long! He shouldn't've been there at all!"

"He said it is an accident. He went to the bathroom and, after, he came into my room by mistake."

"You think he got into your bed by mistake! Are you crazy? He'd probably been lying there, next to his wife night after night, dreaming about you. You've got to leave, go back to the agency and explain to them and tell them you want them to find you a family that isn't so accident-prone. He could've raped you!"

"Nooo," she sang. "He is not so clever."

33

"And you are?"

"I am cleverer than him."

"Do me a favour! Don't be so smart. What did you say to him?"

"I told him if he does not go, I will go to the *shul* in the morning and tell the rabbi!" she laughed.

"You said that?"

"Honestly, darling, and it worked. He is not a bad man. He begged me not to say anything and said I can come back as late as I like tonight. He really likes me."

"Likes you! How can you trust him now?"

"I trust myself. And I don't want to leave the children. They are so sweet."

"Never mind the children. I know how his mind works. He's probably working on plan B right now. Next time he'll tell you he doesn't get on with his wife, they haven't had sex since their last child, and he's in love with you again. I mean wouldn't you rather be somewhere safe?"

"Nowhere is so safe, darling, and if there is such a place I should not like to be there."

"Why not, for God's sake?"

"Because that is like being dead, and if I run when I see a little hippopotamus what shall I do when I see a big one? No, darling, I am not leaving my house for this."

She was plucky, she had spirit and he liked that, but fighting hippos was a dangerous game. "OK, but any more hippos we fight them together," he promised, fiercely, raising his fists tightly clenched one in front of the other.

They returned the boat, and as they left the park and crossed the road into Baker Street she took his hand and squeezed it. Once more the message raced through his body telling him he was the one. He squeezed her hand back. There was no sign of a hippopotamus in Baker Street.

A few minutes later, just before they reached the

Underground station, a large, tall, rather imposing young man emerged from the station carefully studying a street map. The moment she saw him, Leni excitedly grabbed Martin's arm and exclaimed:

"I know this man! He was at my school!"

As the man turned away from them, Leni immediately cried, "Rudi!"

The man turned and called out "Leni!" as she ran towards him.

He swept her up in a great bear hug and swung her round. They spoke in German for what seemed to Martin several minutes. He felt excluded. Finally, Leni introduced him.

"I thought you two probably knew each other," said Martin lightly, concealing a stab of jealousy at Leni's ardour for the man from the homeland.

"Everybody knows Leni," said Rudi. "She is famous at our school."

"Do you mean for her arithmetic or for her biology?"

Rudi laughed. "Her chemistry!"

Rudi told them he was looking for No. 221b. Baker Street, Sherlock Holmes's house. Martin quickly pointed him in the right direction, glad to have seen him off. The big man was about to depart when Leni suggested that, as they were off to the concert that evening and Rudi was flying back to Munich in the morning, the three of them should have lunch together. Martin was not happy about having to share Leni's coquettish smile with another man and ever since bumping into Rudi, she'd done a lot of smiling but he went along with it. Five minutes later they found a tourist pub that served steak pie and cheese rolls and real ale. Rudi instructed Martin to find a table, while he gave in their order at the bar. Leni informed Martin that Rudi was from a very distinguished family called the Von Becks, that he'd been in the class above hers, and that he was the youngest student to study law at Tübingen

University. Then she laughed and added cheekily, "And he has lots of girlfriends."

As Rudi returned with the drinks, Martin wondered if Leni had ever gone out with him but he decided to impress Leni with his magnanimity.

"So you're an admirer of Sherlock Holmes," he said.

"*Natürlich.* He is the most famous detective in the world. He is very logical and can solve every case and catch every criminal. But actually I am more interested in the Moriartys of this world. They are not always so easy to recognise. They are masters of disguise, and speak every language. They can be anywhere, even here." Rudi scanned the customers nearby. "The man over there by the window with the orange beard, pretending to read the newspaper: KGB." He grinned.

"Your friend Rudi is very imaginative," said Martin.

"He is a show-off!" Leni scoffed good-naturedly. "And full of mischief!"

"What is wrong with the KGB?" Martin asked, coolly. "Don't the Americans have the CIA, and England MI5? Aren't they all just spies doing their job?"

"Of course, and the Russians want us all to be communists, and we just want them to be democrats. But nobody in West Germany is trying to escape to the East. Yes, it is true I am a show-off and I will tell you why. A few years ago, all Germany is flat on its back. We are the sick man of Europe. Some doctors do not think we can ever recover. But after the war we in the West did recover, better than anybody can imagine. We took our medicine and worked hard. Now our shops, that were empty, are full, there is plenty of work, and we have the fastest growing economy in Europe. We are in NATO and we have the Treaty of Rome. Our Chancellor Adenaur has brought back all our prisoners from Siberia. We have cleared our debts, paid off the Jews, and most important, four years ago, we won the World Cup. Now we are the champions of the world; and

36

with Helmut Rahn back in the team, this year," he raised his glass of ale like a trophy, "we will win it again!" He swigged his glass of beer down in one. "And what do the Germans in the East have? They have only the wish to one day live like those in the West, and," lowering his voice, "Mr KGB wants to be Mr Bond."

All this had been rather amusing and Martin would've seen the funny side of it if only Rudi hadn't mentioned the Jews.

"Well, this year, I am going to be an England supporter," Leni announced boldly.

Rudi smiled and cried, "Wunderbar! This is excellent for international relations. I think she likes your English captain, Billy Wright."

At that moment, the boy from behind the bar arrived with the pies. Only Martin's appetite had deserted him and his mouth was dry. He had been amused by Rudi's little political rodeo, but something was wrong; and it wasn't the football result. He looked across at Leni, but she seemed unperturbed. True, she said she was going to support England this year, but he didn't care about the World Cup. Six million Jews had just been paid off like a laundry bill; a two-second clean-up between the Treaty of Rome and a football trophy. She'd noticed nothing.

He turned to Rudi and as politely as he could said, "Yes, I'll support England, but I'll support Maccabi too."

Rudi looked puzzled. "Maccabi?"

"They're in Tel Aviv," he said.

"Ah, so they are a club team," Rudi replied, amiably.

"They're top of their league."

"Better than second." He laughed agreeably and turned to Leni. "*Er ist ein Jude, nicht wahr?*"

"*Ja, er ist aber ehrlich und sensible.*" Leni placed her hand on top of Rudi's, smiling. "*Und nicht so taklos wie du!*" she replied.

"*Gott sei dank!*" Rudi said and blew her a kiss.

Martin now recognised a hippo, moving in on the other side of the table, and wondered how long it would take Rudi to finish his pie.

"Did you ever know another German girl speak so good English as Leni?" Rudi said brightly, as he changed the subject. "She is the best in our school."

"Ah, you are crazy?" She slapped Rudi lightly on the forearm.

"You know, for two years Leni won the English prize. The only reason she is not winning it a third time is because another girl made a cheat."

"Really, that is enough now! You don't know this," Leni exclaimed.

"Ach, everybody knows it, but she is your friend, so I will say no more about this, because I know you will defend her; but if I may quote the great English philosopher, John Stuart Mill: 'a person may cause evil to others not only by action but by inaction, and in either case he or she is accountable'."

"You don't know her, and you don't know the truth," Leni said, obviously uncomfortable.

"You will never make a good enemy, Leni." Rudi smiled. "Because you will never let your enemies down." He turned to Martin. "She will never let anyone down."

"Not like me, then," Martin said.

"Ah, so now you are making a good English joke."

"No, I mean it. I think I could let everyone down, friends and enemies."

"Maybe your enemies, but I am sure you are too good a friend to let down your friends," he said, dismissively.

It didn't take much for Rudi to rub Martin up the wrong way. How did he know what kind of friend Martin was? If only he hadn't sounded so condescending.

"No, friends as well. I've done it before. I was eleven. I was one of a hundred and fifty Boy Scouts on a week's camping and canoeing trip. I'd been on holiday with my family in Brittany and was looking forward to it but somewhere between Brittany and driving to the campsite in England, I developed this terrible headache. I said nothing, but by the time my father dropped me off it was really bad. My friends tried to cheer me up, but in the evening my vision was affected; everything seemed blurred. I thought I was going blind so, without anyone noticing, I left the camp, phoned my father, told him I was ill and asked if he could collect me in the morning. Next day the Scout master sent for me and told me he'd heard my father was coming to collect me and asked how I was feeling at that moment. I said, 'I still have this terrible headache and feel sick.' He put his hand on my forehead. He was very calm. He said he was pretty sure he knew what the problem was and if I gave myself another twenty-four hours, he was certain I'd recover completely. 'If you stay, Martin, every Scout will cheer you for it, but if you go, you will not only let down all your fellow Scouts, but also your father and certainly yourself. I am asking you, for the sake of all of us to remember your Scout's promise and see if you can do your duty.' Unfortunately this talk of doing my duty for the sake of the entire troop only made me feel worse. When my father arrived he didn't try to persuade me to stay on. All he said was, 'If you don't feel right, we'll go. It's up to you.' As soon as I got home I went straight to bed."

"But this is not your fault. I do not think this master is very kind. I don't believe you let anybody down," Leni said, rushing to his defence.

"So, how do you see it, Rudi?"

"I think perhaps you are a little homesick."

Of course Rudi was right if only he hadn't sounded so superior.

"Are you crazy? Martin is two years in boarding school

39

when he is only seven years old. He is ill." Leni rallied once more to Martin's aid.

"Was I? What if Rudi is right?" he asked turning to Leni. "What if I panicked? What if I didn't care a jot about the other boys? What if the real reason I left the camp is because I wanted to sleep in my own bed? What if I woke up the next morning wishing I had double pneumonia? What if I never had a headache? What if I invented the whole story because I was too ashamed to admit the truth?"

Leni looked bewildered. Martin smiled grimly looking straight at her.

"Captain Marvel wasn't on duty that day." He turned to Rudi. "Have you ever had a headache like that, Rudi?"

Martin was convinced that Rudi had really enjoyed hearing about his old dilemma. It probably confirmed some deep-seated prejudice he held about Jews.

"No, I have never had a headache like this, Martin. But you must not feel so bad. There is a cure for every headache. So, yes, it is true, you left the battle, but it is only one battle. Next time it will be different and I am sure that your friends had plenty of fun without you. Nobody is hurt, are they?"

Martin felt wretched. He didn't want Rudi to save him, he wanted them to drown together. The strange thing was he'd never confessed this shameful episode to a soul before, but now here he was telling this tale to the big German of all people. But wasn't this what he'd wanted? For in some perverse way, in nailing his shame to his front door he might at last begin to say goodbye to it, better still it earned him the right to shame Rudi and his compatriots for opting out of something far worse.

"No, nobody was hurt, Rudi, but what if some Scouts had've been hurt? What if they hadn't been having fun? What if they'd been in trouble? What if it had been a question of life or death, not just for one Scout but the whole Scout movement?

What if everyone who could've helped went to bed? What if the whole country had gone to bed? I'd be accountable then wouldn't I?"

"I'm not sure exactly what question it is you are asking me, Martin," Rudi, said cautiously.

Martin was in deep now and dragging Rudi down with him. "Do you really think Germany can settle up for Auschwitz with a few Deutschmarks?"

He knew he'd gone over the top and now felt embarrassed but being an insensitive bastard was still a better option than the feeling of being a diplomatic coward. Leni looked confused and troubled.

"Auschwitz?" Rudi asked looking puzzled.

Martin, who didn't believe for a minute a clever lawyer like Rudi could not have heard of Auschwitz, announced firmly: "It was a concentration camp in Poland where they killed Jews."

Rudi remained calm and detached. "I know things are not good for Jews in the war but in Germany now we do not talk of these days. So, I cannot answer your question so honestly as I would like. But today in my country it is good for everybody, even you Martin." He wiped his mouth with a serviette and put it down decisively. "Perhaps one day we will meet again and I will give you a better answer," he smiled, "but now I really must go. Later, I must meet some friends in Knightsbridge. It was very interesting to meet you. I think you and Leni will have some good discussion. I hope you enjoy the concert."

The three of them left the pub, together. Rudi asked Martin if he knew that the father of the Weimar Constitution, Hugo Preuss, was a Jew. "It was not always so bad for the Jews in Germany," he said. "They had a good life."

"Maybe that's why so many made the mistake of staying," Martin suggested cynically.

Leni now flashed Rudi a big reassuring smile and once more spoke a few words of German to him, to which Rudi responded warmly, also in German. Then they embraced and the big man gave her what appeared to Martin to be far too warm a hug before he headed off in the opposite direction. Leni flashed Martin the same reassuring smile and he had the feeling of favours being shared equally and was repulsed by her animated neutrality. That's what did it for the Jews: the neutrals.

They started to walk back to the car. They soon came across some students bearing banners in support of nuclear disarmament advertising the Aldermaston march setting off from Trafalgar Square over Easter.

Leni asked Martin if he believed in that cause.

"I've always admired people who stand up for what they believe to be right."

The joy of their carefree hour on the boat had definitely passed. In those last few minutes, listening to her say goodbye in German, he was convinced she'd apologised to Rudi for something he, Martin, had said and he was furious with her. He didn't like anybody apologising for him, especially when he wasn't sorry and especially one made to a neo-Nazi. Rudi had revealed his true feelings about the Jews right from the famous *paid off* moment. Anything after that had been simply to appease him and amuse her. He hadn't liked the way they'd spoken in German at the table, nor how they'd looked at each other when Leni had taken his hand.

Back in the car she told him what a fun person Rudi had been at school and how good he was at seeing two sides of a problem. Martin commented drily that unfortunately he'd missed the funny bits. It's strange how often two people can have an apparently pleasant chat about one thing, and yet, going on underneath is something much less pleasant that may remain concealed behind discretion or self-preservation for years or could jump out in an instant.

"You know it wasn't just a few Jews who died; it was millions."

"I do not know what you are talking about," she replied.

"But your father's a teacher, isn't he? Didn't he ever talk about his Jewish pupils – the ones who disappeared? Didn't he wonder what happened to all the people with yellow stars on their coats?"

"I don't know any of these stories," she said. "Is this what you talk about with your other German girlfriends?"

"I have never talked about this before."

"Then why are we talking about this now?"

"Because Rudi talked of paying off the Jews like a laundry bill and if I don't speak now I'll be ashamed."

"I don't want you to be ashamed."

He knew she didn't want to hear about the camps but his shameful experience at the Scouts had induced her to open the door. "They were dumped into trains and cattle trucks from towns all over Europe and carted off to places like Auschwitz and gassed to death. That's what happened. Men, women, children and babies, all of them gone up in smoke just because they were Jewish!"

Leni looked at him and bit her lower lip, numbed and in shock.

"It's impossible. I never heard this."

"No, I don't believe you did. How could you if it is like Rudi says and in Germany nobody speaks of it?"

"Martin, I am sorry. If this is true, it is terrible."

"True? They've got films of it – records, witnesses! Haven't you heard of Anne Frank? Didn't your father tell you anything?"

"No, Martin, he did not. Maybe he is protecting me and saying nothing is the best he can do, like your father."

She was defending her father, he understood that, but couldn't she see what her father covered up was different from his father? It was the crime of the century. "It's a big thing to say nothing. Rudi knows that."

43

"I do not know what Rudi knows, but he cannot change this. Nobody in Germany can do this. These people are no more and Rudi cannot help them now."

They were in a dark place and he'd've liked to get out of it. But her support of Rudi rankled.

"Nobody can help them if they pretend like he does they never existed," he groaned.

"Rudi is not pretending anything," she said, defiantly.

"Why do you keep defending him? He said that winning the World Cup was the most important thing, didn't he?"

"He is making a joke."

"Some joke!"

"What is the matter with you? Do you think he is not ashamed for Germany? Do you think now I am not ashamed?"

"He wasn't ashamed. He was more interested in his football trophy."

"I do not think we can ever have enough shame for you. What do you want Rudi to do? You go on and on with this. You know nothing about him. He is a good man. You do not know anything he does and you talk to me like a policeman. If you hate Germans so much why do you go out with German girls?"

"You've been out with him, haven't you?"

"Why do you want to know this now? Why are you always asking me about other boys?"

"You said he has a lot of girlfriends."

"Are you crazy? What has this got to do with the Jews?"

He knew she was losing patience but he brushed the question aside.

"You have, haven't you?"

"Is this the most important thing now?"

"Did you make love with him?"

Martin was not sure whether he was getting more bitter satisfaction dumping the Jewish tragedy on her or torturing himself about her relationship with Rudi. She in her turn was pitiless in her response.

"What if I did? It does not matter. It is not your business. I know him for many years and he has not such a little mind like you," she cried victoriously.

"My God! What an idiot I am!"

"Yes, you are an idiot and I am glad at last you can see this."

"Is that what you apologised to him for when you said goodbye?"

"No, I apologised to him because you are a *Jewish* idiot!" she flung at him.

The passion and sincerity of these last few words sent Martin into a bitter cold rage.

"Well, you don't want to go to a Beethoven concert with a Jewish idiot, do you? That would be a disaster, so I'll take a girl who does!"

"Good, make sure she is a Jewish one."

Martin slammed the car into gear, jammed his foot on the accelerator and screeched off, taking her straight home, just like any good Jewish idiot would. That first ten minutes of the drive were hairy. No car passed him and no car could stop him passing, as he recklessly faced down the oncoming traffic. He wanted to hear her scream in terror, but she sat impassively calm and still, saying nothing. He braked hard at a red light and looked across at her. Only two hours before he'd been so happy yet now he only wanted to hurt her.

"Have you got your key?" he asked icily.

She turned to him out of her stillness. "You don't have to take me home, Martin, you can take me to the next station," she said firmly.

"Excellent!" he said cheerfully, as if he couldn't wait to be shot of her. "I'll drop you at Golders Green. I'm going that way."

There's a little bit of an SS general in everybody, he thought. He was enjoying this a little too much, or was he? Her face, when he glanced over at her, was full of sorrow, and that was good but she was also very calm, and that was bad. It disturbed him. Martin, who'd raced away from the lights, now found himself driving progressively slower. The problem was, as much as he was hurting her, he was starting to hurt himself more. If only he could've expressed everything he felt about Germans and Jews without sounding like the Reich prosecutor Roland Freisler at the People's Court. Suddenly, he missed her calling him *darling* in her deep, sexy voice. All those cute little moves she'd make – taking a handkerchief out of her handbag, straightening her skirt, raising her eyebrows – he wanted to see her do them all again. How could he have behaved so absurdly jealous over Rudi? He'd only been dating her a couple of weeks. What had it to do with him what she'd done with him in the past? As for the Jews – he'd just wanted her to understand. How could it have gone so wrong? Meanwhile, in the next ten minutes if he wasn't careful he'd lose her for good. He was helping her make up her mind to do something he didn't want her do at all! They passed Golders Green Station and he swung into a side road, turned the car around and started driving back the way they'd just come.

"What are you doing? Where are you going?"

"To the concert."

"Are you crazy? I thought you are going with another girl."

"It's too late for that."

"I am sorry it is so late. Can you stop the car?"

He stopped the car in the middle of the road and pulled up the handbrake. "Look, I'm sorry. It's nothing to do with being too late. I was wrong and I don't blame you for wanting to go. Don't you understand? The truth is you're right, I am an idiot! I'm a small-minded Jewish idiot, but I don't hate Germans and I don't hate German girls. How could I when the only girl I want to go with to this concert tonight is you? And unless you come with me I'm going to feel an idiot for the rest of my life. Don't you understand, the only person I want to listen to Beethoven with is you?"

A driver in the car behind now kept his hand on the horn.

"For Christ's sake, I don't want to go with any other girl and if you don't come now we'll both miss it."

A man's voice shouted from a passing car, "Prick!"

"I think you must move," she said.

He put the car into gear and moved off wondering if she was going to open a door and jump out at the first opportunity.

Moments later she responded, "You are not an idiot, darling."

"Yes, I am, and you were right to tell Rudi that."

"I did not tell him that," she smiled.

"What did you tell him then?"

"You never thanked him for buying our lunch, so I thanked him."

Her voice now had that punchy uptick back on *lunch* and he was overflowing.

"Oh no!"

"You are not angry with me for thanking him, are you, darling, because I don't think I want to fight with you any more today."

"I don't deserve you."

"You don't know all the truth," she said mischievously.

"What now?" he asked her.

"I never made love with Rudi. I have never made love to anyone. I only talked like this because you wanted to hear this crazy talk."

"You're joking!"

"Nobody has ever touched me like you have and that is the truth. No matter how much they wanted this."

He could've wept with relief. How close he'd come to losing her. Imagining others trying to touch her as he had only made him desire her more.

"Why did you let me talk you into going to the concert with me again?"

"I liked your Scout story," she said smiling. "I like sad stories."

Martin took her hand and all the warmth between them returned. They were two gulls flying over a lake. Far away a hippo's head disappeared beneath the waterline.

"Now I know I'm a lucky idiot," he said.

She squeezed his hand.

"I am glad you are lucky."

There was a terrific buzz in the auditorium as the first violinist bowed and acknowledged the audience applause before taking up his position. Suddenly, there was a hush and the side curtain was pulled back. A very tall, distinguished figure appeared and made his way, with a tortuous gait, to the podium. He gave a gruff, cursory nod to the audience, turned and sat down on a stool. The giant eagle that was Otto Klemperer, with one glance at the orchestra, now took control. The lights dimmed and Martin watched intensely as the conductor at last raised his right fist and shook it jerkily downwards to conjure up the opening four hammer notes of the famous first movement. Martin was immediately gripped by a sense of foreboding. He snatched a quick look at Leni. As closely as they were seated, and as close as he felt to her now, she seemed transported to a different zone. Dark forces were at play. The world was in trouble. The engine was breaking down, beset by all manner of problems. The outcome was still uncertain at the end of the movement. Then the andante began and slowly, as if out of nowhere, he heard an oboe sing out reassuringly: *Don't worry, I know what's going on here. We can do this. I've just got to find my screwdriver.* When the other instruments joined in he didn't know whether to laugh or cry. Then once more at the end of the third movement the ominous opening notes were back in a dead drumbeat. Then, magic! Out of nowhere there arose, unmistakably, irresistibly, the swirling sound: first of the violins, then of the whole orchestra rushing to the rescue, screwdrivers and spanners flying. Big ones and small ones! There was no screw or nut they could not tighten. Against all the odds Beethoven was fixing the engine and the world was going round again.

By the time the symphony had raced to its triumphant conclusion he was standing, clapping, crying 'Bravo!' along with Leni and hundreds of others. The world would never be the same. For the first time in his life he knew, for absolute certain, that there was nothing in the universe that he couldn't overcome. He looked at Leni. Her face was aglow, her eyes glistening. Now he knew that, without touching, they were as one.

They had been among the last to leave the auditorium. It was a beautiful night and as they walked along the embankment they stopped to look across the Thames where the lights of the city lit the Houses of Parliament and further away the dome of St Paul's.

"What are you thinking?" she asked.

"We first know we exist when we recognise ourselves in another," he said.

"This does not sound like you, darling," she said accusingly.

"You mean it doesn't sound like an idiot."

"I told you, you are not an idiot."

"Aren't I?"

"No," she smiled, "only sometimes I think you are a little boy who must say anything he thinks."

"And this time?" he laughed.

"They are beautiful words."

Then he admitted to her that the words were from a letter Goethe once wrote to his lover. He'd come across it in the library. He'd gone there, like any good businessman, looking for a line that would sell. What he hadn't known was how much he would grow to mean them.

"I hope you are not disappointed," he said.

"If you mean them it does not matter who wrote them," she said.

"I mean them," he said and he kissed her.

He knew she loved him and that he loved her.

He drove over to Hampstead Heath and parked the car and they walked into the trees and lay under an old oak.

Then he took everything she really wanted him to take and, in the fever, it was all. Even when the unendurable moment of pleasure had gone in a whoosh, a deep longing for her persisted. Now he knew that he was her first love, and he loved her like no other. She was his German and he was her Jew and there was nothing bad between them. Beethoven had knocked out Hitler forever.

Later that night, when he finally arrived home, he reflected on the Beethoven concert and particularly the *Fifth Symphony*, and he wrote on a piece of paper over and over, again and again, at the sides, at the top, and then all over the page: *There is nothing a man cannot do! There is nothing a man cannot do!*

The following morning he walked round to the local record shop and listened in a sound booth to every recording of Beethoven's *Fifth* they had in stock, before finally settling on Klemperer's unforgettable recording.

CHAPTER 6

For the next nine months they wandered through art galleries, and went to the proms, and when his father was away she played him the *Waldstein Sonata* on the piano at his house. She learnt about dog racing and cricket, and he sang, '*Once you have found her, never let her go*' on a riverboat on the Thames. They went for a walk on Hampstead Heath and agreed the only difference between Germans and Jews was the same as existed between individuals everywhere: some believed all men were brothers and some did not. Most of all they danced the way two people do when they are oblivious at the edge of a cliff and believe such a dance has no end until the music suddenly comes to a stop.

At Waterloo Station they said their first serious goodbye as she was on her way home to Germany for Christmas. Even when the train had long gone he could see her waving from the carriage window, like him, full of hope for now they both had presents to keep them close. She'd asked him for a book by a Jewish writer for Christmas, something to keep him near when he was not there. So while she was on the train home reading Sholem Aleichem, he'd be on a train back to work reading *The Sorrows of Young Werther.*

He couldn't wait to meet her in Basel in three days' time. The story to his father was that he and Nick were to go skiing together, but in fact he was going to Engelberg with Leni and Nick to Kitzbuhel in Austria.

On the way to work the day before his trip his father raised an issue.

51

"You're receiving a lot of mail from Germany."

"Oh, you mean Leni. She's just a friend," Martin replied nonchalantly.

"Three letters in three days? Don't give yourself a problem, Martin."

Martin recognised the censor. He needed a new letterbox.

Boxing Day, 4pm and Martin, having crossed the Luxembourg border, was standing with his case at a bus stop outside Trier in Germany. He was waiting for a bus to the Central Station in order to catch the next train to Koblenz. From there it was on to Basel and then skiing with Leni.

When a bus finally turned up he was tired and fed up and a little uneasy. It was his first steps on German soil and he was about to have his first conversation with a German bus conductor, who was short and stocky with a little moustache and looked to him like Himmler.

"I want go Trier catch train chuff chuff!" he explained, shunting his elbows backwards and forwards like pistons. "Chuff chuff to Koblenz! *Verstehen*?"

"*Ja! Ja! Trier! Das ist gut!*" said the conductor, knowingly.

Too knowingly, Martin thought, not at all convinced he'd been understood. "First Trier then train, chuff chuff, to Koblenz!" he said seeking further assurance assisted by his piston impressions. "Then chuff chuff to Basel and Switzerland skiing!" he exclaimed, sweeping his arms forward and back like a seasoned downhill skier.

"*Ja, ja,*" the conductor agreed amiably. "Bahnhoff! Trier! Koblenz! Basel!"

Martin looked at him suspiciously; some of the guards had been amiable enough when the trains arrived at Auschwitz. Why was he suggesting Martin go to Bahnhoff first? Bahnhoff might be a nice place to visit, maybe they had a statue of Horst Wessel there, but it was not where this boy wanted to go.

52

"Nein Bahnhoff!" he insisted. "I want to go straight to Trier. Then chuff chuff Koblenz."

By now several of the passengers were glaring at him for holding up the bus. A tall, thin middle-aged man pointed to an empty seat and said: "*Setzen.*" Martin wondered where he served during the war. Then the conductor took over. "*Ja ja! Trier! Bahnhof! Chuff chuff Koblenz! Skifahren in der Schweiz! Alles gut. Setzen, Setzen!*"

Martin hadn't seen Bahnhoff on the map, but logic and fatigue and faith in German attention to detail told him it couldn't be far away. So he sat down to a sigh of approval from his fellow travellers determined to find an English speaking person in Bahnhoff and make his way on to Trier as soon as he arrived. It was only when the bus finally pulled into Trier Central Train Station and he saw the word BAHNHOF written in large letters on top of the railway station and everybody on the bus turned and shouted, "Chuff chuff!" that Martin finally got the message. As he grabbed his case and left the bus Himmler doing his own impression of a skier repeated: "*Skifahren in der Schweiz! Ist gut!*"

The next morning he was standing at the top of a slope on a snowy Swiss mountain next to Leni with a toboggan at his side. Wearing dark glasses, a smart, thick cable-knit jumper, beige gabardine trousers and black suede shoes he imagined he looked the part. But Leni who had her blue woolly hat pulled down over her ears and was dressed in a smart blue sweater and black ski pants said:

"You would fit better in a nightclub."

"Are you going to come with me or not?"

"No, I am not, and I don't want you to do this," she said.

One hour ago as they'd watched some kids sledging down some nursery slopes he'd decided to hire a toboggan. But he didn't feel the nursery slopes offered a suitable challenge. "There!" he'd pointed up at what looked like an advanced slope on the mountain. "That's the one for me!" Reluctantly she had walked up the mountain with him trying to dissuade him. She told him he hadn't tobogganed before and it could be dangerous. But the fact she thought it could be dangerous only emboldened him. This was a golden opportunity to really impress her. He assured her he'd glide down like a master, no special skill being required as there was needed for skiing. Now, standing together at the top of the slope, he noticed a few people who had gathered at the bottom were looking up at him. How could he possibly back down now? "Look," he grinned, "I've got an audience."

"You are crazy. I told you, I don't want you to do this. It is true that when God wants to punish you he takes away your good sense."

"Where did you get that from?"

"Sholem Aleichem," she said.

Martin had never read a word of Sholem Aleichem but the sound of the famous Yiddish writer's name on her lips overwhelmed him and he immediately grabbed hold of her and kissed her.

"You're my favourite reader of Yiddish writers," he said, "and when I get to the bottom I shall shout 'Sholem Aleichem!' and blow you a big kiss."

"Please, Martin, more experienced people than you have been badly hurt doing this. You could be killed."

The idea of possibly breaking his neck and drowning in the icy pond that stood to the right of the slope at the bottom with Leni watching made the whole experience even more enticing. When he pulled it off it would be truly a moment she'd never forget.

Martin, drawing on his twenty-year-old ignorance of tobogganing, bravely cast off, shouting, "See you later!" Now, transported at forty miles an hour downhill in a car with proper steering is quite a doddle, but hurtling down on a few struts of wood with just a mangy old rope to guide you was definitely more of a test than Martin had realised, and the gathering speed of the toboggan set alarm bells ringing. It quickly struck him that this little trip might be a mistake. He needed to slow down. He needed to brake. He thrust his right leg into the snow to act as a drag. He felt a sharp pain in his groin and his leg rebelled, shooting up in the air. As a result of this last manoeuvre he now found himself leaning back as far as he could, buttocks clenched, his right leg waving about like a flag, as he veered off to the right heading straight for the icy pond. Luckily, rescuers were at hand and he was pulled out dripping wet and shivering uncontrollably, the humiliation complete. But he didn't die, neither was he badly injured and when he eventually gasped out a lip-shivering, teeth-chattering, barely audible whimper 'Sholem Aleichem,' nobody heard. After Leni surefootedly made her way down through the thick snow and checked nothing was broken she thanked the rescuers and they made their way back to the ski lift.

"What is the ma-tt-er with you?" she said, angrily. "Are you really such an idiot? I told you not to do this!"

His feet squelching in his soggy suede shoes and his clothes still dripping wet he tried to joke his way out of it by blaming her. "Yes, of course I am an idiot. That's why I did it. I wanted to impress you. That's what idiots do when they're in love. They do idiotic things. You think I'd ever do anything like this for anyone else?" He went on in this same tone all the way back to the hotel. He told her ever since he'd met her at the station the previous evening he'd had this crazy urge to do something that would amaze her. "Look, I know I'm an idiot, and I know it didn't all go exactly to plan, and I know you didn't hear me, but I did say Sholem Aleichem!" he grinned.

Back inside their hotel room with a half smile on her face she said. "Get into the shower and put on some dry clothes."

Later that evening, when they came down for dinner, they sat by a window overlooking the valley and the range of mountains that guarded it.

"They are our protectors of a good week," he said, feeling cocooned in a pocket of bliss.

"This book you gave me… it is interesting, but so sad."

"I haven't read it."

"You should. It is about a Jewish milkman in Russia under the Tsar. He has so many troubles with his daughters. One of them has exactly the same problem like us. She falls in love with a Christian boy and her father is not very happy so one day when he sees them talking outside his house he asks her what he is doing there. She says, 'Nothing. We are just talking.' He asks if she knows who she is talking to and she tells him he is not an ordinary person, and that he is going to be a second Gorky." Leni took his hand across the table. "He didn't even know who the first Gorky is, darling!"

"Neither do I," Martin admitted.

"But he is a famous writer."

"Go on with the story," he said, wondering where all this was heading.

"Then her father tells her not to forget who she is, where she comes from and where he comes from. So his daughter tells him: 'God created people equal.'"

"He must've liked that."

"He doesn't like it at all, and when she carries on arguing with him he tells her: 'Everyone must go with their own. That is how it has been since Creation. And when a hen crows like a rooster it is time to take it to the slaughterer.'"

"Poor hen," Martin said, thinking that his father was definitely educated at the same school.

"When the priest tells her father they are married he tells his wife that from now on their daughter is dead. Nobody can even say her name. At the end of the story all the Jews are forced to leave their towns and villages and go into exile. What do you think of the story? Do you think your father would like it?"

"I think he'd love it, especially the bit where his daughter gets married by the priest."

"I have the answer to this. If Jews and Christians have to be separated, then I can become Jewish like you!" she exclaimed triumphantly. "I can read the Talmud!"

"That's a bit of a jump, isn't it?" he said, hesitantly.

"I want to jump!" she said. "Only I did not think of this until I read Sholem Aleichem! Thank you, darling, for giving me this wonderful present."

Leni's smiling, happy face looked at Martin across the dinner table, eagerly awaiting his response. *Just a friend!* That's what he'd said.

"What do you think, darling?" she pressed him.

"Becoming Jewish isn't easy you know. We Jews like to make it difficult. It's a tradition."

"I want to be with you always."

She was looking to him for encouragement and he was struggling. They'd never discussed the route to a Jewish marriage before, and now she was suggesting it. What an incredibly generous offer! She'd give up everything in the world to be with him. Alarm bells rang. Always was a long time. Yes, now he too wanted that but what if one day he didn't? He was still young. He'd be swapping a romantic, fantasy headache for a real one. Her beautiful, tragic eyes looked deep into his heart and he felt she knew every secret.

"Perhaps it will not be enough for my Tevye!" she said, sadly.

"It is enough for me," he said instinctively, his voice full of bravado. Then he took her hand, and with dessert not finished, they climbed the stairs to their room. All he wanted was to embrace the fantasy and make love to her for as long as he could, for he knew in five nights the spell would be broken.

They were lying on the bed in the moonlight as she massaged his bruised leg, now bandaged courtesy of the hotel's first-aider.

"Darling, you have a beautiful body, but you have one really nasty wound here," she said, gently caressing his right ankle.

"That is what you get for showing off," he said.

In the dim light she raised her eyebrows and her eyes twinkled as she said: "Then this wound is for me. Now I am the bad wound in your life, but if I kiss it, it will bring you good luck when I am not with you."

Thereupon she kissed his ankle, as he stroked her long hair and told her: "Now I know my luck will always be good."

His injured ankle meant that he couldn't ski, which probably saved him from any further embarrassment. Instead, he bought some walking shoes and they took a day trip to Kandersteg, where the steep path led them into the high Gastern valley. After the desolate scenery of rock faces and roaring streams, the view changed as they walked down until they stood by the bank of a meandering river.

"I want to be a river and run though you," she smiled warmly.

"You are," he said.

She'd given up her skiing in order to be with him. On the morning of New Year's Eve he said he knew she loved to ski and it was a memory he wanted to take away with him. From the top of the piste he'd watched, his heart in his mouth, as she swerved from side to side down an advanced slope, her skis, her ski poles, and herself all part of one effortless coordinated glide.

Later that afternoon, just as Leni was preparing for her last run, a tall, rather plump girl called out her name. Engelberg was a popular resort and Leni wasn't surprised to run into someone she knew. Erika, who'd arrived the previous evening for a one-night stay at the same hotel, was with her fiancé who'd already zoomed away down the mountain. Leni introduced Erika to Martin as an old school friend. The girls agreed they should all meet up in the bar that evening for drinks but he noticed Leni was not wholehearted as usual.

"It's her, isn't it? That Erika – she's the cheat, isn't she?" Martin said later, as they were changing for dinner.

"Yes, it is Erika, but I did not say she is a cheat and I do not want you to talk about this in the bar."

"So long as nobody else does," he grinned.

There was the sound of clinking glasses and the hum of chatter in the bar as Leni and Martin sat drinking their Coca-Colas at a small table near the window. She was teasing him about his skill on the toboggan and his bus ride to Trier.

Martin had only met Erika briefly on the piste, but he resented spending any more time with her, especially as it was to be Leni and his last night together. When they finally made their grand entrance, Erika flounced over to them like a large Sugar Plum Fairy and sat down. Gunter was a balding, dapper, middle-aged man several inches shorter than Erika. He bowed formally to Martin and kissed Leni's hand but seemed unable to release her. Erika immediately ordered him to fetch the best champagne for everyone. Then speaking in her best English she told Leni how wonderful it was to see her again.

"I am so pleased to see you one time more, Leni. You must like London, no? To be au pair in this city you must be so excited and interesting. Did you see the Parliament on the Thames? I am told it is beautiful. I am so jealous."

She did not sound jealous or terribly interested in what Leni might've thought, and before Leni could reply she whispered loudly in German:

"*Er ist sehr schön, nicht wahr?*" Martin rolled his eyes.

Returning with the champagne and four glasses, Gunter poured drinks for everyone while Erika continued in her less than excellent English:

"What a big chance meeting this morning with you and Martin! You know, it is only one year, this same time I am meeting with Gunter on this same piste and at this hotel." She blew Gunter a kiss. He blushed. "Now here we are together, one year later, and we are drinking champagne at this same bar with you. You think it is not *fantastisch*?"

"Amazing," Leni agreed sweetly.

Erika told them that she and Gunter had fallen in love instantly and that she could see immediately Leni and Martin, too, had something special. She apologised that she and Gunter were not able to spend more time with them but they had to rush off to this fantastic party at a five-star hotel in Lucerne. If only Leni and Martin were not leaving tomorrow, if only there was a way they could somehow stay longer.

"I hate people who break arrangements." Martin butted in. "You must go. You look fantastic. That really is a very pretty hat."

Erika, who was wearing a red velvet pillbox with an absurd arrangement of artificial fruit on it, was delighted.

"It'll look great in Lucerne," Martin said stifling a laugh.

Naturally, she missed the point and concentrated on the compliment. For if Erika was going to be stopped when in free flow it was obvious there was nothing she appreciated more than being stopped by a compliment.

"Thank you, Martin. Gunter has bought it for me when he is in Paris, *nicht wahr, liebling*?" she said.

"Martin, I think you know about hats," she said adjusting her pillbox.

Leni smiled. "He should do. He makes them."

"Martin, you make hats! Is this true? *Das ist wunderbar!*" she said, as she mentally elevated herself by association with Martin, whom she presumed must, at least, own a celebrated fashion house.

"It's just a small family business my grandfather started," he replied, seeking to crush any elevated thoughts she might have.

"This is the same with Gunter. His grandfather is also in the family business."

"What do you make, Gunter?" Martin asked.

"Oh, I think you will know us by our medicines."

"They are the first ones to make *aspirin*," Erika said sitting bolt upright.

"So we both make something for the head then, Gunter," Martin said.

"We make people feel better," Gunter agreed.

"What a coincidence," Erika said, delighted that everybody was getting along so well.

Martin asked Gunter the name of his company. It was Bayer. He'd heard of them. They'd been part of I. G. Farben during the war. They'd been hand in hand with the SS and he knew what they made, and he knew it wasn't good for Jewish heads.

"Didn't they make Zyclon B?"

"Yes, of course, but thanks God these days we make other things," Gunter assured him, trying to keep cool under the not so innocent fire.

"When are you getting married?" Leni asked Erika, rescuing a tricky situation.

Erika was delighted with the change of subject reverting to her wedding plans and went into overdrive telling her all about it. They were to be married in the spring in Rothenburg. Her greatest joy was that they were being married in the beautiful old Gothic church of St Jacob with

61

the famous Heilige Blut Altar that was said to contain drops of Christ's blood. By now she was completely swept up in her own parade and wanted everybody to celebrate and be as happy as she was.

"Maybe you will marry too, Leni. Wouldn't it be wonderful if one day you are married in the same church?"

Martin was at a loss. He couldn't believe how stupid and insensitive this girl was. She wasn't satisfied with her own wedding; she wanted to celebrate two weddings and one of them, his. Not only that, but how did she know, after just meeting him, that he wanted to get married anyway, and in a church? He was on the verge of giving her a little Jewish education when Leni entered the fray.

"Oh, I don't know if we will be married."

"And if we were it's unlikely it would be in Germany," Martin added. "I mean, we couldn't very well, could we?" he said turning to Leni. "Not if we were getting married in a synagogue."

"A synagogue!" Erika exclaimed.

"Well, there aren't too many of them left in Germany today, are there?"

"Then, then... you will be Jewish," she said to Leni, shocked.

"Yes, like me." Martin grinned.

"But do your mother and father know this, Leni?" she persisted.

"Yes, they know this," Leni said, without flinching.

"Oh, I am sure when they meet Martin it will be *alles gut*," Gunter said, trying to smooth things over.

"It is not so easy, Gunter. They are two different kulture."

"Yes, I know this, but I am sure Leni knows what she does. She has been au pair in London. She is *kosmopolitisch* now."

"Gunter! I am not au pair in London but I do not know

anyone who is more *kosmopolitisch* than me and I must tell you sometimes you see the truth most clear when you are not so close to these problems. When you are up on the mountain you must be careful. The air is clear and beautiful but it can be dangerous. Is it not so Martin?"

"It certainly can be, Erika. Thanks for warning us. We will be careful. Your English is really superb."

Gunter smiled and put his hand on Erika's knee. "That is why she is winning this English prize in her last year at school."

Without batting an eye Erika removed Gunter's hand and generously said: "I am lucky. Leni is sick for a very important test."

Martin glanced across at Leni. She was silent and without any sign of upset. He could not believe she was prepared to let Erika get away with this. Erika, it was obvious, was in complete denial.

"Funny, but Rudi had a completely different take on that story."

Erika blushed. "You know Rudi?"

"I met him in London, with Leni. We all had a drink together in a pub. He's quite a character."

"I am glad he makes the good impression, but I must be sorry to tell you his character is not so good," she said, wriggling in her chair.

"Really?" Martin exclaimed, acting the innocent.

"The truth is he does not like me and does not like me getting this prize. So he told me the head teacher wants to speak with me. I am very worried *natürlich*. When I go to see her she does not know why I am there. I do not tell her who sent me. I do not like to tell stories. But I do not think this is a very nice thing to do."

Martin smiled broadly. "I wonder why he would do a thing like that?"

Erika seemed stuck. Gunter took her hand and Leni immediately rushed to the rescue.

"Because he likes to play tricks, and sometimes they are not so funny but he is a good man, Erika," Leni said firmly. "Only sometimes he talks too much and he is not the only one to do this," she continued glaring at Martin.

"Ah, Leni, you are so sweeeeet, always making excuses for him," Erika purred. Then, looking at her watch, she quickly jumped up as if something was about to boil over in the kitchen. "Gunter, we must go. We will be late for the party. We must leave immediately!"

She swiftly hugged and kissed Leni, politely nodded at Martin, and before he could say anything more to upset her, she said, "I do hope you will have true love and be sooo happy together as we are."

She wished them Happy New Year and swanned away into the night with her Gunter. Martin wanted to laugh, but Leni looked cross.

"Well, that got rid of the pudding and the jelly," he grinned.

"They would've gone soon enough without this," Leni said.

"I'm sorry if I upset your best friend."

"She is not my best friend," she snapped.

She seemed disappointed in him but all Martin could think of was after ten minutes of trying to arrange their lives for them her preposterous friend had finally snuffed out any sense of credibility with a blatant lie.

"Then why didn't you say something? Were you sick that day?"

"No, I was not sick."

"Then you knew she was lying?"

"Yes, I know this."

"Then why? What on earth did she ever do for you?"

"It doesn't matter what she did for me or did not do for

me. She is stupid, and I do not need to make her look more stupid in front of Gunter and neither do you. You know nothing about this person."

"I know she's a phony!" Then, mimicking Erika: "'Oh, Leni you are *so* sweeeet, always making excuses for Rudi'. And 'I do hope you will be sooooo happy together and find true love as we have.' She is ridiculous!"

"Yes, she is ridiculous. Everyone in the school knows this. And I did not expect her to get this prize. But I do not care so much about it as you do. She was the most unpopular girl in our class. She is fat, and she never had any boyfriends and she was not very happy. Now she has found one who is much older than she is, and maybe he is a jelly, but he thinks she is wonderful, and that is good for her. Why do you have to spoil this for her when she has so little?"

"Because she was making a fool of you."

"She was only making a fool of herself."

"Her talk about the truth. It's a joke!"

"Yes, it is a joke!"

"So why do you have to keep defending her?"

"Because she is an injured bird and knows I will keep her safe," Leni finally exclaimed.

"Is that why you stay with me?"

"Yes, darling, you are injured too. But one day you will heal. And I don't know if I will see this. But I want too."

She said she didn't want to argue any more. She wanted to be happy; she would have plenty of time to be sad. So he apologised sincerely for his overblown reaction and being as stupid as Erika, and they laughed at each other for arguing their last few hours away. Later they joined in the celebrations at the hotel, where an accordionist and two violinists played throughout the evening. They danced, and as a girl sang 'La Paloma' in German she told him that if ever he were naughty when they were apart she would be like the little dove in the song and fly in through his window and flap her wings so he would remember. Then he told her he didn't want to be so naughty with anybody else because there was nobody else like her. She laughed heartily and told him he really was a good storyteller. There followed 'Parlez-moi d'Amour', and endless Strauss waltzes, as they made love only with sad eyes till twelve o'clock, when the balloons flooded the room and everybody shouted "*Prosit*! Happy New Year!" The little band finished up with 'Auld Lang Syne'.

Later, in the early hours of the morning, they lay on the bed watching the snowfall outside the window.

"Isn't the snow beautiful, darling? Don't you think we are like two little snowflakes falling together? If only we can *land* together," she said, with the old familiar uptick in her voice. "But soon the wind is going to blow you far away, back to London."

"For five days I did not feel the cold," he said.

"Except when you fell through the ice," she smiled. "I shall write to you."

"And I to you."

"My letters will be your blankets. I shall write every day, so each night I can be near and wrap you up in them, and kiss you, so you will never forget me," she said.

"I'd like that."

She said no more and as he turned to look at her her eyes were shut.

"What are you thinking?"

Her eyes opened and she smiled cheekily. "I am not thinking, I am making a wish."

"Tell me!"

"Not now, I will tell you later."

He guessed what she'd wished; marriage, and children. Once more remembering his father's words: *Don't give yourself a problem*, he gripped her hand tightly.

"What is it, darling? Tell me! It is your father, isn't it? He can't forgive Germans."

"He needs time," Martin said. "It might be best, in the beginning, if you send all your letters to Nick. I can pick them up from him."

"Oh, darling, I am so afraid that I am going to lose you."

She looked sad, and he felt ashamed that he couldn't console her without lying.

"It will only be for a little while," he said.

She explored his face wanting to believe him but he could not conceal his doubts, either in his voice or in his determined stare.

"Oh, darling, it is really all so terribly sad. Last night I dreamed your father is a policeman and he came to take you away from me. He said I am a thief. I was so angry with him. It is so unfair. Hitler is dead so many years now. You know, in my whole life I have been punished for two bad things: I stole this stupid pencil, and I loved you. Honestly, darling, I don't know which one is the worst. I have given the pencil back. But I can't give you up. If I give you up then I shall have nothing but a dream of you falling in the snow, and the mountains, and the memory of our wonderful days in London. Why must we give up our life? Do you think I am a thief, darling?"

She looked so terribly sad and tragic. This picture of her would never leave him. Nobody smiled like her, nobody laughed like her and when faced with tragedy there was no one more beautiful than her. "It's not over yet," he said. Then he put his arm round her and kissed her head. The following day they left the mountains and took the train to Basel where they had lunch at a hotel. He would never remember what they ate, or whether the restaurant was empty or full, but 'La Paloma' played on the radio, and they made promises to meet up again, somehow, either in the spring or the summer.

They had devoured each other's bodies and minds for

six days, and now it was fast coming to an end. Outside, all around the hotel, the snowflakes fell together.

"It's true," he said, at last full of passion and conviction. "You're right. You are a thief for you have stolen my easy life and left me with a difficult one! And I am glad, glad, for now I am stuck with Goethe, Beethoven and you and I wouldn't part with any one of them, least of all *you*. Don't you see, what you have taken I don't want back. What I have now is far better than anything that was mine before. And one day I'm going to tell my father this!"

"Oh, darling, do you really think you can do this?"

"This little snowflake is going to fall where it wants."

This was a revelation not just to her but himself. For the first time he'd spoken of telling his father exactly who Leni was and what she meant to him. This was no fantasy-headache. This was for real. Her eyes filled with tears as she held his hand across the table.

"Oh, darling," she cried. "Just to hear you say this is the best present you could give me. I just wish we did not love each other so much – then we would not have to hurt anybody. No, this is not true! I do not wish this. I just wish there was no history! No, that is not right either. The world must remember."

As he boarded his train at Basel she cried: "Take care of you, darling!" She was wearing a thick light-blue winter jacket that matched her eyes. He waved from the window and clung to an image of a blur of blue as she disappeared from view. When he eventually sat down he noticed that an elderly gentleman, smoking a pipe, was staring at him, smiling.

"*Guten abend,*" the man said.

Martin had just waved goodbye to six of the happiest days. He wondered what the future held for them both. He remembered a line from a book by Hermann Hesse she'd once given him. *Alas, love does not exist to make us happy. It exists to show us how, through sorrow, we can be steadfast and endure.* Well, their love would endure. They would be steadfast and if there was to be sorrow, they would endure it together. It wouldn't be easy, but not everybody knew they had a Walter to call on. Martin smiled back at the man with the pipe.

"*Guten abend*," he replied.

CHAPTER 7

Whenever Martin's father was troubled a build-up of phlegm would cause him to clear his throat repeatedly. So, when back home the following morning over breakfast he cleared his throat three times before enquiring if he and Nick had a good time in Switzerland, Martin sensed something was wrong but he wasn't sure what so he slipped in a happy half-truth.

"Yes, great until I tobogganed into an icy pond!"

"Monty's not been very well," Albert said. "He's got bronchial pneumonia. As soon as he's well enough he's going away to recuperate. You're going to have more to do."

Oh, so that's it, Martin thought. Well, in two weeks when his uncle had recovered and everything would be back to normal perhaps they'd talk about Leni then. But when two weeks later *normal* succumbed to a life of chain-smoking and forty-nine-year-old Monty died, it was a shock. Now any mention of Leni would have to be put on hold. At first he was concerned for his father. It was a blow. The brothers had both left school at fifteen to go into their father's expanding business, working together for more than thirty years. He needn't have worried; coping was in Albert's DNA. Lost orders, divorce, death – he'd just sign on for another tour of duty.

Martin stood next to his father in the crowded prayer hall listening attentively as Albert neither rushed nor struggled annunciating slowly and clearly each word of the *Kaddish*. Then the doors to the cemetery opened and they escorted the coffin to the grave, family and friends following.

There was a chill wind and Martin shivered in his duffle coat at the graveside as he watched his father's steady arm shovel the first earth onto the coffin. During the seven days' *shiva*, sitting on the low chairs, standing to pray, or talking with the endless stream of family and friends who came to pay their respects, he was always calm.

On the first Friday evening service to welcome in the Sabbath, Martin waited on the edge of his seat inside the prayer hall. Suddenly the chanting rose up, the doors swung open and the congregation rose as one as they welcomed the lone mourner back into the fold.

His father was not one who ever courted attention. He didn't bob and bend in ecstasy when he prayed – he was still. He was not a scholar and didn't understand the Hebrew text he read so fluently. God was the Jewish itch he scratched every Sabbath with the same routine devotion to duty as a day at the factory. That's how Martin saw it. But that Friday, as Albert walked down the aisle in his smart grey suit and took his place next to his son, he seemed to Martin uplifted. When he joined the congregation in prayer and sang 'Lecha Dodi' he was transformed His voice rang out like a *shofar*. This smiling *hello* was no routine. It was as if grief had been dropped into a magic hat – scarves pulled out – joyous colours – one after another. When the solitary mourner recited the final *Kaddish* Martin watched and listened in awe – then trembled as he wept in silence for his father's fortitude.

The band was playing 'Mack the Knife' and the room was sultry and smokey as usual. Nick was seated at a small table opposite Martin inhaling deeply on a Gauloise.

"You quite sure there were no letters for me from Leni?"

"Not today," Nick said downing his scotch. "Got it bad, have you?"

"I've just got this urgent feeling to be with her nearly all the time."

"Have you?" Nick said, eyeing a pretty girl, who glided by.

"If only I'd had a chance to talk to him."

Nick raised his eyebrow dubiously. "You said that a couple of months ago."

"Ever since my uncle died he's at the *shul* every morning and evening. It's difficult. And there's another ten months still to go."

"You really are living a dream, aren't you, Solomon?" Nick always reverted to schoolboy surnames when he was thinking of dropping a bombshell. "Shall I tell you something? I think you're kidding yourself here. The truth is you'd've found it pretty difficult to talk to your father before your uncle died and you'll find it just as difficult when he's finished mourning. Truth is when your uncle died I think you were relieved."

"So Monty got me out of a hole, did he?"

"Look, I've seen your father a few times since we've been back but not once has he asked me about the holiday. I'd say that's unusual for him. And another thing: remember what he said to you before you left? *Don't give yourself a problem!* Well, I'll tell you what, it doesn't take Einstein to work out which relativity theory he was talking about. He saw those three letters from Germany and decided he didn't like the idea you might be paddling in the Rhine. Mind you, I don't think he's got a clue you might be over your head in it."

Martin helped himself to one of Nick's cigarettes in the blue packet on the table and lit up using the book of matches on the table. "That's why I need to be honest with him."

"Shall I tell you my theory on that? You tell the truth when you can and when you can't you duck down low, dodge any temptation to be honest, and jab a good lie. Bit like a boxing match: you've got to learn to wait, pick the right time to throw your punch. And right now seems to me a good time to wait 'cause I reckon if you don't you might well be looking for another job. I think Monty might've just saved you a lot of trouble here. I mean, if you think about it, the I-want-to-marry-a-German-*shiksa* story isn't every Jewish parent's idea of a dream wedding and certainly not your father's. Of course you could always go Reform if she's willing to convert, but I don't believe it would help one bit. This is not the future he's been dreaming about for you these past twenty years. You've hardly known her a year. If it wasn't for him you might not even've had the money for a week in Switzerland." Nick looked directly at Martin for his reaction. Martin was quiet. "Interesting, isn't it?" Nick said.

"Yeah, very. So, what are you suggesting?"

"All I'm suggesting is why not give yourself a chance. A year's not such a long time, and at least you'll buy some credibility because right now all that your father's going to be thinking is you need to learn how to say goodbye the way he's just done to his brother. Then if it doesn't work out, well… "

Martin grinned, "I could come and work for you. Sell a television."

"We've got a few," Nick said.

Nick had entered the family radio and television business when he was sixteen. Always ambitious and quick to learn he soon had plans to expand the small chain of four radio and television shops. When his father had died suddenly a couple of years later everyone was amazed when he succeeded in persuading the bank to support him in the purchase of another three shops whilst he bought two vans, expanded the service division and started installing car radios.

Just then a pretty girl with long brown wavy hair and a cute figure tapped Nick on the shoulder and speaking with a French accent asked, "May I have one of your cigarettes, sweetie? I like Gauloises and mine are all finished."

"Sure," Nick said. "Go ahead. What's your name?"

"Jeanne," she said as she helped herself, leaning further over than she needed to reach the packet.

"You can keep the pack if you want."

"Thanks," she smiled, and put the rest of the packet in the pocket of her full polka-dot skirt.

"Are you boys waiting for someone?"

"No, nobody at all. Why don't you sit down? I'm Nick and this is Martin."

"Do you mind?" she asked Martin.

Martin shrugged and nodded his head indifferently as Jeanne completely unabashed sat between them.

"Your friend is very quiet, Nick."

"Don't worry about him, he has girlfriend problems; but I don't," he leered.

"If I have to think about a problem more than two minutes it must be a tragedy, and I do not like tragedies."

Martin, who was amused by her audacity, wasn't quite sure if she was sympathising with his single state or trying to provoke him into a reaction.

"So what do you do after two minutes if you still have a problem?" Martin asked.

She grinned. "Maybe I will blow it away in a balloon."

"Like to dance?" Nick asked her.

Jeanne stubbed out her cigarette in the glass ashtray and she and Nick drifted onto the crowded dance floor.

There was something about Jeanne that fascinated Martin. For the first time in weeks he found himself tapping his fingers on the beer mat to the slow beat of 'Autumn Leaves'. He wondered what line Nick was spinning her or she him for they seemed to be in deep conversation and danced more than once. Finally they returned to Martin at his lonely table, Jeanne leading the way.

"Nick has told me all about you, Martin. And you look so like Monsieur Hamlet. It is very cute. Too dance or not to dance. It is a difficult question when you see Leni everywhere."

Nick looked guilty. Martin guessed he had his own self-interested motives to look after. If she was going to give one of the boys her telephone number at the end of the evening it was sure to be to the one who wasn't attached. There was something of the Puck about her – full of mischief. She wanted to knock him off his chair, that's all this was.

"I haven't flown a balloon since I was six."

"Then I must remind you," she said. "Come!" With that Jeanne took Martin's hand and led him directly on to the dance floor.

Things weren't going too well for Martin at work. Leni was constantly on his mind. He'd turned down an urgent order for dozens of sizals becase they didn't have the hoods in stock but forgot Albert had told him he could borrow them from another manufacturer. Then worse than that he gave instructions to make up an order that wasn't due until the autumn instead of one that had to be ready in two weeks.

"You need to pay attention!" Albert exclaimed, his eyes flashing dangerously. He never joked about work and Martin imagined he'd read his mind and knew the cause of his lack of focus.

The first time he had the opportunity to telephone Leni was at the end of March when she started her new job as a receptionist at a hotel in Karlsruhe. She wrote asking him to call on the Thursday at 4 pm as she'd be on her own. Martin saved up a pocketful of shilling coins. The same day he was due to call her he had appointments in town to show a new range of samples. Before he left the factory Albert told him he was getting a lift to his grandmother's after work and Martin should pick him up from there not later than 6 pm as he didn't want to be late for the evening service. His last appointment was at 3.30 pm. He reckoned this would still leave him with plenty of time to make his call to Leni. The buyer was impressed, had one of the girls try on the hats, asked about delivery times, reached for his pen and started writing out his orders. It was a slow process as there were six different branches to account for and the quantities of the different styles varied. The grand total was for 500 dozen hats. It was the biggest order Martin had ever received. The only downside it was 4.30 pm before he got away. He didn't want to be late for his father but he knew Leni would be waiting for his call. Fifteen minutes later he was rifling his coins through the public telephone booth trying to reach her. Just his luck the line was engaged. When he did finally get through his heart was booming. "I'm sorry I'm late. I was afraid I might've missed you."

They spoke quickly trying to catch up on all the days that they had not shared. Then she asked him if he could visit her in the summer holidays. "I want see you," she whispered.

"And I you," he replied like a man drowning in his favourite bottle of Liebfraumilch.

When Martin finally ran out of shillings and put the receiver down, his head was still counting *eins zwei drei*. He looked at his watch. It was almost 5.30 pm. Well, he told himself, even if he should be late and it meant his father missed the service, it was only one and they had the order, didn't they? He drove to his grandmother's house as quickly as he could, but the traffic was intense. By the time he arrived his father was standing at the front door waiting with Martin's grandmother standing behind him. It was five minutes to seven.

Martin raced up the drive. "Sorry I'm late, Dad, traffic was murder. An accident at St John's Wood, ambulances, police, the lot! I was held up for ages."

"Your last appointment was at three-thirty," he said with bite.

"I got here as quick as I could."

"Did you?"

Martin felt his face turn the colour of a baboon's arse. He'd been found out. He banked the only positive result he had. "I've got an order for 500 dozen hats."

Martin tried to press the precious orders into his father's

hand but in response Albert furiously waved the pages on to the floor.

"It's five minutes to seven. I told you to be here at six!!" he thundered. Martin scrambled on the ground picking up the orders. "I did it for you!" he said, once more trying to give him the orders.

"I don't need anything from you," his father snapped. "Just give me the car keys!"

That stung worse than a hard slap. Disappointment and humiliation in front of his grandmother overwhelmed him.

"Great! You drive and I'll take the fucking bus!" he exploded. With that he thrust the car keys into his father's hand and stormed across the road to the bus stop.

As Martin watched his father drive off at speed he was barely able to stand erect. His legs trembled. He'd never imagined missing one night's prayer could've provoked such a devastating reaction; all this because of his telephone call to Germany. Shame and guilt now harassed him. He winced at his elaborate lie about the traffic and his exhibition of foul temper. He knew all that his father had wanted in the world that evening was to be able to say *Kaddish* for his brother in the company of ten men at the synagogue. It would be a long time before he could talk to him about Leni now.

In the morning, at breakfast, he glanced at his father. He wanted to tell him how desperately sorry he was, but he couldn't bring himself to speak. They drove down to the factory in silence. He even wondered if he'd ever be forgiven, if he would ever ask him to do anything for him again. Then when they arrived at the factory Albert looked him in the eye.

"Check we've enough stock to meet that order you got yesterday, Martin. I think we might need to buy some more material."

There wasn't much given away in the tone, it was business-like, but their eyes had met and Martin felt embraced.

"Okay, Dad," he said and ran downstairs on his two strong legs to check the stock. It was back to business as usual.

Nick said while you're waiting for one thing to happen you do another. It was human nature. To do nothing was unnatural. In the warm spring evenings Martin still collected his letters from Nick, only now he was writing to Leni that he'd met a French girl called Jeanne. She wrote back saying, *I have been to see the Beggars Opera with a boy I know, but I cannot stand anybody else kissing me. Do you kiss her? I do hope we can still meet up in the summer.*

Jeanne didn't mind listening to Martin talk about Leni but she never offered any advice. She was perfectly happy with their casual arrangement: he was her Tuesday and Thursday Man. The other nights were given over to middle-aged Frank who let her drive his Alfa Romeo Spider and kept her in clothes, and Bob the stand-up comedian who kept her in jokes. One Thursday night as Martin was about to drop her off in Tavistock Square where she shared a room with a friend his frustration got the better of him.

"And what do you do for Monsieur Monday, Wednesday, and Friday?" he asked, pulling up the handbrake and turning off the headlights.

"They are my friends too."

"Perhaps they are more than *friends?*"

"No," she grinned, "I am only more than friends with you."

"I want to be your Saturday Man."

She laughed. "You are too greedy."

"I am not very good at sharing."

"Why not? I am happy sharing you with Leni who you see everywhere."

"I don't see Leni so much these days."

"But you can see her whenever you want," she said indifferently.

"What I want is to see you when I want."

She pouted, exaggerating her sympathy for him, "Oh, la la la la! So perhaps we will meet next Saturday then." She promptly kissed him quickly on the cheek, and said: "Or perhaps not." With that she leapt out of the car, closed the door behind her and was gone.

Even when Martin became a Saturday man, Jeanne wouldn't give up her other appointments and when he complained if she missed the occasional Tuesday she would tell him only pencil and paper are ruled by plans. The fact she didn't think too much of Goethe and Beethoven, or anything that smacked of tragedy only served to enchant him. Ballooning was a midsummer night's trick performed by Puck that hid the light from Leni's star.

He wrote to Leni the letter he never believed he'd ever write. He told her: *I still love you, but it's probably for the best that we write less often for a couple of months to see how we get on. It'll be hard, but the truth is I believe it's better for both of us to be disappointed now than later.*

A few days later Martin collected a letter from Nick.

27ᵗʰ June 1959

Hello, darling,

A couple of months! And you say you love me! Are you crazy? I read this and thought I would die. I am so depressed. I miss the days you have forgotten. If we really shared this disappointment you would not write of it like a lost tooth and grow another so quickly. I understand if you have met someone else. But please do not let us break up like this. I cannot bear to think we can no longer be friends. I will be happy whatever you do if we can just write to each other what is in our hearts. That is what is better for me!!! I have started a new job at a hotel in Karlsruhe. I hope still I shall see you this summer.

Love Leni.

Martin immediately wrote and told her not to be depressed and said he'd not forgotten anything, but it would help neither of them to act as if they were living a Greek tragedy. He was glad she'd turned down his rash proposal of a more leisurely correspondence. It'd never been what he'd really wanted.

For the next couple of months Martin saw Jeanne regularly until one day he phoned to find out from the landlady that she'd been arrested and taken to Holloway Prison on a drugs charge. So Mr Saturday went to visit her at her new abode. It was a grim, overbearing Victorian building and seeing her behind bars in prison uniform with no make-up was a shock. But she was as upbeat as ever. Yes, she'd been charged with drug trafficking. It hadn't helped that her visa had run out.

"Don't look so worried, sweetie. I am innocent. I do not take cannabis. Bob asked me to keep this big packet for him for two days; that is all. Now they want to deport me."

Martin knew she was innocent; cheeky maybe but she was no druggy.

"Why do you look so sad? It is not so bad here. Except there is no jam for breakfast," she grinned. "But believe me, I have been in worse hotels. On the ship I will be a guest of the British Government and the captain will let me have all the jam I want. And when I am back in Paris you will come and visit me."

A few weeks later Martin wrote to Leni telling her he'd been on a short trip to Paris with Nick and that he'd seen Jeanne. Leni wrote back telling him how hurt and dreadfully upset she was that he hadn't driven the extra few miles to see her. *I am so jealous. Are you kissing her?* she'd asked.

She'd wanted him to tell everything that was in his heart and he liked the freedom of being able to tell even the most painful truth without their being a penalty. Testing her excited him. Her resistance to all others and undying loyalty proved

80

her worth to him. It's a lucky man who can clear the air on those terms.

So he wrote to her:

It was Nick's car; Nick was the driver and Nick wanted to see Paris. And it's not just a few miles to Karlsruhe; it's 350, a seven-hour drive one way. We only went for twenty-four hours. But I will not lie to you, the truth is I have been with Jeanne, but however bad this sounds she could never mean to me what you do. Comparing her to you is like trying to compare a light bulb to the Great North Star.

She wrote back of her disappointment that he could not control himself with Jeanne. Then forgave him as always.

In the end Martin never saw Leni that summer. He wrote that as they were so busy at work, his father had decided to keep the factory open. Meanwhile, by the autumn Jeanne had found herself a new Tuesday and Thursday man in Paris and he'd found an au pair called Katya from Nuremberg.

In the months that followed, the tone and frequency of Leni's letters changed and he felt restless. She'd used to write three or four times a day so he could virtually trace every step she took. There used to be a pressed flower pasted on the right-hand corner. Now she wrote only once a week at most and with no flower. At Christmas Leni wrote about a young Greek man at the hotel she'd met who was homesick for Greece. It wasn't the first time she'd mentioned him, but it was the first time she'd mentioned he played the guitar and that he was popular in the hotel. He wondered how popular the Greek was with her. She wished him the best New Year ever and hoped perhaps they might one day meet up again as the best of friends. The desperation of her earlier letters was gone. Was it only a few months ago he'd actually criticised her for sounding depressed and mourning days gone by as if she were living out a Greek tragedy? Now she had the Greek, and he had the tragedy. She sounded so calm and resigned and her calm unsettled him. What a fool he was. Suddenly, he was missing all the *Sturm und Drang*, and he was missing her. The brightest star in the firmament was disappearing.

Then came the cold February evening he collected a letter from Nick that really unsettled him.

February 18th 1960

Hello, darling,

It is cold but very sunny and I have been lying in a meadow of wild flowers in the middle of winter. Can you imagine? How beautiful nature can be when the smallest and most inconsiderable things can grow into such things of wonder. I have read some beautiful words by the poet Rilke:

'Be patient with all that is unsolved in your heart and try to love the questions themselves, like locked rooms, like books written in a foreign language. Do not seek answers that cannot be given you because you would not be able to live them. The point is to live your questions now, and perhaps, without noticing it you will live some distant day into the answer.'

Kisses Leni

What did Rilke mean? What did she mean? Wait for a distant day?

And what about the present? Did that spell a Greek day in a field of flowers?

Was that what he'd sown? He drove home listening to the last movement of the *Waldstein* Sonata playing on the radio, Rilke's words storming his brain and tears streaming down his cheeks.

In March he collected a letter from Nick's. He hadn't heard from Leni for more than a week and his heart was jumping, but the handwriting was not hers, and when he opened the envelope he was amazed.

March 11ᵗʰ 1960

Dear Martin,

As you will now know, Germany did not retain the World Cup. That will teach the arrogant German, you will be thinking, and maybe you are right. Since we last met, many months ago, I have often thought of our talk in the pub that day and my silence when you asked me about Auschwitz. I am not usually a quiet person, but I could not answer the question you put to me because I never asked myself this question, and somebody who does not know all the facts of this terrible time cannot give a good answer.

Since then I have read much on this subject and asked myself many times how did Germany ever arrive at such a place? Bismarck, our first chancellor, granted Jews equal rights. He did much business with Jews. He had a Jewish banker, he had Jewish tenants on his land, gave them credit when they were in difficulty, and he was a great admirer of Disraeli.

He was at the inauguration of the great Oranienburg Synagogue in Berlin. I cannot say he was a lover of Jews, but he was not a lover of Catholics either, or anyone whose policies were different from his own. But in 1878, for his support of equal rights for Jews in Romania, he received many letters of thanks from Jews around the world. Unfortunately, as we have learned not all chancellors are the same. So how do we respond to these terrible days? Perhaps when I spoke of the settlement between Germany and the Jews you thought I was not so serious as I should be. What happened was a catastrophe for every Jew and every German. But I do not believe any country should be judged as a whole in a situation like this.

When I think of all those Germans who could not bring themselves to speak against this terrible crime I ask myself how can this be? But perhaps I too could be one of those who turned away at Kristallnacht, and the burning of the books. Perhaps I too could be one of those who did not want to discover the terrible fate of the disappearing Jews. It is always safer to go with the majority and wait for the next man to be the one to act. But I like to think, today, I shall be one to walk in trouble's way, and be, myself, like Pastor Bonnhoefer a spoke in the Devil's wheel. Finally, I have seen Leni and I can tell you she is quite well and sends you a kiss.

Your friend, Rudi

Leni had been right about Rudi after all. Martin felt a pang of remorse for judging him so harshly.. Here was a German chancellor who'd been a wonderful supporter of the Jews even if he didn't always love them. Here was a chancellor he could talk about to his father. Here was a moment he could stop the lie in his heart and start being honest. If he could persuade his father about Bismarck surely one day he'd be able to persuade him about Leni. But the first day he mentioned him driving home from the factory all Albert said was: "The best thing about *Bismarck* is they sunk it."

CHAPTER 8

Nick, who now had seven shops, had bought himself a brand spanking new Vauxhall Cresta PA that was parked right outside his house. It was a showstopper: red with a white rooftop, sun visor, chromed tail fins, four portholes either side of the engine and whitewall tyres. But most importantly, it was fast. Nick stepped back after he'd finished polishing the car.

"What do you think? Not bad, eh," he said, addressing his friends Martin and Lionel.

Martin, who'd been inspecting the splendid exterior, was now running his hands over the luxurious red leather bench seats.

"Not bad, and this one's all yours? Bet you won't miss the old Buick. Eighty-nine miles an hour, you say. Not bad at all!"

Lionel was standing kerbside watching. He was tall and dark with a somewhat pallid complexion. A slight smirk played on one corner of his mouth.

"I'll bet that cost a few televisions," Lionel quipped.

"Just over a grand's worth. Nought to sixty in sixteen seconds," Nick boasted.

"Wouldn't mind going for a spin," Martin said.

"Have you taken it on a decent run yet?" Lionel asked.

"I'm still running it in, aren't I? Where do you want to go?"

"Well, personally, I wouldn't mind going to Karlsruhe." Martin grinned.

"Karlsruhe!" Lionel exclaimed.

"How many miles is that?" Nick asked, buffing up a smear on the bonnet with his elbow.

"Only about 440 miles from Boulogne."

"Round the corner then?" Lionel jeered.

"That's where she is now, is it?" Nick asked.

"Yes. So we were discussing what to do over Easter, why don't we pop over? You two could drop me off at Karlsruhe, go on to Salzburg for a couple of nights then pick me up on the way back. I mean, you've both got girls out there, haven't you?"

"See that, Nick? That's what I like about Solomon. He's never just thinking about himself," said Lionel.

"That's right, it'll be a joint enterprise; my idea, your jokes, and Nick's car."

Nick smiled. He was used to the banter between his two friends.

"I'll tell you something, Lionel, it's not such a bad idea. Traude and Heidi are bound to be around then."

The boys had been going out with the two Austrian girls until Christmas, when they'd returned home. Martin knew Nick would fall in, and if he did Lionel would.

"I suppose I could go for a couple of nights," Lionel said, slowly coming around to the idea.

"That sounds perfect," Martin said. "We take the six o'clock ferry Friday morning, and arrive at Boulogne around nine o'clock French time. Allowing a few minutes to drop me off in Karlsruhe, if you two can do an average speed of forty-six miles an hour you could be singing *Figaro* outside Mozart's house by six in the evening – well in time for dinner."

"Isn't he wonderful?" Lionel glared. "He's done all these calculations to save us the trouble. I'll bet he's bought a map."

"It so happens I found this at home," Martin said, taking the map out of his pocket and spreading it open over the car bonnet. The other two gathered round.

"We might have to push your car a bit," Lionel warned Nick.

"I reckon we could do this," Nick said, ignoring the warning.

"So long as I'm back for Monday night," Lionel said. "Easter's a busy time for us."

"Don't worry, you'll be back," Martin reassured him.

One hour later Martin was in a call box phoning Leni at her hotel, his heart thumping. He confirmed he was coming to see her the week before Easter. She hesitated for a split second but told him she was pretty sure she could get the time off. He could tell from her voice she was excited, but somehow he didn't feel she was excited enough. Nevertheless, as he hung up he started counting down the number of days until he'd be seeing her again. He told his father they were all going to Brighton for the weekend.

The day finally came around for the three friends to set off on their journey. They laughed and joked and Martin hummed tunes from *South Pacific* as the engine purred and the miles rolled by. The Cresta pulled up in the early evening outside the Schloss Hotel. Lionel told Martin to enjoy himself and make the most of it; he had thirty-six hours until they picked him up on their way back early on the Monday morning.

It is quite extraordinary. Somebody tells you: *This you cannot have! That is impossible! But you can have this, that, or the other!* A thousand choices but that one is *verboten*! Immediately you want the one you can't have a thousand times more than any of the others, and when you wait fifteen months, travel nearly 600 miles to see your wonderful *verboten*, and your name is Martin Solomon, you know that for you there's more at stake than a bit of fun. The moment Martin entered the charming old hotel he was looking for her. It didn't take long. From behind the reception desk across an uncrowded foyer she smiled. 'Some Enchanted Evening' played again in his head. Only some of the enchantment disappeared when Martin noticed on the other side of the desk, leaning over, was a tall, lanky, dark, good-looking guy, who glanced round at him almost immediately after she did. Then he turned back to Leni, who spoke a few words to him before he tiptoed away like a burglar. She looked amused. It was harmless enough... or was it? He had signalled a knowing look. Martin knew instantly this was the lonely Greek boy, only something told him he wasn't so lonely any more. He had a strong feeling that this boy knew something about Leni he was not supposed to know, something only he, Martin, was supposed to know. He felt all his old jealousy rising up in him. Before he even greeted her he was obsessed by the image of the two of them unravelling loneliness together.

Leni called out, and another girl appeared from the office at the back and indicated to Leni that she should go. She immediately came over to him and kissed him on both cheeks. Then she told him she was off duty for the next two days. She went upstairs to change out of her dark blue suit and reappeared in tight black trousers and a black T-shirt. They went to a smoky, crowded taverna a few minutes' walk away, ordered a forgettable meal and listened to an unforgettable 'Cry Me A River' by a soulful girl singer. Leni asked him about the trip down with his friends, and his work. She tentatively asked if he had received Rudi's letter and he said he'd found it really interesting. She obviously knew all about Rudi's research. Martin still had the Greek on his mind.

"Tomorrow I want to take you to Heidelberg. It is very pretty. It is on the river and has the oldest university in Germany. It is especially known for its democratic and liberal ideals."

"Liberal is good. Liberals have most to lose, they have the most freedom. They have to be on guard for disruptive forces. Are you a good liberal?"

"I am a good Democrat," she said.

"Tell me nothing important has changed?"

"Nothing important has changed."

Then he told her his friends were great! The trip was great! Business was great! Rudi was great! Julie London was great, and he was sure Heidelberg would be great too. He tried hard to sound light so she wouldn't notice he was still afraid they might've lost something. So he never mentioned the Greek at all; instead, he reassured her wherever they went that it would always be great. How could it not be? He waited for her to reassure him but she did not speak.

Later, when they returned to the hotel, he slipped, unseen, into her small single room, none the wiser. He was convinced she was holding back. On a plain wooden shelf above the bed was a row of books: Sholem Aleichem, Hermann Hesse, Heinrich Bohl, Homer, and a book of Rilke's poems.

"'The Trojan Horse'. That's one of my favourite stories," he said, flicking through the *Iliad*. "You've got to hand it to them; those Greeks certainly knew how to sneak their way in."

She said nothing.

"How about your Greek friend? Has he been to Heidelberg?"

"Yes, I am sure, he must've been."

"That was him you were talking to when I arrived, wasn't it?" His tone was so roomy. "How good a friend is he?"

"He is a good friend."

"Did he play you his guitar?"

There was nothing subtle about this; she knew what he meant. She turned to face him, tense and tight-lipped.

"In the summer you told me we should not write so often then you told me you saw Jeanne and could not see me because you are busy. Then you told me about Katya. I felt I was losing you. One day before Christmas I was sick and Skevos brought me some hot soup. He was very kind and sympathetic. He was lonely too. He said he had never met anybody like me, that he was in love with me and wanted to marry me, so I told him all about you and how much I loved you."

"How was the soup?" Martin interrupted. "Was it hot?"

"It is not as you imagine."

"No? How different was it? Did he stay the night?"

She didn't reply.

It's not much fun driving 600 miles to find the great girl you want to see has been enjoying her liberal democratic rights with another guy, no matter how lovely or lonely he is.

"You said to tell you everything, so I did. I trusted you! I was counting on you to be strong!"

"I thought I had lost you."

"And you thought that fucking him would find me?" he cried, exasperated with her. "When was it?"

She hesitated. "Before Christmas."

He'd guessed it. That was when she'd left off the pressed flower in the top right-hand corner of her letters.

"A romance in the snow," he said bitterly.

"It is not a romance."

"No, then what?" he snapped. "A study in a minor feeling? A rush of 'Jingle Bells' that always goes down a treat at Christmas."

He grabbed her and kissed her, burying his tongue in her mouth. Then suddenly she thrust him away so forcefully he nearly fell over a small blue case by the bottom of the bed. "Not like this," she said.

"Then how?" he snapped. "You want me to fetch a bowl of soup and tell you a sad story! I can do that. I can read you the *Iliad*. I can sing an aria from *Traviatta*," he laughed manically. "You like tragedy, don't you?"

"That is not what I want."

"Then what?"

"I want you to look at me so I can see you and not a madman."

"I'm here, look! Can't you see? Feel?" He took her hand and held it to his chest. "That's my mad heart beating for you!"

He embraced her again and this time she responded with equal passion. They tore at each other's clothes until they fell together on the bed, his hand between her legs, his fingers searching for a way to escape. He jammed into her crying out as he came too quickly, his face contorted in blissful agony as she rocked him gently until the pain went off.

They made love through the night with her constantly reassuring him that she didn't know or remember any other touch than his. What she gave to him she couldn't give to another. They exhausted each other until there was no pain. Then, just before the dullness of sleep finally overcame them, she asked him if his father knew where he was. He told her his father thought he was in Brighton.

When he awoke in the morning his mind was soon back on the case of the unfaithful lover. He didn't believe for a moment that his own dancing around in any way justified her soupy night with the Greek; or was it soupy nights? She had wanted them to tell each other everything and he had done just that, but if she thought she could reward his frankness and honesty by betraying him at the first hurdle she was mistaken.

As the sun streamed into the room he watched her sitting with her legs crossed, a cup of coffee in her hand watching him.

She was wearing the white skirt and green jumper and her hair hung down to her shoulders to please him. He thought she looked troubled and guessed it was because of the Greek. He knew she wanted him to have a good time. His trouble was, the only way he could do that now was by seeing her hurt more.

"Are you all right?" he asked stretching his arms.

91

She smiled. "It is a beautiful day to go to Heidelberg."

"It's a beautiful day to go anywhere," he said, with some edge.

"You must get up, darling. It is eight o'clock."

"How many times was it?" he asked slipping his trousers on.

She paused. "Must we discuss this again?"

"This question is important to me," he insisted.

"If you have to know this… it was two times."

"For Christ's sake! I thought you couldn't bear the thought of another man touching you. How do I know you aren't still with him?"

"I finished it weeks ago."

"You expect me to believe that? What if he's lonely after I go back to London? Why didn't you write and tell me? Because you knew I might not come? Is that it? What happened to 'Tell each other everything'?"

Her silence in face of this onslaught only infuriated him more.

"You're too easy," he said, bitterly shaking his head. "At least Katya isn't weak. I didn't realise how different we are," he damned her.

"You are right," she said firmly. "We are different. I do not hate like you, I do not love like you, and I do not forgive like you."

Her passionately controlled swipe infuriated him and made him feel cheap. He didn't want any further exchange of blows. He wanted to knock her out. "I'm going to Nuremberg," he said, blithely.

He was daring her to respond more vigorously. He knew she was hurt but she remained calm and unruffled and showed no sign of a knock-down when she spoke. "I hope she will be at home over Easter."

"She'll be there," he said matching her insouciance. "Do you know how long it takes on the train?"

"About two and a half hours," she said.

"Not too long then," he said, stabbing her with the words.

He was irritated she didn't plead with him to stay, and although he'd caught a glimpse of pain when he first mentioned Nuremberg she now concealed her feelings too well and he wouldn't be satisfied until he saw real misery and devastation scrawled all over her face. Her quiet defiance was harder to stomach than any sharp verbal response.

"I'll aim to be back around ten tonight. Perhaps you could meet me at the station, or shall I come straight to you? If it's too much, I could stay at a hotel."

"I shall be there," she said.

Half an hour later, as they neared the station, Martin was becoming increasingly uneasy. She'd cheated, and cheats deserved to be punished. He'd started off enjoying his revenge, only she was still not responding in a suitably humble, downtrodden way. She was obliging, up to a point, but her head was still held too high. True, she had apologised for not being open with him, but what about the fucking bit? She had not yet asked him to forgive that. Nevertheless, he still thought the odds were pretty good that, before reaching the station, she would beg him to reconsider going to Nuremberg. But she said nothing before they reached the station, and when she finally mentioned Nuremberg she didn't try to discourage him at all. On the contrary, she encouraged him. She said, very agreeably, that he must ask Katya to take him to the International Toy Fair for which Nuremberg was so famous.

"There are lots of beautiful wooden dolls there that you can bend, stand or sit, just as you like," she said. "I am sure for you this will be perfect."

She had said it without sarcasm and without any expression of real regret over what had happened between them, and he wondered if she was glad he was going. *Of course,* he thought, *she knew the Greek would be on hand.*

"Will you still go to Heidelberg?" he said, concealing any trace of concern.

"Why should you care where I go?" she asked. "You did not come here to see me. You came to see someone who is strong, like Katya. Not someone who is weak and who cannot control her feelings better! Well, I am glad you are going to Nuremberg, because you are cruel, jealous, and you are the most selfish boy I have ever met, and I am glad to take you to the station so I can make sure that you find it, and I will be there to meet you when you come back, because I am weak and stupid like a donkey."

At the station she told him to wait in the queue while she checked the train departures. On her return, she had a strange far-away expression on her face as if he'd already left.

"You have just sixteen minutes. The train is leaving from Platform 4," she said as she joined him in the ticket queue.

"Fine."

Martin's brain was a throbbing melee of contradictory thoughts and feelings, all rolling over each other, first one on top, then another; anger with himself, anger with her, and sorrow for both of them. *Love isn't there to make us happy but to help us endure.* So said Hermann Hesse!

He didn't know where it would all end. Worse he was beginning to worry he might find the wrong ending. Meanwhile, his body didn't move from the spot. His feet seemed to have understood something that his brain was only slowly coming around to. Whatever else was going on, he loved this girl, and Nuremberg was in the wrong direction.

"Wait!" he said, as the queue slowly brought them nearer to the ticket office window. Suddenly, he grabbed her arm and pulled her out of the queue, and they watched as it closed up, their places gone forever. Her blue eyes now were pools of hurt and defiance.

"You will miss your train," she said.

"It's going the wrong way," he replied.

Then, very firmly she asked him: "Are you sure, Martin?"

"Only a Jewish idiot would say goodbye now," he said.

Her facial expression no longer far away she smiled and took his arm.

"Now we are both weak, darling," she said.

Hours later they stood on the famous Alte Brucke Bridge in Heidelberg. On the right bank of the Neckar a mountain of green looked down on them. On the other side the old castle ruins.

"Heidelberg is much prettier than Nuremberg," she said.

"And you are much prettier than Katya," he smiled.

"Am I?" she asked, her eyebrows unforgettably arched above a broad smile, teasing him with the question.

"What would you have done if I'd let you buy my ticket?" he asked.

She laughed heartily. "That would have been a disaster! Then I should put you on the train to Berlin, and that is more than two hours. It is six!" she exclaimed.

He smiled. "I don't believe you."

"Believe me, darling. I would do it. Platform 4 is not going to Nuremberg!"

"No!" He looked at her incredulously.

"Of course! I was so furious with you. All you can talk about is *you*, what *you* feel about this, what *you* are going to do about that and where *you* are going. Not once did you ask me what I feel about this crazy idea. You talk to me like I am your servant. Well, this servant has planned for days what we are going to do in Heidelberg, not in Nuremberg!"

A few minutes later they crossed over the old bridge and walked into the Old Town. Now standing outside the Church of the Holy Spirit in the centre of the Marktplatz, she told him the extraordinary story of Pastor Hermann Maas who had been minister there at the time of Hitler.

"It is true, darling, every Sunday he is preaching in the church and every Saturday when the Jewish rabbi has left he is taking the service for the Jewish people in the synagogue. He can speak Hebrew and he is a Zionist. He is taking the service at all the Jewish weddings and funerals. He helped hundreds to escape from the Nazis and go to Palestine. What do you think, Martin? Can you believe this? Isn't it amazing?"

"Can't have been easy being a Jew-lover!"

"He even put a *mezuzah* scroll on his door so all the Jews can know they will be safe in his house. Then the Gestapo arrested him and he is sent to a labour camp. In the end the Americans freed him. After the war he is first German welcomed to Israel."

Martin opened his arms in amazement. "Leni Meister, you win the history prize!"

Leni laughed. "Everybody knows about The Rabbi of Heidelberg."

"Is that what they call him?"

"That is what the Gestapo called him."

"It's an unusual story."

"He was not the only German pastor to do these things. Bonnhoeffer was hanged for plotting to kill Hitler."

They left the church and she took him to Galleria Kaufhof, a department store, where she led him straight to the millinery department. Her eye fell on a floppy white cotton sun hat with a lopsided crown and a dip on one side of the brim.

"Don't you think this one is fantastic?" she said holding it up for him to see.

"Try it on," he said.

She arranged the hat on her head, looking in a mirror and struck a pose like a model. "Do I look chic, darling?" She grinned and stuck out the tip of her tongue. "I can be a model for your factory."

"It's pretty fancy. Do you like it?" he asked.

"I love it," she replied looking at the price tag, "but it is very expensive."

"I'll make you one myself and send it to you. Then when you wear it you will always think of me."

Martin drew a quick sketch of the hat and she smiled and hugged him as he put it in his pocket. "Good as done," he said.

As they walked back to the town centre they passed a gift shop with a soft toy tiger in the window.

"He is beautiful," she said. "I like cats."

Martin instantly told her he didn't like wild animals that were locked up at night and kept behind a shop window all day. Then he went in and bought it.

"Now he's free and he's yours," he said handing it to her.

"Thank you, darling. What shall we call him?" She had no sooner asked herself the question than she came up with the answer. "I shall call him Mr Now because he came to me so quickly."

They sat outside at Max's Bar in the Marktplatz, each with a salad and a coffee. They had seventeen hours before the boys would pick him up to go home. He thought about the hours he'd wasted raging at her.

"What is the matter, darling? You look so angry."

"I am angry. I'm angry with myself, angry for being jealous, cruel and selfish."

"Don't worry, darling, I forgive you."

"You do?"

"Of course, because I know after you are so angry you will change and become quiet and peaceful and be my sweet Martin again."

"It won't last you know. It's in my genes."

She smiled cheekily. "That is all right, darling, I will wait. Only it will be great if next time you can change quicker," she teased with a real snap on the *quicker*.

"And if I can't? What if I take longer?"

"Don't worry, darling. If you are longer I am going to kill you."

"I was only going to Katya to hurt you. Sad, isn't it?" he smiled.

"For me it is only sad your father thinks you are in Brighton."

"It was the only way."

He'd told Leni about Katya because he thought she could take it. He hadn't told his father about Karlsruhe because he knew *he* couldn't.

"Was that what you were thinking about this morning when I woke up?"

"I had a very bad dream. You are standing across from me in a big cemetery. I ran towards you trying to reach you but I couldn't. I called and called your name. It is terrible."

Martin guessed they were Jewish graves and that his father was at the back of it. He knew it was a cry for help but what could he do? He couldn't bring himself to tell her that he didn't have an engineer's know-how to build her a bridge across that particular cemetery.

"Don't worry, darling," she went on. "It is only a dream."

He said nothing. If they were not equal before, they were equal now! Equal in joy and equal in sorrow.

They walked up the hill to the famous castle and wandered around the ruins. From the courtyard they entered the cellar where the largest barrel of wine in the world lay. They looked out over to the town from the Belvedere Terrace. From there they walked into the magnificent garden where the ginkgo biloba tree stood.

She smiled mysteriously as they stood under the tree. Natural history was not really Martin's passion, but he was curious as he watched her reach up and pick off a leaf. She held it in her hand and drew his attention to its flat heart-shape that appeared to be divided into two parts while still

98

remaining one. She told him that when Goethe had been an old man he'd fallen in love with the young wife of a friend, Marianne Willemer, and she with him. They too had visited the garden. He'd been so inspired by the strange shape of the leaf that he'd dedicated a poem to her. In it he'd unified his love of Eastern poetry and culture with his love of poetry and culture of the West.

"Perhaps one day even enemies can come together. What do you think darling?" Her excitement reached a peak. "This leaf could be you and me, German and Jew. Don't you agree?"

She gave Martin the leaf and, as he looked at it, he thought, *She's right. We should be together.* It had never struck him so clearly before.

"I agree," he said stowing it in his wallet for safekeeping. "Do you think they were lovers?"

"Yes, they are lovers I am sure but only in the eyes," she smiled. "But I know once he did kiss her. He is very gallant."

"Not like me then. I don't think I could be so gallant even if I am hundert unt nayntsek," he said with an exaggerated German accent.

She laughed, "That is because you are so selfish, naughty one."

"How did it end?"

"I do not think they met again, but he sent her a poem about the tree with two leaves stuck at the bottom of the page."

Before they left he took a photo of her standing under the tree. Then they meandered past the Goethe monument. They made their way down to the Grotto and stopped by a pond where the sandstone sculpture, *Father Rhine,* reclined on a bed of rock surrounded by a fountain of water. He appeared to be watching them.

"He wants us to make a wish, darling. You must close your eyes."

He watched her close her eyes then glanced at his watch.

It was five o'clock. They'd barely twelve hours left together and then he'd be gone. Martin closed his eyes and wished that he was an engineer. When he opened them she was smiling at him.

"I hope you made your wish, naughty one."

"Yes, I have made my wish. I want you to come back to London with me!"

"Are you crazy?"

"I'm not crazy, I'm serious. I'm not going to send you the hat, I'm going to give it to you. And then I'm going to talk to my father. I should've talked to him months ago. I mean it. I've put this off long enough. I'll find you a place to stay. You said we are meant to be together, well, I believe this too."

"Oh, darling, I really think you do believe this. But what about my job? I'm on duty tomorrow, and the hotel is full! My boss likes me, but I do not think he will let me have a week off at this time."

"There must be other staff he can call on."

"It is im-poss-ible," she said slowly and deliberately, almost to herself.

"But what did we wish for?" he cried. "Remember your dream? Well, it doesn't have to end badly. Maybe we can make it end well! Maybe making it end *well* is how this is meant to be! This is our chance," he insisted. "I love you. Don't you understand?"

"Oh, darling, you make me so happy, but I am afraid when love is so great it must be doomed."

The words were tragic, but hope was in her eyes.

"Why do you always imagine a tragedy with a miserable ending like Werther? I told you I would change the end, didn't I, and I will! Believe me, this story is going to be one where, just when you think everything is lost, right at the very last moment, there's a beautiful ending."

"You really mean it!" she said.

"I mean it."

"Then I will have to tell my boss I am not well."

"You've got to convince him. How do you feel? You look terrible!" he laughed.

She grinned. "Oh, darling, I am going to take time off – for Walter!"

They both laughed and held hands as they made their way back down the hill through the woods and took the train back to Karlsruhe. She left Martin in her room while she went to the hotel to talk to the manager. When she returned she announced, "I'm going to pack!"

"Tomorrow is for us!" he cheered.

CHAPTER 9

Nick and Lionel left Saltzburg that Monday around 1 am but they had a flat tyre on the way and didn't pull up at the hotel in Karlsruhe until four hours later. Leni and Martin were waiting for them.

"Any room for an extra one for London?" Martin asked Nick.

"Always room for a pretty girl," he smiled.

Martin grinned as he loaded the two cases into the boot and joined Leni in the back seat.

"Well, seems like you two had an interesting holiday! What's next then?" asked Lionel who was driving.

"I'm going to make Leni a hat."

"What sort? A little white one with a veil?" Lionel laughed.

"No, it is a big white one to keep the sun out of my eyes so I can see what I want to see," she smiled.

"Trouble with hats like that is what you don't want to see can be just what you need to see."

Martin knew what Lionel was thinking; *great girl but once a Kraut always a Kraut.* "We've seen all we need to see," he said reassuringly squeezing her hand.

"They've had a year to think about it." Nick winked into the rear window. "Take no notice, Leni. You'll look a picture."

Leni had an easy relationship with the two friends and everybody soon settled down for the long journey ahead. They had been travelling barely an hour when they had their second puncture, only this time there was no spare and they were miles from anywhere, save for an old farmhouse about

200 yards away across a field. As they pulled off the autobahn into a lay-by, Nick heaved a resigned sigh: "Something'll turn up."

Lionel, increasingly frustrated, told him that the only way something ever turned up was when someone like him did something about it. Then, taking Leni with him, to act as translator, he made for the farm.

Lionel worked at his father's sweet factory and he was under pressure. They had a fifty-ton order for humbugs and deliveries were due to start the next day. The problem was the new sweet-wrapping machines from Germany hadn't arrived yet, and the twelve sweet-wrapping machines they had were constantly breaking down because of broken bits of boiled sweets jamming up the works. Lionel was due to open up the factory at seven the next morning and take charge. He was the only one who had the knack of freeing the clogged-up machines quickly enough to maintain production. He was determined to be back that night.

The trip to the farm proved fruitless except for the fact they found out the nearest garage was more than ten miles away. Lionel positioned himself at the side of the main road hoping to get a lift to the garage or better still stop a car with a spare tyre that matched. Their luck was in as a few minutes later another Cresta pulled up that was exactly the same model as Nick's.

"Need any help, chaps?" asked the knight in the shining white Cresta.

"Bloody hell! Are we lucky to find you," Lionel said. "We've got a puncture, and we've already used our spare. You don't have one you could loan us do you?"

"Glad to be of help," the knight said.

The tyre was a perfect fit. They followed the knight to the garage, where they managed to buy a new spare and returned him his. By the time they'd sorted everything it was well past 10 am.

They now had less than seven hours left to make it to the Port of Boulogne 300 miles away. That required an average speed of 43 mph. Not impossible, but with some slow-moving farm vehicles, a flock of sheep on a D road and various traffic jams along the way they finally arrived at the docks just in time to see the last ferry pull anchor. The three friends and Leni hurried straight to the ticket office to find out from the girl behind the desk that there were no more boats departing that day.

"That does it!" said Lionel in a state of despair.

"It's not a disaster," Nick reasoned. "We can sleep over and get the first boat tomorrow morning. We'll be back by nine."

"The whole bloody world could be there at nine. I'm expected at seven," Lionel ranted.

"Nothing's impossible!" Martin assured him. "We mustn't lose hope now."

"Who's losing hope?" Lionel exclaimed with his usual sarcasm. "I've got lots of hope. As soon as Nick and I have grabbed a bite, I'm going to come back here and hear you tell us the *Queen Mary*'s docked."

"We haven't eaten or drunk anything for twenty-four hours," Nick sighed.

"You might not notice starvation when you're in love but for your information, we're not in love," Lionel glared.

With that Nick and Lionel disappeared through the swing doors heading for the cafeteria.

Martin, who'd still not given up on miracles, returned to the girl at the ticket desk. "Are you quite sure there's no way at all of getting out of France this evening?"

"I did not say there is *no way*," she replied. "It may be possible to take the plane from Le Touquet. Silver City has an air ferry service there."

"An aeroplane!"

The heavy cloak of fatigue hanging over Martin immediately fell away.

"Call them now," he insisted, *"s'il vous plaît!"*

The girl made a quick phone call and confirmed that the last air ferry was due to leave in thirty-five minutes, at six o'clock. There were still places, but she did not believe that they could possibly make it to Le Touquet in time. It was at least thirty kilometres away. Martin told her to page his two friends immediately.

"They were just bringing the bloody food," Lionel complained. "You'd better have a good reason for this Solomon."

He looked tired and hungry and was dragging his feet, but as soon as Lionel heard about the aeroplane renewed hope recharged him with energy.

"Well, what are we waiting for? Let's go then. We've got a plane to catch!" As the freshest and the fastest driver it was agreed Martin should take the wheel. No sooner had they set off for Le Touquet than the car spluttered to a halt. In their eagerness to reach Boulogne, they hadn't noticed they were out of fuel. Fortunately, they were but a few yards from a Total petrol station! The three passengers pushed the car to the nearest pump while Martin steered, and they filled up.

Once more they set off with Lionel leaning out of the left-hand window barking instructions as to when it was safe to pull out to overtake. They'd barely twenty minutes left on the clock and at least seventeen miles still to cover. They couldn't be sure how long they'd be held up at customs, nor were they assured of a place on the plane. The Bristol super freighter only took three cars but Lionel was intent on their catching that plane no matter what. Martin put his foot down. They were doing a steady 85 mph. He constantly had to brake because of the vehicle in front and oncoming traffic prevented overtaking.

"Solomon, it's a new car!" cried Nick.

Lionel's head popped in and out of the left side window, bellowing like a sergeant major: "Go! Go! Pull back! Stay! Stay!"

Martin responded blindly to every order. It was a hairy drive, but the hairiest moment came when, with about eight miles left to go, he found himself rapidly running out of road as he gained on a huge articulated lorry.

Lionel, his head still hanging out of the window, shouted:

"You've got one chance to get past this bastard, then there's a stream of fast oncoming traffic. Wait! Wait for it! Waaiit! Okay! Go! Go! Go!"

Martin started to pull out fast, but the first oncoming car had accelerated suddenly and was almost on top of them.

"No! No! There's a car! Pull back! Pull baaaaack!" Lionel shouted desperately.

Martin swung back in behind an articulated lorry. He now had two options. He could stay behind the lorry and so lose valuable time – or there was a second option: immediately to Martin's right, there was a field with only a raised mound for a border. A small copse lay ahead at the end of the field. He quickly calculated that if he turned into the field he should be able to get round the lorry on its nearside and pull back onto the road before he hit the trees. His mind fixed, every muscle in his body tense, he gripped the wheel, swinging it right-hand down, flattened his foot on the accelerator and hit the field. The parched brown, furrowed soil was hard through lack of rain. Leni screamed as the car bounced up and down over the ridges of ploughed earth. As Martin pulled level with the lorry the driver leaned out of his open window screaming: *"Putain de fou!"*

Nick moaned: "My car! My car!" But Martin was deaf to all. Then came the second shock. In front of them there wasn't just one articulated vehicle to pass. Unseen by Lionel and Martin, horror of horrors – there was another.

"There are two of them!" Martin yelled.

"Oh, my God!" Lionel gasped. "This is it!"

Once past the second lorry, the trees were now very fast approaching, and as if the situation wasn't dangerous enough, the field, at this point, was edged by an extra high mound of hard earth. The speedometer read 89 mph. The Cresta was going flat out.

Nick cried, "*Shema Yisroel,*" the ancient Hebrew prayer before dying, Lionel sighed "Goodbye world!" and Martin remained silent leaning forward like Stirling Moss over the steering column with one last hope. At the very last moment he swung the car to the left, just avoiding the trees, the car rearing up as it hit the mound before bouncing safely down on the road.

"My God, we've made it!" cried Lionel.

Martin burst into song:

> '*On the road to Mandalay*
> *Where the flying fishes play*
> *And the dawn comes up like thunder*
> *Till the angels hear us pray.'*

"I've never prayed so hard in my life!" Nick said with relief.

The car was now making a cacophony of rattling and squeaking noises. Nick was convinced Martin had killed it. However, the others were all upbeat. There were only four miles to go. They arrived at the airport with two minutes to spare. They passed through passport control, but were told by officials they were too late – the plane was preparing to take off. Lionel now reacted as though his spirit was under the spell of an African witch doctor.

"They can't," he said. "They can't! They can't do that!"

"It's not even six o'clock," Martin cried.

"But the pilot must leave at precisely six o'clock," insisted the official.

"They can't do it," Lionel mumbled, speech almost deserting him. "They can't do it!"

"We've got to stop it," Martin cried – then pointing to Nick who was still mourning his clapped-out car, shouted: "His mother has just died for Christ's sake!"

Nick, miserable, and unshaven, arched his thick black eyebrows and rolled his sad brown eyes, looking as bereft as Bambi as he gazed mournfully at the two officials, opening his arms in a helpless gesture.

Martin turned to Leni in desperation. "Can't you get through to them?"

Leni was no actress, but she was a sucker for tragedy and this was a tragic situation. She jumped out of the car, slamming the door behind her and in a deep Dietrich voice of grief and fury cried:

"*Sa mère est morte! Nous avons conduit cinq cents kilomètres! Sa mere est d'être enterré demain! Vous n'avez aucune pitie? N'avez vous pas de coeur? Alors*, we are going!" Then as though washing her hands of the matter she opened the car door and jumped in, slamming it shut and told Martin to, "Drive!"

Nick, inspired by Leni's performance, now worked himself up into some bizarre hypnotic state of despair and moaned: "*Maman! Maman!*"

The officers were stunned into sympathy. The engines on the plane were firing up. The official quickly waved Martin through. The car raced up to the plane as it started to taxi to the runway. Lionel leapt out of the car and raced onto the tarmac to head it off, flagging it down waving frantically, shouting: "Stop! Stop! His mother has died! Stop! Stop!"

The official, flag in hand, arms extended, chased after Lionel attempting to stop the plane using semaphore. The plane halted. The official spoke to the pilot and explained the sad situation. The mouth of the plane opened and to everyone's relief there was room for just one more car and four passengers.

They were on their way.

CHAPTER 10

First thing the following morning Lionel arrived at his father's sweet factory ready to unblock any misbehaving wrapping machines. Nick, without blaming anyone, shook his head and made up his mind to sell his car. Meanwhile, Martin found Leni temporary accommodation in a bed and breakfast in Belsize Park, near the station.

At the factory, Martin made his first attempt to recreate the hat he and Leni had seen in Heidelberg. He decided not to say anything to his father about her until he had first spoken to his mother. Ellen had arrived in London a few days before he'd left for Karlsruhe. Her husband now had a great job as area troubleshooter for a large discount store group in Memphis, so she'd taken the opportunity to visit her parents in London. Unlike Albert who'd an uncompromising attitude to romantic liaisons between Germans and Jews, Ellen who'd heard all about Leni delighted in taking a contrary view and thought Heidelberg a far more attractive choice than Brighton, where Albert thought Martin had been away. When Martin told her about his crazy drive and that he'd brought Leni back to London with him, she was neither upset nor surprised. When he told her he was thinking of getting married, she immediately invited him round for a chat and told him he should bring Leni too.

On Saturday morning Martin collected Leni from the B & B at Belsize Park and drove round to his grandmother's house in Wembley. On the way, he stopped off to buy a nutty brown bread. A pretty, old lady with dyed black hair wearing a black skirt and white lace blouse met them at the door.

"Oh, Martin, dear, you're here, and you've got the bread. You are a good boy. He never forgets," she said to Leni. "You're German, aren't you? You know we've still got one of your bombs in our garden."

"It's not a bomb, Grandma, it's a piece of shrapnel. And we're all friends now."

"Oh, I do hope so," she said, smiling. "I always liked the Germans before the war. All that beautiful music! Who would've thought it? How do you like being in London, dear?"

"I like it very much. And I'm glad to be here," Leni said with the familiar uptick.

"You don't talk like a German. Not like the ones in the films. Besides, everybody deserves a second chance," his grandmother said decisively like she clearly had somebody else in mind. "Your mummy is in the back garden, dear. I'll tell her you're here and put the kettle on."

A few moments later, Ellen joined them in the glass-roofed conservatory next to the kitchen at the back of the house. Black tape criss-crossed the glass roof, and a couple of buckets had been strategically placed to catch any rainwater that managed to drip through. On one of the sideboards lay some old sheet music and his grandfather's old dice-shaped maracas and wooden xylophones with their 'light bulb' sticks, for a stagey effect when the main lights were switched off. He had been one of the leading society bandleaders of the twenties and thirties, and Martin told Leni, on the way to the house, that he'd written a famous party song at a Soho club during the war. Dance bands had now been superseded by rock 'n' roll and his grandfather's band reduced to one fiddle player, himself playing at a Hungarian restaurant in town which was where he was now.

As she sat across the table, there was nothing of the girl about Ellen. She was strikingly attractive with her high cheekbones, black eyes and pitch-black hair drawn back off

111

her face into a chignon. She looked more elegant and hard than the gypsy he'd described, but when she spoke she was far warmer and more welcoming than Leni had expected. Nevertheless, as she leant forward, there was no disguising it: her voice had a strikingly rough and commanding edge to it.

"Sounds like you two had one hell of a drive to get back here," she said, studying Leni closely. "If that's how my son is going to take care of you, you'd better be prepared for a bumpy ride."

"I do not mind the bumps." Leni smiled.

Martin told his mother he couldn't go on deceiving his father about Leni. He was sick of the lies and the fake stories, and he intended to sort the whole thing out once and for all and tell his father they wanted to get married. He knew it would be a difficult discussion.

"Guess there's a little bit more of me in you than your father would like. You tell that to your father, and there won't be much discussion."

"He'll know what I feel, and I'll know exactly what he thinks."

"Let me tell you something, honey. You don't have to talk to him to find out what he thinks; I can tell you that right now. He'll think this is the biggest mistake of your life, and when you've finished explaining to him all about Germans and Jews, and how much you love her, it won't make the slightest bit of difference. The only thing you're going to find out is exactly how much you really want her, and if that's not one hell of a lot, you'd better forget the whole thing right now."

Martin, who was accustomed to Ellen's usual no-holds-barred approach, gave Leni a reassuring smile, and calmly addressed his mother.

"There's more than one way of dealing with this," he said.

"That's right, there is, but if you think you're going to persuade your father to be Mr Imagination here, you're in for one big surprise. I've known this man since I was fourteen and I'm telling you, he only reads one kind of book and it only has one kind of ending and it's not your kind. He has your story all written out for you in his head, just like he had mine. Well, I decided to write my own, you know that, and he didn't like it so I paid the price, and so will you. You're a good son, Martin, and I don't want to put you two kids off, but this isn't going to be easy."

Then, turning to Leni, "Do you really believe you can't live without him?"

"I shall never live without him because he will always be with me." Leni smiled confidently. "But I would like it much better if I don't have to dream it," she added.

"I suppose you feel the same," his mother said to Martin.

"Exactly."

"Well, I can understand two young people feeling that they can't give each other up," she said, radiating empathy; though she, herself, had told Martin she'd never felt that way about any man. "But I don't know if you two realise just what you're up against here. Have you thought how you're going to live? Don't think you'll be able to carry on at the factory. Even if he let you stay, this isn't going to work! You won't be able to look him in the eye, honey. I saw the pain there when I disappointed him. I know that look. He never wanted me to leave, you know. The judge said he thought we should stay together but the rabbi told him what a man can do and what a woman can do are different. He never gave himself a choice. He's a good man, but he's as predictable and reliable as a Swiss watch, which is fine if you want to know the right time and you can agree where to meet. But it's not so fine if you want to meet him somewhere that's not on his map, and Leni, honey, you may look good, and you may sound good, and maybe I can see what my son sees in you, and maybe you really are the loveliest girl in London but you are nowhere on this man's map, honey. Nowhere!"

"You think I should say nothing?"

"All I'm saying, sweetheart," she warned, "is that you two have a mountain to climb. If you come to the States I'll help you all I can, but you'll have to make your own way. So before you do this, you be sure when you talk to your father that you mean every word you say, otherwise it's not fair to put either him or Leni through this."

"I'm always fair," he said, smiling at his mother's use of the word fair.

Ellen turned to Leni. "Are you happy for him to give up everything he has here? Because whatever you do is not going to be Jewish enough for his father."

"I know what happened to the Jewish people, and I am happy to become Jewish. If Martin's father is not happy with this, only Martin can decide what to do. Whatever he decides I will still love him. And I am glad I can meet at least one parent."

"Nobody can know what another person will accept until they're put to the test," Martin spoke reassuringly.

"There's only one result to this test, honey."

"Then if it doesn't work I'll get a job. I'll open a stall in a market. It was good enough for Marks and Spencer. Or I could work for Nick selling televisions."

"You mean that?"

"Why not?"

Suddenly, the cobra, as Martin had once described her, perhaps prodded by what she perceived to be a flippant response, quickly reared up her head and lashed out in a rasping voice,

"Then you tell him, Big Boy! You forget about your father right now! Leave the factory! Do it! Do it today! And don't look back! Or aren't you ready for that?"

Martin was not to be intimidated. "That's what we're here to find out," he replied.

"Then you go right ahead and find out. You've been driving yourself crazy over her long enough. If you really want to marry her like you say you do then do it. You said you don't need the factory. Well, giving her up isn't something you owe to anybody. It's your life, Martin. You don't have to discuss it and you don't have to *ask* your father. You just have to *tell* him."

His mother had made it all sound so simple, and maybe she was right. Why shouldn't it be? Give up Leni? He didn't owe that to anybody. Not even his father. He didn't agree with her about a lot of things, but she was spot on with this one. As they were driving away he felt fired up and optimistic.

"She's great when she's on your side."

"Yes,"she said, "and your grandmother is very kind."

"She lives in a world of her own."

"She is very pleased you brought her this bread."

"Before the divorce my grandfather threatened to have my father 'duffed up by a couple of heavies' if he didn't stop the case and take my mother back. It was a hollow threat but it didn't help their relationship then and didn't help it afterwards. The only time I remember seeing them was one day on my way home from school. At the top of our street I saw these two old people waving to me from across the road inside an old Wolseley. 'Don't tell your daddy you've seen us,' they said. They missed out on a lot. Whenever I drop round now I take a loaf of nutty brown bread, it's her favourite."

"You have a big heart, Martin."

"He paid more than he needed."

When they stopped at a red traffic light he turned towards her and saw she looked troubled. He began to wonder if Ellen's outburst over his father had undermined her.

"Don't worry about me losing the job at the factory. I told you, there are plenty of things I can do. I can do something with Nick any time I want. There's a lot of money in that game. By the time he's finished he'll have at least a hundred shops."

"Yes, darling, I know you can this and you do not need Nick."

"Then what?"

"It is your father. If your mother ir right about him I think it will be hopeless. He is so important to you. He is the one who brought you up. You must try and talk with him and make him understand. Then one day maybe he will talk with me. Oh, I want to believe you can do this. If only I am not doubting so much. But I am afraid he will not listen to you. Believe me, darling, I want so much to be wrong."

He squeezed her hand tightly. "You are wrong," he said emphatically.

The lights changed, he slipped the car into gear and drove off. They ended up agreeing it was better to have one parent on side than none, and he assured her that one day it would be two.

That Saturday afternoon Martin joined his father for a trip to White Hart Lane to watch Tottenham Hotspur play at home to Manchester United. His father was in good form and when a Man United player fouled a Spurs man and 30,000 supporters stood up shouting: "Foul! He could've broken his leg! Off! Off!" Albert sat stubbornly silent biting into his crisps. But when half an hour later a Spurs man fouled a Manchester player and when the crowd was silent he immediately jumped up furiously waving his bag of crisps bellowing: "Foul! Send him off! What about legs in Manchester? Don't they count?" Then he sat back down again crunching his crisps in satisfaction.

Nobody said anything. They were obviously used to this maverick behaviour. Martin smiled to himself. His father was always a man prepared to stand up for fair play especially when the crowd ganged up on the opposing side. On the way home, even though Spurs lost 2-1, Albert was in excellent spirits and Martin was emboldened.

"I thought you were a Spurs supporter."

"I am."

"Half the time you were cheering Manchester."

"They were the better team. They taught us a lesson. I was showing my appreciation. Don't you appreciate your lessons?"

Martin smiled and encouraged by his father's free and unbiased spirit decided to test the ground.

"Did you know they wear more ladies' hats in Germany than anywhere else on the continent? It was in the *Draper's Record*?"

"Was it?"

"Apparently their economy grew at eight per cent last year. That's four times as much as ours. We could learn a few things from the Germans."

"Why are you so interested in the Germans?"

"I'm just keeping an open mind and thinking of the business."

"There are plenty of teams to learn from. We don't need lessons from the Germans."

"I don't know, Dad. The facts speak for themselves. They're doing all right. All I'm saying is there's a great export market out there. One that we could be tapping into."

Albert didn't argue the point further and seemed more concerned with the amount of traffic on the road. Martin took it as a good sign. The Germans were still on the field. And so were the Jews.

Monday evening at the greyhound track Nick and Lionel were busy studying the form of a dog running in the fourth race called Solomon's Girl. Leni and Nick were chatting together as the dogs paraded in front of them before the race. Nick had called Martin earlier in the day to tell him about this coincidence, and said he was convinced that Solomon's

Girl would win tonight and that Martin must bring Leni to the stadium, so they could all celebrate together afterwards. The dog was a 25 to 1 outsider, so Nick's confidence seemed bizarre. Martin wouldn't normally have been tempted, but there was something in Nick's clairvoyant tone that compelled him to go along. What had he got to lose? Nick was a lucky punter, but a choosy one. He could look at a racing card with eight races on it and still bet only on the one race, with the one dog that took his fancy, and win! This always created a little extra tension because everything would depend on that one race. Lionel was not impressed, and as he looked up from the card at the brindle dog in the black-and-white-striped jacket, with a red number six, he asked Nick how much he'd placed on the mangy-looking hound.

"Twenty quid at 25 to1! Not bad, eh?"

"You must be out of your mind!" Lionel said. "Haven't you noticed it's been raining? Haven't you read this dog's form? She hasn't finished in the first three in her last four races. She doesn't like the wet, and as a fast starter she favours trap one, and not trap six, where she's drawn. Meanwhile, this favourite, Lucky Dancer, in trap three, has won three races on the trot and loves the wet. So where does that leave your tip?"

"I'll tell you where. It leaves me very happy, because if any one of those circumstances were different, it wouldn't be 25 to 1. It would be a lot less."

"Have you had a tip for this dog?" Lionel asked caustically.

"You could put it that way. Look, can I tell you something, Lionel? Most bookies and punters only know one thing and that's the form. That's how they calculate the odds. They study the racing history, the statistics, and all the different conditions; they may even talk to the trainers. These are all logical things to do, but the fact is if statistics and logic were always right, then the favourites would win every time. Outsiders wouldn't get a look in, but they do; and I'll tell you why. Because there's always the day when the best dog doesn't run according to his best form, and for some reason a rank outsider does. That is why, after the race, the punter who put his dosh on the even-money favourite tells you his dog never turned up, while the punter on the outsider collects his winnings because his dog did. The trick is knowing when the outsider is going to perform."

"And you know this dog's going to perform." Lionel grinned sarcastically.

The dogs were whining. There was a roar from the crowd as the mechanical hare passed the traps. The gates went up and the dogs leapt out. The chase was on. Lucky Dancer, the favourite, was first away, with Solomon's Girl last round the first bend, but she gradually started to make ground, coming down the back straight. Then round the last bend the favourite was badly buffeted by the number four with number six, Solomon's Girl, seeming to find a second wind. Down the home straight, Nick suddenly cried out: "Come on, The Girl!" Then Martin, and Leni, joined in crying out for all they were worth: "Come on Girl!" Even Lionel couldn't restrain himself. It really was touch and go between Solomon's Girl, and the number one dog in the red jacket, who suddenly seemed to appear from nowhere to join her, but Nick's luck held, and she finally won by a short head. Cool as a cucumber, Nick turned to Lionel.

"I told you she'd perform."

"What a clever friend you are!" Leni said excitedly and congratulated him with a big kiss.

"All we're waiting for now is Solomon's Boy to turn up, and if he performs anything like Our Girl we'll have a real party," Nick said, glancing at Martin.

They all laughed together. Nick walked over to the bookmaker to collect his winnings and then treated them all to dinner.

But things were not going as well for Solomon's Boy as they'd gone for Solomon's Girl. Martin had been back at the factory for more than a week. The hare had passed his trap again and again, and he still wasn't running. It was one thing talking to his mother or Leni, or even his friends, about his father; it was quite another talking to his father. It began to look as if his moment might never arrive.

At the factory the cotton fabric was in stock, but the cutter's patterns never seemed to be quite right, so whenever the machinists sewed the pieces together for the crown something was always wrong but he didn't know what.

"Are you building a pyramid or making a hat?" his father asked, as Martin, once more, examined a faulty sample.

Martin swallowed hard. "I saw this hat in one of the department stores when I was away. If I could just get the pattern right I know we would sell loads."

"Which store in Brighton was it? They must have a branch in town."

Martin hesitated. It wouldn't be his father's first trip to the West End to buy a hat that he could unpick and copy but Martin knew this hat wasn't from Brighton and wouldn't be in any store in town.

"I'm not sure," he said.

Albert asked him to describe it. Two and a half hours later, after his father had cut his own patterns, machined them together and given the result to the trimmers to finish off, he provided him with a perfect sample. Martin was delighted with the hat. He'd give it to Leni that evening. But when his father asked him on the way home how he could possibly have forgotten the name of the store in Brighton he'd seen the hat; he was silent.

You don't have to discuss it, and you don't have to ask. You just have to tell him. That's what his mother had said. At home after dinner Martin said he had a problem. They sat facing each other, father and son, nothing between them except the white Formica kitchen table and the sniff of a bad dish.

"I didn't go to Brighton, Dad."

"So where did you go? Paris?"

There was a pause then Martin served it raw and fast before it could be sent back. "Karlsruhr – in Germany! Nick and Lionel dropped me off at a hotel where she works and then drove on to Saltzberg. I couldn't tell you because I knew you wouldn't like it." There was no ducking and weaving now, just a quick flurry of blows that weren't meant to hurt but he knew they would. "I went out with other girls, Jewish girls too, but none of them came close to what I felt for her. I tried to end it. We broke up. I wrote to her and told her to go out with other boys. We stopped writing. Then I wrote to her and we agreed to meet. We went to Heidelberg and she saw the hat in Kaufhof and loved it so I promised I would make her one. I wanted to tell you." Albert looked uncomprehending and Martin took a deep breath. "She's the girl I went to Engelberg skiing with last January."

He searched his father's face for some sign of hope but his lips were tight – his expression now grim.

"Is that it?" The tone was sharp and uncompromising.

"Dad, not every German is a Fascist. There was this pastor during the war; he put a *mezuzah* on his front door so every Jew would know there was a safe place to go. He saved thousands of Jews' lives. They called him the Rabbi of Heidelberg. Don't you see she's not the kind of German you imagine? She loves the Sholem Aleichem stories. She wants to convert. We were standing under this tree in a park that has this incredible leaf. It's called a gingko. It looks as if it's made up of two parts but really it's just one. Goethe, he's a famous German writer, wrote this great poem about it. It says how customs that divide people can actually bring them together. Maybe this is how it's meant to be?"

121

When Albert abruptly stood up from the table Martin knew the fight was far from over. It was only round one.

"Don't talk to me about Mr Git! I'm not interested in him! Or his poem! Or his tree! You think because you spent five minutes looking at a tree with a fancy leaf this is *meant to be*! I think you want your brains tested. There's something else that's *meant to be*! This isn't just about you and the girl!"

"Dad, I know this is a problem for you."

"It's not a problem for me," Albert interrupted. "You think the hat's a problem? I'll tell you what a problem is: it's when six million people lose their hats. That's a problem. You don't have a problem. For a Jew it's straightforward. You took a trip to Germany, you met up with a girl, and you had a good time … fine. You said you'd send her a hat, so send her the hat and let her get on with her life and you get on with yours. Next time you want to take a trip? Go to Israel! That's what a Jew does."

His father was sounding like the official spokesman for the entire Jewish people. He hadn't even *registered* the possibility of her converting. He knew what he was afraid of: not only that she was a German, but that she'd be a Reform Jew and never be a member of his Orthodox club where men and women sat separately and the prayers were all in archaic Hebrew. But Leni never did anything by halves and Reform Judaism was not half of anything. It was Judaism reborn. He felt a volcano of frustration rising.

"I won't have to send it to her," he said, standing up. "She's at a guest house in Belsize Park."

Albert's look now hardened into a slab of biblical wrath.

"You brought her back here?"

"She's been here a fortnight."

Martin now saw the Prophet Samuel's sword raised in both hands above King Agag's head just before his execution. God's message: *All the Amalekites to be killed. No mercy for any man, woman or child*. But what if Samuel had got the message wrong? People had been getting the message wrong since time began.

"Dad, it's fifteen years since the war. She knew nothing about the camps. None of her friends did. She was horrified when I told her. She wasn't even four years old. She's as innocent as I am. You can't condemn this generation. It's not their fault. How long do you want to go on with this? They can't bring the dead back. Nobody can!"

His father's stony silence only made him more determined to overcome the terrible impasse.

"I know how you feel but if you'd just meet her!" Martin pleaded. "If you'd just listen and talk to her like a normal person. If you could forget she's a German and forget you're a Jew just for a few minutes I know you'll see what I see!"

"What did you say to me?" His voice was low, his jaw set. "You want me to forget where I come from – forget where she comes from and you know what I feel?"

"Dad…" Martin appealed.

"You're telling me to forget I'm a Jew and you understand that. You don't know what it means to be a Jew!"

Don't ask him – tell him. He couldn't do that. It had never been that way between him and his father. It never could be. "I'm not *telling* you to do anything," he said, his voice trembling as he felt his and Leni's life together slipping away. "All I'm *asking* you to do is give her a couple of minutes."

"For what? To see what you see? Not if every German family called their first child Abraham. You want to know how dead men breathe? Forget her!"

All his life he'd wanted to please his father – to see his warm, embracing smile. Where he stood was a place of safety, a place where no harm could ever befall him and whatever he did was blessed and right now more than anything else in the world he wanted that blessing.

123

"I want to marry her!"

"I'd rather you were dead." The voice was icy.

Martin was stunned. The words hung in the air like a hangman's rope.

He searched his father's eyes for a sign he might be mistaken, but all he saw was the unyielding Prophet. He could barely breathe in the oppressive silence.

"Then I'd better tell her it's over, hadn't I?" he choked.

Did he believe what he'd just said? He didn't know himself. They weren't the adult words of a free man. No warrior he. They were the words of a small boy who'd been sent to his room.

Without glancing at his father Martin picked up the hat from the table, left the room quiet as a ghost and walked out of the house. He sat in the car despising himself and shamed not for just giving in but for not once having referred to Leni by name. He took out his work notebook and angrily wrote down all he remembered of what had passed between them. Then he slammed the car into gear and drove round to Leni, fighting back his tears. The only good thing about all this was he'd at least be able to keep one promise: to give Leni the hat.

CHAPTER 11

London Hospital 16th April 1960, 10pm

My wonderful darling,

    As soon as I woke up I phoned Nick and told him I was in hospital. He said you are trying to contact me. Do not worry I will be all right. I still cannot believe that I fainted in the street. I was so upset about what your father said and so worried about us. Please come and see me soon. I knew immediately you gave me this wonderful hat you had a big problem, even though you tried to hide it from me. When we are in the cafe and you told me this sad story I could not imagine anything so dreadful. How can your father speak these terrible words to you? I cannot even write them. When you told me this news the sky dropped a black curtain and you are on the other side of it. I was so afraid. Then your lovely face peeped through and said that this is not your father's true voice. I hope the next time you speak to him it will be different as you say and one day we are going to be together. Oh, darling, why must people we love be like this? I cannot believe I must once more write to Nick for you to receive this letter. You know, darling, I think I must have written more than two hundred letters. My God, can you imagine what your father will say if he knows this? Isn't life crazy! I did not tell you this, but when Solomon's Girl won this race I even thought, one day, I am going to write a letter to your house again; not to you, darling, but to your father and thank him for being so understanding. What a crazy dreamer I am!

    Kisses

    Leni

P.S. Nick just came to visit me so I am giving him this letter.
He was so sweet. I said sometimes I feel God is against us, and
Nick said sometimes God performs best in bad conditions. He
made me laugh. He talks like God is in one of his races. He
is really quite funny. You are lucky to have so good a friend,
and so am I.

Martin kept the letter, in its NHS long envelope in his inside
jacket pocket. On the third day he visited her he wore a
different jacket. She told him all the tests had proved negative
and they were discharging her the next day.

"Do you know, darling, I am famous? My boss called my
mother looking for me so when I didn't go home she reported
me missing to the police and they told Interpol. Now, for three
days, everybody has been looking. Can you believe it they put
my picture in the newspaper? Isn't it amazing? I am only away
two weeks. I had to promise that I am going home as soon as I
leave the hospital. Please will you book me a ticket?"

"But you told your boss you were sick and he agreed to let
you have this time off."

She smiled. "Yes, darling, I told him I am sick but he did
not give me this time. So I took it."

"You crazy girl. You think that was wise? You could lose
your job!" But he knew she'd never let such caution tamper
with matters of the heart. She'd put her trust in him and risked
all! He was fired up by her spirt. He clenched his fist. *Come
what may they were going to make it!*

As Martin put the key in the lock and entered the house
that night his mind was made up. Then he noticed a light on in
the kitchen, the door ajar. He walked in to see his father sitting
opposite him wearing a *yarmulke*, leaning over the kitchen
table reading a prayer book. Martin hit the brake bracing
himself for the crash. His father looked up and slowly pushed
a letter in a long NHS envelope across the table towards him.

He didn't speak but waited silently for Martin to pick it up. He stared at the letter and reckoned his stepmother must've found it in his other jacket. He looked back up at his father. There was no sign of the Prophet, just a look of a man in deep disappointment and sadness. He knew Martin had lied, knew exactly how deeply he was involved with Leni. He knew about the hundreds of letters. He knew that she was a decent girl in hospital because of her turmoil over her love for his son. He knew all this and Martin knew it could make no difference. He picked up the letter.

"I thought you said it was over," Albert said quietly.

There was no chastisement this time and no accusation of deceit yet through the pain in his father's eyes he saw the demand. It was silent – but still there – and insistent. He'd rather have dealt with the wrath of the Prophet. Antipathy grew and he hated his father – hated him for wearing a *yarmulke* and holding a blackmailer's prayer book. He hated his stepmother for shopping him and doing what she imagined was right. He searched his father's face for some sign of judgement but saw only a man shackled to tradition who could act in no other way. But Martin could – and he would. He'd go into business with Nick, prove he was his own man. He was gripped by a profound sense of injustice. His father's sad green eyes, gentle and knowing, only infuriated him. He glared back – striving to wrestle control. They were locked in a terrible fight eyeball to eyeball. In a last desperate attempt to throw him to the ground Martin thought of slamming the door – walking out of the house and out of his life forever. He saw his father fall – down on his knees, crawling on the ground. He'd won!... But as he stared down at the beaten man he saw the demand still there and the eyes though weary – were still insistent. As he watched him struggle once more to raise himself up pity and shame and an old protective urge everwhelmed him. Martin was a six-year-old child again.

"It is over," Martin said softly, putting the letter in his pocket. "Leni is flying home tomorrow." At least he'd spoken her name. "Goodnight, Dad," he said and trudged heavy-footed upstairs.

At 8.30 am the following morning he collected Leni from the hospital.

"How do you feel?" she asked.

"Better!" he said, with her memorable uptick on the exclamation.

It was a beautiful day and she looked radiant. He'd picked up her small case and the hat from her room at the bed and breakfast place. Shortly after 9 am he pulled up outside a large electrical shop in Soho's red-light district.

Nick stood in the doorway in a suave light-grey pinstripe suit, a cigarette held aloft in his left hand. He smiled as Martin pulled up.

"Solomon, how wonderful to find you here so early in the morning and not on your own, I see!"

Martin wound down his side window. "I'm taking Leni to the airport this afternoon. Is there any chance your upstairs room could be free for an hour or so?" he asked, knowing Nick loved being part of any subterfuge.

"Leni, how are you?" Nick said, leaning through the open car window, his expensive aftershave wafting through. "I knew he didn't come here just to see me."

"I did not know we are coming here at all," she replied warmly.

"So you two have some last-minute business to discuss," he smiled. "Thinking of joining the Common Market, are you? Well, so long as you are all signed up by eleven o'clock, I've sent the secretary off for a couple of hours."

"Nick, you are very sweet," she smiled.

"No, I'm very jealous," he said opening the door for her.

Nick led them past rows of televisions and radios on either

side of the floor to the back stairs. "I'd've given the place a dust up if I'd had more notice you were coming."

They climbed up to the office on the first floor. It was a small room with a desk, a couple of chairs and an old sofa. A window looked out over a strip joint on the other side of the street.

"Have you been here before?" she asked him.

"To the shop – many times. Up here – never."

He walked over to the window and pulled back the half-drawn curtains. A beam of sunlight lit up the room. Across the street, from the window above the strip club, he watched an attractive young girl leaning out wearing a red silk slip. She saw him watching and waved. He closed the curtains and turned back to face Leni but as he did an image of his father stood behind her.

"Is it a very difficult question, darling?" she asked, smiling.

The question was easy. It was the multi-choice answers that were difficult because they were all wrong. Leni still didn't know about the second encounter with his father. She didn't know he'd read her last letter and Martin had told him it was all over between them. Now, if he changed his mind again it would be wrong for his father, and if he didn't it would be wrong for Leni; so he didn't ask himself any question that might be right for tomorrow. He only asked himself the question that was right for now.

"I have a little ache," he said.

He put his hands around her beautifully shaped bottom and pulled her into him pushing his erect penis hard against her. They fell onto the sofa and lived the moment.

Twenty minutes later the sound of an aeroplane roared overhead and he wondered if it was the one landing at Heathrow to collect her.

"I hate planes," he said, "especially the one that's going to take you away from me."

"You are worried about your little ache. Naughty one. But you will soon find someone else to help you with this."

"Not true," he protested.

"Perhaps the girl in the window you were watching," she teased.

"I see girls every day who offer that. I've seen them since I was twelve but I've never experienced an ache like the one I have for you with any girl I've ever known, and I never will."

The clock on the mantelpiece chimed eleven times.

When he'd told his father for the second time that it was over, he'd meant it. But now, as they said goodbye to Nick and drove to the airport, the terrible sense of hurt that he felt at losing her once more quickly overcame any concern he had for his father. Pain can change anybody's mind, and the truth now was he couldn't bear to lose either Leni or his father. His only honest option was to drift for as long as he could and persuade both of them to drift along with him, while he waited for times to change, or for one of them to force a decision. After all, drift was what he was good at. He was driving slowly and must have seemed a little quieter than usual or worried about something, for she suddenly turned to him:

"I know your father is not one to change his mind quickly, but neither am I. And I hope that you are not either."

"At least you have the hat," he said, evading the question.

"And it is even better than the one we saw in Heidelberg. I am sure that you will sell thousands. Perhaps I shall send you another one," she teased.

He could've laughed and agreed and settled into further evasion as he'd planned for his father. But for two weeks now they'd shared the good and the bad and now somewhere deep inside he felt an overwhelming need to bare his soul to her.

"I'm not sure that would be such a great idea," he frowned.

There was an old Ford in front, travelling even slower

than he was but he couldn't overtake it. He couldn't increase his speed.

"You know I don't love you, don't you?" he said.

"I know this, darling. This is because you are a selfish one." She joked.

"I'm serious," he insisted.

She asked him what it was that was troubling him. So he told her about the second encounter with his father, how he'd found her letter.

"He wouldn't talk to you if every German gave their child a Jewish name!"

"Oh, darling, it is so sad but if you want us to finish you must tell me."

As he glanced across at her the little moment of joy that had wrinkled from the sides of her eyes had gone.

"For God's sake, I never want us to finish. But if you stick with me I'm going to let you down."

"No, you will not let me down."

"Don't you see? You'd risk everything for love, but me – steal a weekend in Heidelberg, risk our lives in a car and I'm a warrior, but give me time to think and I go with the crowd."

"No, darling, you go with your father."

"If only you could've stayed," he said wistfully, afraid to let her go.

"Don't worry, maybe one day I can come back to London. When I am twenty-one I shall see if I can get a work permit and get a job in a hotel near you."

Her voice was firm and decisive; she was still not prepared to lose him. He squeezed her hand tightly.

He knew Leni was glad he'd told her the truth, and would've seen this as a gesture of true love. By the time they'd arrived at the airport, parked the car and queued at the check-in, her mood was transformed. She was wearing the hat.

"What do you think, darling? Do I look dishy?" she pouted, posing as she faced him.

"Amazing," he smiled.

Then suddenly she cried: "Oh God, if only everything was not such a bloody mess, and a muddle!"

"Don't worry," he laughed bravely. "Somehow we'll make this bloody muddle work."

Her flight number was called so they kissed and quickly made love with their eyes. "Darling, I think if we are together in a muddle this is much better than a marvellous solution and we are not, don't you agree?"

"I agree," he said, sadly wondering if she would ever come back to London.

"Don't be sad naughty one, we are not saying goodbye. You will hear from me very soon."

They kissed once more then she tore herself away and walked into the departure lounge where he saw a young man offer to help her with her small case. She turned and smiled her wonderfully cheeky smile and waved.

CHAPTER 12

A few days after Leni had left for Germany he received her first letter.

22 April 1960, 8pm

Oh, my darling,

Once more we are apart. I cannot tell you how much I am already missing you. Your face wakes me every morning. It wakes every sky. What am I to do? Sometimes I despair of your father. My mother thinks you will never be able to overcome this and my friends say to continue with this is not reasonable. It is so sad. Sometimes I feel this cold reasonableness will kill me. It is like ice in my heart. If I listen to this then I shall become a shadow of me. Oh, darling, I do not want to be this shadow. If I must be a shadow it is only to you. Then I shall always be near you wherever you are, and my reason is love, love for you. So you see, darling, I do not give up and neither must you. In September I shall write to the British Embassy for a work permit. We must make this bloody muddle work. It is funny when I think of this. I suppose we were always in a muddle but I never thought of it so much till now.

I love you so terribly, and much more.

Kisses, Leni

For a few weeks Martin immersed himself in books on German history, literature and philosophy and studied the differences between *Halacha,* Jewish law, and *Haskala,* Jewish Enlightenment, as expressed in a book of essays by Martin

Buber. But he read nothing that would sway his father and soon as he was treated to a company car it was back to the port of least resistance.

She was tall, dark and pretty. Her name was Julia and she came from Sweden.

"You look Italian?" he said.

"No," she smiled. "Only my mother is Italian. You like Italy?"

"Who doesn't? It is warm and sunny, with beautiful sandy beaches, the people are friendly, and they have great ice cream."

"And in Sweden there is too much snow, we are cold, and not so friendly," she mocked. "But this is not true. In Malmö we, too, have beautiful sandy beaches; we are very friendly, we have great gelato and we have a beautiful forest!"

"Do you? Do you have the ginkgo biloba there?"

"You know this tree?" She seemed pleased.

"It's the oldest tree in the world."

He felt uncomfortable about mentioning the gingko to any other girl than the one he'd discovered it with. Then that Saturday Martin took Julia for a drive to Brighton where they sat on the beach. When she laughed and wiped the white gelati from around his mouth and sucked her fingers Leni slipped into the wings. They went out a few times until one day Nick passed him a letter from Leni. She'd written she was more than two weeks late. He wasn't particularly alarmed. She'd been that late before. Besides, he was getting a lot of sunshine in Malmö that made him forgetful and lazy. When he did write back he told her he was sure it would all work out but to let him know in the next few days if it didn't. Then Nick informed him he was going to New York for a couple of weeks and had left instructions with his new secretary to call him if she got any letters. Ten days later, not having heard, he phoned Nick's office to discover that the dozy girl had mislaid his number and that she'd been hoping he'd call as she had three letters for him put aside. She suggested sending them on, but Martin told her he'd collect them himself.

On his own in the car he opened the first letter.

20th May 1960, 10pm

Darling,

What are you doing tonight? I wish I could be with you. I miss you terribly. Yesterday, I was having coffee with a friend in Strasbourg when I was asked out by a famous actor Jean Marais. Do you know him? He made a film of Jean Cocteau called Beauty and the Beast. It is quite famous, but I was not interested in him at all. I am only thinking of you. Now I am so worried about my period. I did not want to worry you but I really think this time we are unlucky. I am now four weeks late! What shall we do? Please, darling, write soon! I am going to sleep dreaming of you.

Many thousand of sweet kisses and caresses,
Leni

Martin's first reaction was one of shock. Four weeks was a long time. He couldn't remember her being quite so late before. He was furious with the secretary for mislaying his phone number. Leni must've been desperate to hear from him. Now she was asking him what to do. It was obvious she must get some pills to bring her period on immediately. He put the first letter down and tore open the second with his thumb giving himself a paper cut.

Thursday, 26th May 1960, 8pm

Darling,

What is the matter with you? Why do you not write to me? Did you not promise to write every week? Please, this is not very nice of you. Tell me what we should do. I am sure I am going to have a baby. I know it. Now I am five weeks late!

I am so worried, and tomorrow I am going to Baden-Baden to start my new job. Are you out with another girl? Write to me at once at Hotel Muller. You have the address.

Kisses, Leni

He was in a cold sweat. What if she really were pregnant? They wouldn't like that at the hotel. No wonder she was upset and she thought he was out with another girl. Christ, what a mess! What had he put her through? She was again asking him what to do? How could he tell her he'd love to have a baby with her one day, but not just now? As much as he'd like to it was just impossible. Frantically, in trepidation he opened her last letter.

Tuesday, 31ˢᵗ May 1960, 8.30am.

My darling, Martin,

You just don't know what I have been through. You really are not a gentleman. I went to see a young doctor who made a test and said that I am definitely pregnant. I really got a shock. The next day when I still did not hear from you he said he would help me and gave me an injection. Since yesterday I have had such shocking stomach pains you cannot imagine. Then late last night at last I had a very heavy period. It was really terrible. This doctor told me there is even a chance I may not have children again. I cannot tell you how terrible I feel knowing there is the smallest chance of this. I must tell you I will never do anything like this again. What have we lost? This little life of our love that now will never breathe! It really is the most depressing experience of my life. Write soon.

All my love and kisses,

Leni

His head fell back against the headrest; closing his eyes he exhaled heavily. His hand, still holding the letter, flopped to his side slowly dropping it to the floor. She'd gone through the full gamut of emotions on her own and then made the decision for both of them. At first he felt relieved but that didn't last. How she must have anguished over what to do. Suddenly, he was gripped by an intense sense of guilt. He licked the blood oozing from his cut thumb. The days that she'd needed him he'd written himself out of her life and into Julia's. In a rage he disowned every second of his absence and blamed his father for putting Leni in this dreadful place. But how could he blame his father for his own crippled spirit and for not following his heart. He lashed himself with self pity. It was he and he alone who'd put her there. Outside the sky was dark and there was a crack of thunder.

Then he drove home and immediately wrote her a letter of abject apology.

5th June 1960

Dear Leni,

Forgive me for not writing sooner! No, forget me! I am a worm who wriggles away on a rainy day. In my defence, I must tell you Nick was away and the girl in his office was supposed to tell me when I had letters and she didn't. I know this is not a very heroic excuse, and the truth is I should've phoned her to check. Now I am really sorry I did not. At least I should've shared these terrible days with you and you would not have had to go through this on your own. I can't imagine what you must've felt. I really hope you will understand and give worm another chance. Please write to me soon. I do hope you are feeling better now.

All my love,
Martin

It was nearly two weeks before her next letter arrived enclosing a copy of Goethe's gingko poem, with two leaves drawn at the bottom.

For my dear Martin,

In my gardens care and favour
From the East this tree's leaf shows
A secret sense for us to savour
And uplift the one who knows.

Is it but one being single
Which as same itself divides?
Are there two, which chose to mingle
So that each as one now hides?

As the answer to such question
I have found a sense that's true
Is it not my song's suggestion
That I am one and also two?

*How can it be that our lives drift so far apart and now I
must live in time without you? No matter whatever happens
in the future, even if I am one day with someone else I shall
always remember these sweet days. But today I am feeling
much better; the doctor has been very kind.*

Love Leni

Martin was touched by the poem, but her words had the hint
of a goodbye: *How can it be that our lives drift so far apart?* How far
had she drifted? *Even if I am one day with someone else!* One day?
When? Maybe she already had somebody in mind. There was
no sanctuary in Malmö now.

Her letters over the next few weeks became less frequent
and his jealousy grew. The doctor had now become 'a good
friend', so was no longer just *kind*? He wondered how good a

friend. Reason and patience were swept away by a tidal wave of suspicion. You can't abort suspicion.

In his next letter he asked in the most casual way if she was going out with the doctor. When she didn't reply he felt sick. He couldn't concentrate on the simplest task. He needed reassurance so he telephoned her at the Hotel Muller.

"Leni, I need to see you. I'm thinking of flying over for a day. We need to talk."

"If you want this. It... will be wonderful. Let me know when you are coming."

If you want this! What was that about, and there'd been a moment's hesitation before the *will be wonderful*. But how could he blame her?

He booked a Friday night flight to Düsseldorf and told his father he was going to the Turkish Baths in Russell Square with Nick and staying over with him until Sunday morning. His father said nothing as once more a beautiful lie took root between them.

On the way to the airport Nick read Martin his form-card.

"Your trouble is, Martin, you're fast out the trap all right but round the bends you keep looking over your shoulder when really you should be looking straight ahead; let's face it, on current form you don't like heavy going and you're not a great finisher."

But Martin was in a confident mood. It was as if he'd rubbed up against a piece of orange kryptonite and the world had suddenly lost all its complexity. Under the penetration of his new found super–vision there were no bends.

"No bends today, Nick. It's a straight road ahead. I'm going to marry her."

Nick grinned. "And my Bubba's gonna climb Kilimanjaro."

"No, your Bubba's going to tell you to give me a job."

Martin took the night flight from London to Düsseldorf and the following morning the train on to Baden-Baden. The

139

Hotel Muller was just fifteen minutes' walk from the station. As he entered the lobby he saw two elderly American ladies talking together at the reception desk. He stood silently behind them, waiting. Then she suddenly appeared from a back office. Her hair was pinned up and she looked wonderful. She was holding some papers, and the moment she saw him her hands shook so badly she dropped them, and he felt like a magician.

"The concert starts at seven thirty in the Kurhaus, I am sure you will enjoy it," she said to the two ladies, as she retrieved the papers from the floor trying to hold her composure.

"I'm sure we will. Thank you so much for your help. I've always loved Beethoven. He never drips," said the lady with a camera around her neck and she and her companion turned to leave the hotel.

"You crazy man! I didn't think you'd really come," Leni said.

"I like Beethoven too," he grinned.

She asked him to wait a moment and disappeared into an office behind the reception where he heard her talking in German.

"How long are you staying?" she asked him, when she returned.

"I have to leave Baden-Baden by nine o'clock latest."

"Good, I am on duty till four," she said.

"Don't worry about me, I'll find something to do."

She hesitated as if thinking something over then told him that a band was playing in the park that afternoon. She referred him to a popular restaurant nearby and marked other places of interest on a street map.

He had a buttered croissant and a cappuccino at Kaffe Konig, visited Brahms' home, and sat on a hill listening to the band in the afternoon playing Franz Lehar: 'Girls Were Made To Love And Kiss' and 'You Are My Heart's Delight'. He couldn't wait to see her again yet he was uneasy. What was she really thinking when she asked him what time he was leaving? Maybe she was weighing up what she'd have with him at four o'clock, against what she'd have with the doctor at nine. She was doing her sums, and that was fine, but when two people are in love they do their sums together, don't they? He left before the concert had finished.

When they met up at the hotel again she'd changed out of her uniform into a tight grey skirt and matching blouse and seemed much more relaxed. He wondered if that was because she'd satisfactorily rejigged her arrangements with the doctor. Either way, they had barely five hours left and he wanted to be alone with her.

They left the picturesque Old Town and made their way up the steep Florentinerberg, hand in hand. Through the botanical gardens the scent of oranges and lemons wafted around them.

"The castle is not far," she said.

"I'm sorry," he said with a jerk, "about the baby." She didn't reply so he pressed on. "I don't blame you being angry. If only I'd known. I can't imagine what hell you must've gone through. It was Nick's lousy secretary. As soon as I read your last letter I felt sick and confused. Well, I'm not confused now. I want to marry you." She smiled. "I mean it. I love you," he cried, dramatically, as she laughed out loud. "Why are you laughing?"

"Darling, you always mean it."

So that was it; she was no longer taking him seriously. This was far worse than her being upset with him.

"Is it the doctor?" he asked gruffly.

She withdrew her hand. "I do not like to talk about this. Be good, darling, you are not here very long. It is soon five o'clock. We do not have so much time. Look, how beautiful it is," she said pointing out the view over the river. "There is so much for you to see!"

"I'll be good," he said trying not to sound irritated.

141

A bird with deep red plumage and long, narrow black-tipped wings flew overhead. They both looked skyward at the feathered glider.

"Is that an eagle?"

"No, it is a *rote milan*. I think you call it a red kite. They are not unusual here. She can stay up there like that for hours, not using her wings, and turn with just a twist of her little fork tail."

"I didn't know you were interested in ornithology."

"I am interested in nature. After these sad days I saw nothing. Then one morning I looked up in the sky and I saw this beautiful bird. Now I see many things."

He'd always loved the sound of her voice but now he felt a distance.

"What is wrong?" she asked.

He frowned. "I miss the girl who wanted to put me on the train to Berlin."

"I am not so angry any more," she smiled and took his arm.

After a while they came to a narrow path with some steps leading up to the castle. From there they could see the Old Town, the Rhine valley and, in the distance, as far as Strasbourg. She told him all about Baden-Baden, and how Dostoevsky had once lost a lot of money at the casino but Martin was only thinking about the doctor.

They walked down the slope, among the trees. Someone had thrown a rope over a large branch of a chestnut tree for a swing with a small plank of wood for a seat.

"See, darling, we are lucky. Someone has put up a swing for us."

She sat on the swing, crossed her ankles and rocked herself slowly backwards and forwards. He was transfixed. She must've seen him studying her. Every time she swung forward she smiled and he wondered if she knew how much he wanted her. He couldn't speak. He calculated he'd barely two and a half hours left. The good thing was, now they seemed to be in tandem: her waiting, swinging backwards and forwards watching him; him standing there, still, waiting, watching her swing. His eyes followed a line from her ankles upwards, feeding greedily on her shapely legs, then up again as they focused on the small dark triangle that had been formed by the hem of her skirt crossing her thighs. He wanted to reach inside for the grape. He wanted to drink the wine. All this he thought as he walked towards her and stopped short. He didn't think who might walk by. He pulled her off the swing and she fell into his arms. Then he kissed her passionately. She responded. Then suddenly she pushed him away.

"Martin, I can't," she said

"You shouldn't look so beautiful. Can't I tell you what I feel?"

"Yes, you can tell me – only with your eyes."

What was she talking about? Didn't she realise he was big as a bull elephant in must.

"You are not very fair."

"Where did you tell your father you are going today?"

"Now you are very cruel," he said. "I told him I was going to a Turkish bath with Nick."

"Nothing changes." She smiled.

"It can change if you want it to."

"We must go soon," she said softly.

"You don't believe me! Oh, how I hate this *soon*. If I obey it soon you will disappear. I do want to marry you."

"I know you do, darling."

"You think too little of me," he complained.

"No, you think too much of your father and he thinks too little of *me*."

"Will you sit with me?" he said.

He lay with his head on her lap under the shade of the chestnut tree and reached up for her hand.

143

"I don't want to lose you."

"You must marry a nice Jewish girl and then you will not think about this."

"And will you marry the doctor?"

"I told you I do not want to talk about Karl."

He was sure she still loved him but he was convinced Karl had persuaded her to think about love in a different way.

"Then I won't ask," he said. "I'm glad he is a good friend. I mean it. Oh, if only life were not so bewildering. One day I should like to write a book with hundreds of pages all about us."

They lay for a few more minutes under the tree her gently stroking his forehead he still holding her other hand.

"Darling, I think we must go."

"Now?" he groaned.

"You will be late."

"I want to be late," he said, once again trying to pull her towards him.

Just then a young fair-haired girl appeared and sat on the swing watching them.

Leni stood, took his hand and pulled him up.

"You must be practical."

"I hate being practical. I want to take you with me!" he said as he reluctantly stood up. He gripped her by the shoulders. "It is still not too late."

"If we do not go now you will miss your train, and then you will miss your flight, and then Nick will think you are dead, and your father will blame me."

"This arithmetic kills love."

For a moment all her facial muscles seemed taut and her expression, tragic, and he saw an icicle in her heart. In this terrible moment of sadness she'd never looked more beautiful. What was she churning over in her mind?

Then calm and reflective as a very wise person who has

discovered a great truth that is only revealed to someone who has undergone a life-changing experience she spoke.

"No, darling," she said. "Only love can kill love!"

He struggled to understand. Could she mean her love for this doctor had killed their love? It was impossible. Suddenly he knew it as sure as apples grow on trees. It was he who'd killed love. He'd abandoned her. And for so long as his father lived he'd abandon her again and again. He'd let it happen. He'd let their one chance of ever having a child together be destroyed, and he knew they'd never have another.

"*Ich kann höher gehen*," the girl on the swing squealed without a care in the world.

Leni smiled at the little girl. Martin hiding his true face behind a clown's fixed smile cried "Higher!" The girl swung higher, and Leni squeezed his hand before they walked down the hill away from the castle in silence. "You know I don't want to go," he said

When they saw the kite again as she flew away from the town she let out a long high-pitched cry, "ee – oww."

Leni looked up. "How beautiful she is saying goodbye."

"It is easy to do beautiful when you know you can come back tomorrow."

They took the bus back into town and she walked with him to the station. She was quiet on the return journey, and when he told her that her hat had been a big success, and that she'd been right and they had sold thousands, her mind seemed elsewhere. By the time they reached the station and stood at the platform he could restrain himself no longer.

"You're doing your adding up again," he accused her.

"Am I? And what am I adding?" she asked him.

"You are adding up all your plans for tomorrow and the day after and taking me away from them," he said, grimly.

"No, darling, this is not true."

145

"Am I still in your sums?"

"You are always in my sums, every day, even when I get the wrong answers," she smiled.

"And what is the right answer now – me with another girl and you with the doctor? Is that what we must do?"

The train was ready to depart. He still stood with her on the platform. He remembered what she'd written about his not being a gentleman when she'd gone through the abortion, and he took her hand.

"The truth is when you needed me I wasn't there."

He kissed the back of her hand. "This is where a gentleman kisses a lady," he said, bravely, then opening the palm of her hand he kissed it as a bee would a rose and said: "This is where a gentleman does not kiss a lady." Then he kissed her on the mouth passionately and said: "I have not been a very brave Walter."

She held him tight and told him one day he would be a very brave Walter. She was completely sure of this. As he boarded the train she called out to him:

"Take care of you, darling!"

The train raced into darkness. Martin searched his mind for anything at all he might've done differently. If he'd had real faith he'd have been open with his father before he left London. He thought he'd planned for a wedding. Who'd he been kidding? He'd been playing with an idea, that's all; playing in Baden-Baden, and this was the endgame. There'd been no real commitment. She'd known that. He hadn't come for a wedding; he'd come for a funeral. He winced. What did they have left now? What a fool he'd been. In the departure lounge at Düsseldorf Airport he was gripped by the thought that in the best movies this was the moment when the hero suddenly realises what he'd got wrong. He knows exactly what he needs to say and just what she needs to hear. So he turns around and catches the next train back to Baden-Baden, walks

146

into her hotel and tells her sod the Scriptures, he isn't going anywhere without her ever again. He grabbed his bags and stood up, and for a few moments he was paralysed and quite unable to take a step in any direction but the effects of the kryptonite had worn off.

Two hours later, thirty thousand feet up, he was mesmerised by a golden butterfly resting on the wing of the plane, luminous in the darkness. *How could it possibly stay there?* He closed his eyes and remembered, as a child, running around the back garden with a net, catching butterflies and letting them go. When he awoke from this reverie, seconds later the golden wonder had vanished.

CHAPTER 13

Back in London Martin had that old feeling of being buffeted by forces over which he had no control. All the familiar treats, the family business, his nocturnal visits to the Moulin Rouge in a company car, the money in his pocket all wove a 24-carat trap. Then one morning, when he was in the bathroom shaving, he looked in the mirror above the basin and saw an angry young man glaring back at him. *Sycophantic! Phlegmatic! And pusillanimous! You need to straighten up, boychick! Whose life is it anyway, his or yours? You need to think for yourself! You're too cosy! You've been too cosy for years! You don't need a pillow! You need a hard place!*

Martin decided there and then that what he needed to do was clean his teeth on a kibbutz. It was an instinctive pull. Somehow, once there, he'd find the answers. He knew his father wouldn't object. After all, he'd told him to go to Israel. Besides, anywhere there was hard work, chopped liver and the natives spoke Hebrew was a step in the right direction; and if this helped him find a more philosophical way of handling the loss of Leni, so much the better. On his last night in London, as the first stage of his quest, he went to the cinema to see *Exodus*, the story of Holocaust survivors trying to enter Israel by facing down the British naval patrols.

On the day of his departure, with his savings in his pocket, Martin took the Channel ferry, then boarded a train bound for Marseilles. Once there he would book his passage to Haifa on the newly commissioned French ship, the 8000-tonne liner *Moledet*. He'd heard about her in London and was looking forward to a luxury voyage. Arriving at the docks the following evening he soon saw her shining white hull moored next to another much older ship, the *Flaminia*. Next to the *Moledet*, the *Flaminia* looked like a barge and he would've passed it up if he hadn't noticed two people standing around talking together. The man looked to be in his early thirties. He was of medium height, had short, brown wavy hair and flint-grey eyes, and a close, sculpted beard followed his jawline and covered his upper lip. The girl, who looked to be about Martin's age, was tall, and, though not obviously beautiful, was attractive and captured his attention. She wore dark glasses and a red triangular scarf had been pulled over her short black hair and tied at the back; plain red cotton slacks and a man's khaki shirt hid her boyish figure. She wore sneakers and a guitar was slung casually across her back. In fact, everything about her seemed casual except for her steady gaze and the proud way she stood that made her look as statuesque and aloof as Garbo.

Martin was curious and wondered if they were a couple. He asked if they spoke English, and when they said they did, he asked if they were going to Israel on the *Moledet*. The man, who introduced himself as Arik, was courteous and direct but his gaze was disarmingly lofty, as if he were someone who knew everything and was picky about the little he gave away. He told Martin, in a detached French accent, that he and Tamar had managed to get booked on the *Flaminia*.

Martin took another look at the old freighter.

"I was going on the *Moledet*," he said.

Arik shrugged. "It is a beautiful ship, and I'm sure you will have a very comfortable journey."

"What made you decide on the *Flaminia*?"

"To cross on the *Moledet* it is fifty-five dollars. On the *Flaminia* it is eight dollars."

"That's quite a saving."

"You share a cabin with six or seven other passengers."

149

"It doesn't sound the most comfortable journey," Martin said.

Arik's smile was as friendly as a crack in a glacier. "If you want to be comfortable there are two boats travelling to Haifa: one carries several hundred tourists who will dine well, and sleep well, take excellent pictures with their cameras and do Israel in a week. If you take this boat you will have excellent service and know what it is to be a good tourist. The other boat carries 500 Rumanian refugees who have nothing. Take this and you will not be so comfortable but you will know what it is to be another kind of Jew."

There was something about his take-it-or-leave-it tone that attracted Martin as much as it unsettled him. Meanwhile, it was absurd to suggest that the only way he could understand what it meant to be this other kind of Jew was to travel on a refugee ship. He'd seen a film.

"I've got a good idea what it is to be a refugee on a boat to Israel," Martin replied. "I saw *Exodus* a couple of nights ago. It gave a pretty unforgettable account."

Arik swooped down like a hawk. "In any film all that you see is with a director's eyes. What is unforgettable are the pictures you take with your own eyes, the smell that you smell with your own nose, and sounds that you hear with your own ears. These become the unforgettable memories. The ones you keep."

It was clear from Arik's tone that he didn't view Martin's cinematic experience of *Exodus* as the ultimate experience of Jewish suffering. Martin asked him about the refugees, and he explained that at the end of the war there were 350,000 Jewish survivors living in Rumania. They were having a hard time but the Communists wouldn't let them leave. Fortunately for the Jews the Rumanians needed dollars, so they offered to sell *a goodbye* for 5000 dollars a head.

"They've emptied their pockets to get here and the Jewish Agency has chartered this ship to take them on to Israel."

Martin was curious about the refugees and he was curious about Arik. The girl hadn't spoken. She'd just stood watching them throughout, like somebody studying a game of chess, and he wanted to know more about her too. When she did speak her question was lazy and she didn't sound overly interested.

"Why Israel?"

He was about to say he was going to a kibbutz to pick oranges and grapefruit because he wanted to know what they tasted like straight off the tree but he thought it might sound flippant when he wanted to win her full attention.

"I'm doing research on a novel."

Arik raised an eyebrow but Martin had the response he'd hoped for. He picked up his Samsonite suitcase.

"See you on the boat," Martin said, as he strolled off to buy his ticket.

It was the way she'd cocked her head slightly to one side and offered him a lazy half-smile that seemed like a lazy invitation to be friends. He guessed he'd made an impression. Although a number of ideas for a book or play had certainly crossed his mind, none had ever stopped long enough for him to write the first sentence of anything. But the moment he'd heard the word *refugee* he'd had an idea, but it was no more than that.

Once he'd settled into his cabin, on the lowest deck, with six circus troop companions who only spoke Hebrew, he quickly escaped the chatter and the smell of fuel to seek out his new-found friends. He learnt that Arik was an Israeli film director born and educated in France. He'd worked with Louis Malle, a director of the French New Wave, and had just accepted an offer to direct a film to be made in Israel. Tamar was an actress who'd had her first starring part in a new film that was being released the very week they were to arrive in Haifa. She'd been living in Paris for the last nine months, playing guitar and singing at various clubs. It was there, at one of these clubs, that she'd met Arik. Were they a couple? It was far from clear. She was quite as inscrutable as he, and her attention to the two men seemed equal and nonaligned. It was not until the second day at sea that all three put down their markers. The conversation began in the bar on the upper deck. They were sitting on bright orange upholstered chairs with a nondescript white rectangular Formica table between them. Three long glasses of Evian were waiting to be downed. Tamar asked Martin what his book was about.

"It is about a refugee, only he's not running away from the bad times. He's running from the good times," he said confidently. Martin had been rather pleased with his answer it being completely off the cuff and having given hardly any thought to the story.

"Interesting – a paradox – the best enemy." Arik nodded approvingly. He settled back in his chair, his fingers intertwined across his chest. "But how did this refugee find himself in this situation?"

Martin, now perched on the edge of his chair, had an overwhelming urge to impress this sophisticated, arrogant film director.

"It is about two young people in love, only one of them has to fight against the customs and prejudice of his family. After a great battle he is injured and goes into hiding. When he returns his lover is gone, she has run away with a doctor. Depressed because he's lost the girl he loves he leaves the comfort of home and the family business to go on a journey in search of answers. That's the general idea." Martin leant back in his chair with a self-satisfied look, thinking *end of story. As if that skimpy outline was going to satisfy anyone with half a brain!*

"Why is he so certain that he has lost this girl?" Arik said pressing him further.

"It seems to him the outcome is inevitable," Martin insisted.

He flinched under Arik's intense gaze as he scrupulously began to unwrap a parcel within a parcel.

"So your refugee is on the run because he sees no alternative?"

"Isn't that how it usually is with refugees?"

"Yes, I am sure it is how it is with most of those who are on this ship. But is this the same for your refugee? Maybe he is mistaken. Look!" Arik now opened a paper serviette on the table. He then drew a large circle on it with his pen, and said, "This cake is all the love in the world this girl has to give to your refugee." Then he looked at Martin and said, "That is what she gives him but his family do not like this cake. They do not like the taste. She does not know what to do." Arik shrugged and drew a line that cut off five per cent of the circle. "This little piece she gives away to the doctor. That is what your refugee has lost. The big piece she still keeps for him. If he does not take it perhaps one day it will grow smaller. But wait, perhaps this story is not inevitable at all. It is a mystery. This refugee is wearing smart shoes! His hair is tidy! He has money in his pocket. This is not someone who has suffered a big loss. He is not someone who has been driven out of his home! He is someone with choices. He is free to travel anywhere. He can go home – he can go on. Why should anyone care for him? He still dreams of this girl but he can save her! He can save himself! Something is wrong." Arik put his finger to his temple, calculating. "He is not a refugee at all! He is a phony!" Arik's voice had risen softly in an unmistakable note of triumph. He pierced Martin with his steely grey eyes. "It is your story, Martin, and this man can be whatever you want him to be. But perhaps it will be better if he knows the true reason he runs away is because he is afraid to pay the price for his ticket!"

"It's an interesting idea," Martin said, trying to recover from the onslaught. "It could be some facet of his character

153

that's let him down – self-deception you think? Perhaps you're right."

It was scary the way Arik read Martin so well. He glanced down at his smart leather, tassled slip-ons, and self-consciously ran his fingers through his hair. Suddenly he began to wish he'd never mentioned his idea for a book. "I will have to find out more about this man," Martin said, struggling to muster his remaining crumbs of self-belief. "There may be some things he's not aware of until later in the story. Love can be a bastard, but I suppose if it wasn't there'd be no *Anna Karenina,* and no *Madame Bovary*. It's not easy to let go of a dream."

Arik took a soft packet of Camel cigarettes from his jeans pocket and gently tapped it on the table until one started to fall out. His delicate, sunburnt hand pulled out a box of matches and struck one. Then cupping his hands he lit the waiting cigarette between his lips.

"If you are calm you can let go of whatever you want. One year ago I was making a film. My wife was on vacation and met a friend. He is a composer and she likes to sing. There was a moment on a lake – a spark – they became close. An arrangement was made – they met back in Paris and became lovers. It is not something they are looking for. It happened. Three months later this friend fell out of love and my wife came home. Now it is over. For three months I lost a little love. Now I have it back."

"Amazing but how will you ever be able to trust her again?"

"Why must I trust her again when I did not stop trusting her before? She is a passionate woman. She is in love. What happened to her could happen to me."

He had spoken in a cool and detached manner and Martin had never met anyone quite so free of resentment. He wondered what Arik would make of his father's attitude to his mother's one-night fling during the war. Clearly marriage for

Arik was not sacrosanct. So long as people had strong feelings he seemed to be saying it was perfectly all right to have a *liaison dangereuse*.

"Well, I suppose there's a difference between serious music and rock'n' roll."

Tamar, who'd been silent throughout the conversation, now engaged Martin. "Why do you make this difference? Nine months ago I am at a party. I met a man. We went out for six months. He knows more about art, literature and philosophy than anybody I have met. He is my life. I am his. I do not want it to end. Then one day he tells me a story about a little girl who is crying in the park because she lost her doll. A man runs to her and tells her not to worry – he knows where her doll is and has a letter for her and if she comes to the park tomorrow he will bring it. The next morning he reads from the letter even though the doll loves her very much she wanted new adventures. For the next three weeks this man reads letters telling the little girl about her new family, her new school and her new friends. Then when he wants to end the story he tells her he has wonderful news – the doll has met a young man. They are to be married and are going to live in a beautiful house in the country. The little girl is very happy to hear this." Tamar casually sipped her water. "The day after he told me this story my *grand amour* is gone."

She didn't enlarge and Martin was intrigued. He wondered: *was her lover a married man who'd gone back to his wife or was he dead*. "That can't've been easy," he said sympathetically.

She shrugged, "A few days later I went to a club and I danced with a man from Casablanca. After, I went back to his place. I stayed for one night. We did not speak. In the morning I left. I do not know his name! He is not my *grand amour;* he is my dancer but on this day I like this music too."

Arik smiled. "Beautiful."

Up until now Martin had been enjoying their discussion.

He'd begun to think of the three of them as the Three Musketeers: *All for one and one for all!*' Now he wanted to ask her more about her lover but at this point Arik began speaking to Tamar in Hebrew. At first Martin was pretty cool about it, and he might've stayed cool if it had lasted a few minutes, but it didn't. It went on for a good quarter of an hour! That's a long time when you're three people around the table and one of them doesn't speak the language and you've spent the last two and a half hours speaking English. Arik did most of the talking but he didn't look across at Martin once. Had he suddenly become invisible? He felt as isolated and forgotten as Dreyfus on Devil's Island. Was this Arik's way of saying goodbye? He thought briefly of saying hello, but he didn't want to appear needy. Then came a split second when Tamar glanced over at him, just a quick flash of her eyes – that's all it was and it was gone. What was she saying? Or was she just checking to see if he could swim?

"I'm going on deck to see the sunset," he said, pushing his chair back with a loud scrape.

He watched the orange sun go down behind the horizon and listened to the gentle slap of the waves against the bow of the ship. Thoughts of the cake drawn on the serviette consumed him. Arik had called him a phony. Maybe he'd a better case than he knew. Only a month ago he'd written to Leni telling her how much he still loved her and wanted her when he knew very well she was trying to build a new relationship with the doctor. There was something else in the story Arik didn't know. He didn't know that in her answering letter she'd told Martin she'd been offered a job with Volkswagen in America and asked what he thought about it. It was clear, however much she loved the doctor, he was still on her mind. It was a test, wasn't it? She'd needed to know if she went, would he follow. And what did he do? He took a ship to Haifa.

He shivered in the cool night air. He wasn't exactly cold – just out in the cold. When he'd left the table to go out on deck neither of the Israelis had reacted. For Arik he, Martin, wan't a person, he was a plaything that'd just been kicked out of play. How he missed Leni. However far apart, he knew they both lived in each other's heads and if one day he too were to marry someone else she'd still be there with him each step he took. Every time he heard the words *German* or *Beethoven* she'd be there, not as as an old snapshot but animate with potential, waiting always for him to come to her once more. How he wished she were there on the ship now and that she would suddenly walk up, put her arms around him and say in her deep, sexy voice: 'Hello, darling', and they would travel on to Israel together.

"Is it very complicated?"

He hadn't heard Tamar approach and was surprised to find her now standing next to him.

"I'm not much good at Hebrew," he said.

"I know," she said, smiling.

"Arik knew it too."

"You do not like him, do you?"

"He's a very interesting guy. It's just – well, maybe I'm one of those who needs extra lessons. Look, I know he was amazing over that business with his wife and that friend of his. He's very clever and generous and somehow he manages to make everything seem so simple – but maybe he just doesn't care about anybody or anything enough to really worry about it."

"You think he does not care?"

"I think he does what suits him."

"If he is a man like this he will take this job in Israel."

"I thought he had taken it," Martin said surprised.

"There is another director working on this film. The producers want to stop him. But Arik will only take it if they keep this other man too."

"If the first man isn't up to it why should two men have to be paid?"

"Because he needs this job as well."

"And if they don't agree?"

"Arik will return to Paris. When we arrive in Tel Aviv I am going to see my agent and he is going to see the producers. He will know then."

Martin knew Arik wanted to do this film and couldn't believe he'd risk the job by insisting they keep on the other director who obviously wasn't up to it. It seemed ludicrous yet he couldn't help admiring him for his absurd moral stance. Suddenly, his little personal problem felt less significant. As he looked at Tamar she was smiling at him as if she knew something he didn't. He was beguiled.

"If you loved each other so much why did this man leave you?"

She shrugged. "Why did you leave your girlfriend?"

"She left me."

"Did she?"

She didn't wait for his answer but said, "*Leila tov*" and went to her cabin.

When Martin returned to his cabin all the clowns were asleep. He lay down on his uncomfortable bunk, still fully dressed, thinking about Tamar and the little girl who lost her doll in the park.

The last night on the ship, Tamar gave an impromptu concert. Hundreds of refugees, with their children, had crowded together at the stern. She strummed away under the stars and everyone joined in the folk songs where they could. He was captivated. Then she led her flock in 'Hatikva'. They followed her boldly as only those can who have lost everything and know that unlike Moses, in the morning they will take their first step onto their own long-promised homeland. When the boat finally docked at Haifa he watched from the deck as the refugees disembarked. Many knelt and kissed the ground, just as they had in *Exodus*; only this wasn't a film. He could see them, smell them and hear them. As they wept he thought of his Russian grandparents and a people wandering from place to place throughout the centuries, caravans of carts laden with worldly goods – children clutching their favourite toy and far into the distance at the end of a long line a young man with a Samsonite suitcase and smart shoes and he swallowed hard.

Once on shore, he knew Tamar was going straight on to Tel Aviv with Arik, but the closer it came to a goodbye the more uptight he felt.

"Well, it's Haifa for me," he said.

If he'd imagined, that in these last minutes, she'd show the slightest disappointment that he wasn't travelling on with them, he was mistaken.

Tamar smiled encouragingly. "It's a beautiful city. You must see the German Colony, Elijah's Cave and the Bahia Gardens," she instructed him.

"Good luck with your writing," Arik said firmly.

"Shalom," Martin said as he shook their hands in turn and determined to leave like a soldier on the way to the Front.

Arik glanced at Tamar. "It is time for me to go," he said, and he left.

Martin waited for Tamar to leave too, but she didn't.

"Let's go," she said.

"Go? I thought you were going to Tel Aviv with Arik," he said, astonished.

"Tomorrow," she smiled, giving him no further explanation.

"But, but, what about your agent?"

She shrugged. "He will wait. I know a very reasonable price hotel. It is not far."

She swung her guitar across her back, they picked up their cases and made their way to the bus station. She was taking over.

Martin couldn't believe his good fortune. They would be

having dinner together, alone, in Haifa, without the masterful Arik; just the two of them. Who knew what might happen after that! She'd taken her pick. He was so excited by this sudden turnaround that he had to force himself not to grin stupidly like Bob Hope in *Road to Morocco*.

They boarded a bus with a Jewish bus driver, carrying Jewish passengers reading newspapers in Hebrew. He began to feel at home as he saw young Jewish boys and girls laughing in the street.

"It's my first time on a Jewish bus. I'm living a Jewish dream."

"You are a tourist in a Jewish dream," she corrected him. "An English tourist; this year you support Israel, next year France, Italy, or maybe Spain."

He felt like he'd got another poor mark at school. "Jews in England do not support Spain the way they do Israel," he reminded her.

"Yes, of course you send us your money and you share our history but you do not make it. The skin on your feet is soft."

"And yours is hard and sore?"

"My brother died in Sinai in 1956."

She did not sound proud or bitter or even disappointed and he did not feel she was judging him but he saw her hurt and he felt guilty and could not look her in the eye. "No, we do not give the same way," he agreed.

As the bus turned a corner and her body shifted towards him, her thigh rubbed briefly against his. He felt a sudden urge to put his hand on her lovely Israeli knee, and stroke her lovely Israeli leg, all the way down to her ankle and up again. The bus stopped and a handsome Adonis stepped on. He greeted her warmly with a kiss and engaged her animatedly in Hebrew. Martin guessed it was something to do with the Eichmann trial then in full swing, because 'Eichmann' was one of the few words he understood.

"Next stop is for us," she told him.

"*Tov, beseder,*" Martin said.

They rose and bid her friend *Shalom*, leaving the bus at the corner of Hertzl and Balfour. Then they stopped at a stall where an elderly, toothless Arab sold them slices of juicy red watermelon.

"Do you think there will be peace here one day?"

"When we can agree what we cannot have then maybe one day we can visit the Western Wall and the Old City again, and maybe one day they will come from Cairo to visit us in Tel Aviv with their cameras and their shopping bags, and not with their guns."

They walked past a falafel stall, and a few minutes later she led him into the foyer of an anonymous plain white concrete four-storey hotel. She spoke to the man behind the desk and then asked Martin how many nights he was staying in Haifa.

"Two," he said.

"Do you have fifteen dollars?"

He gave her the money thinking how reasonable the price was for a single room and filled in the register. The man gave her a key. A single key! He hadn't seen her pay for a room for herself.

My God! he thought. *We're going to be sharing a room!*

She led him up three flights of stairs, put the key in the lock and opened the door. Five minutes later she was in the shower, and five minutes after that she was out. Two minutes later he was in the shower, and fifteen minutes after that he was still there. She hadn't even discussed sharing a room. It was supposed to be 'me Tarzan, you Jane'. He thought he knew a few things about girls, but right now he felt like a novice. He wished they hadn't had that conversation about rock 'n' roll. Now, when he wanted to rock, he couldn't.

"Is the shower all right?" she called from the bedroom.

"Great! Great!" he called back as enthusiastically and as boldly as he could.

161

This was just not how he'd imagined it. It was crazy; six strides away lay this fascinating, beguiling creature, probably sprawled naked on the bed, and his cock was still drooping like a flag on a still day. This was a totally new experience for him. She wasn't looking for *Sturm und Drang*. She didn't want to open a hurt and happy account! She just wanted them to screw each other senseless. And what was wrong with that. The water continued to pour over his shoulders. Why not let her enjoy what they both wanted? But after all that'd passed between them, she had to know he was a serious person and not just a rock 'n' roller. He didn't want to be just another number on her list. He wanted to be a man on her mind.

When he finally came out of the shower it was all of fifteen minutes later. It felt longer. He slowly dried off, wrapped the towel around his waist and walked into the bedroom. She was lying under a single sheet, and the outline of her breasts and legs stirred him, yet he was still hesitant. If only he could leave the moral philosophy to the Scriptures, and pack up this daft idea of setting himself up as a moralist and just settle down to being a grateful immoralist.

"I thought you are writing your book."

"I lost the soap," he explained.

"Oh," she smiled.

He saw her watching him as he slowly closed the shutters, turned off the light, threw off the towel and got into the bed next to her. He lay flat on his back still feeling troubled. What was the matter with him? Why should he feel troubled over having sex with a girl who'd probably had a hundred lovers? What difference could one more possibly make? Besides, if he didn't she'd probably think he was an idiot. Well, if she did so be it; Arik wasn't the only one with principles.

"You think too much," she said, as she leant over and kissed him firmly on the mouth. He felt her naked breasts brush against his chest. Her tongue snaked into his ear driving him wild. Her fingers ran up and down his trunk. The torture was exquisite. It was amazing how quickly he forgot about his troubles. In seconds he had the principles of a slug. The moment she touched home his cock shot up like a flag stiff in a breeze. Before he could say *Hatikvah*, she had grabbed his buttocks and was pulling him deeper inside her and he was happily slugging away until the early hours of the morning.

When he awoke she was gone. For a moment he wondered if she'd really been there and if he were really in Haifa. Then he winced as he remembered his tortured mental gymnastics in the shower. She'd been there all right. He opened the shutters and listened to the chatter of Hebrew in the street below. He wondered if she'd just gone down for breakfast, but her guitar and backpack had both gone with her. Then he saw her note lying on the chair.

He smiled to himself. It was typically brief and no mention of their night together. *Casit... café... Dizengoff... Tel Aviv. Tuesday 7pm... TAMAR.* That was the scribble. No *Great night! Look forward to seeing you!* Or even *Have a good day!* But reading between the words he must've done all right. At least he knew he wasn't a one-night-stand! After a jerky start, he'd left his mark. They were meeting up again tomorrow!

He ran his fingers through his hair and examined himself in the bathroom mirror. He was doing okay. Normally having a girl this easily was off-putting. He missed the chase. But Tamar was different; this wan't just a slug with a pretty girl who'd turned him on. She was a free spirit. She knew what she was doing. This could be a lot more than that. For a few hours she'd actually chased Leni out of his mind. Maybe that was why she'd gone to bed with him, to help him say goodbye to his doll. Maybe that was part of the reason he'd gone with her. Then he heard Leni's voice in his ear whispering '*Naughty one!*' and everything *w*as back to normal.

After breakfast he spent the morning walking around Haifa and early in the afternoon entered the splendid Bahai Gardens that looked down over the German Colony. Then, turning around, he noticed an interesting-looking thickset man, sitting on a bench reading a book.

"Excuse me, do you speak English?" Martin asked, hoping to strike up a conversation.

The man looked up. "What do you want to know? I can tell you in five languages," he said abrasively, with a Mancunian accent.

"I see you're an admirer of Buber," Martin said, pointing at the book the man was reading.

"Martin Buber's a traitor."

"But you're reading his book."

"I read Hitler. It doesn't mean he's a sweetheart. You like Buber?"

"I've heard he's a wise man."

"You're not alone. A lot of young people in this country; every time they scratch their heads they want to knock on his door. Me, I'm not in that camp."

"You mean he lives in Israel?"

"In Jerusalem, in Talbieh. Why? You have a problem? Believe me, if you have I can help you better."

"Why are you so against him?"

"I told you. He's a traitor."

"But you didn't tell me why."

"When did you get off the boat?"

"I arrived yesterday, on the *Flaminia*."

"With the refugees? Good. I'll tell you why he's a traitor. Since the War of Independence hundreds of thousands of Arabs have fled this land, and hundreds of thousands of Jews have fled the Arab lands. But at least we take care of our own. They always have a home to go to. Six months ago the United Nations proposed that the Arab refugees should be offered

164

compensation and resettlement: if they weren't happy with this they should be offered the right of return. Ben Gurion threw out the proposal for return, but Buber supported it!"

"Was that really so unreasonable?"

"Unreasonable? If you're an Arab, it's wonderful. Another fifty years and there'll be three times more Arabs than Jews, Sharia Law, and a monument to Nasser outside the Knesset, and those Jews who survive this blessing will be the same second-class citizens here that they are in all the other Arab countries. It's amazing, since partition, every time they go to war and lose they want back what they lost. What land did we ever get back these last 2000 years? How many houses? Who looked out for us when we were in camps? We moved on. We had to. What about our payback from the Arabs in Libya, Tunisia, Algeria and Iraq, and Egypt? Meanwhile, Buber thinks we can do a deal with them and all live together in a bi-national state. Well, if everybody thought like Buber it might work, but the way I see it, in the world I live in, there's a shortage of Bubers and it's not going to change any time soon. I know the Arabs. They don't want a bit of this or that, they want the lot. What can you do with a genius like this? That's how screwed up you can get if your mother walks out on you when you're three years old."

Wow, Martin thought. It seemed he and Buber had more in common than he knew.

"What are you doing in Israel?"

"Tomorrow I'm going to Tel Aviv then I'm going to work on a kibbutz."

"Which one?"

"I don't know yet. I haven't decided, but I hope an English-speaking one."

"So, go to Kfar Hanassi. I have a cousin there, Shmuel Liebewitz. He'll show you the ropes. You take the bus to Tiberius. It's thirty-five kilometres from the lake. Ask anybody.

You'll find it in no time. Just say Yossi sent you. Here, this is my card. If you need a cab sometime, give me a call."

"Thanks," Martin said, looking at the handwritten card.

"By the way, what did you want to ask Buber?"

"I wanted to know if he had a cure for prejudice."

"You're wasting your time. We enjoy it too much. You may as well ask a monkey to stop scratching his armpits."

"I'll remember that," Martin grinned. Then putting the card in his pocket he left Yossi from Manchester to his book and walked on down towards the German Colony chuckling as he remembered again his dillydallying in the shower. How Leni would've laughed and he could hear her saying *Naughty one!*

The following afternoon Martin took the bus to Tel Aviv, checked into a small hotel, and walked up Dizengoff. The Casit was a cafe where a lot of writers and artists met up and was not difficult to find, and he arrived a few minutes early just before seven, the appointed hour. They weren't particularly busy; no more than a dozen people sitting around outside and a guy playing softly on a guitar. He ordered a coffee and cake, watched the people walk by, read about the Eichmann trial in the *Jerusalem Post*, while keeping a regular lookout for Tamar. Forty-five minutes later he glanced at his watch once more. Something was amiss. Maybe she'd been held up with her agent, maybe she'd had an accident, or maybe he just wasn't quite as relevant as he'd thought. Maybe he was a quickie-Moroccan after all! At eight o'clock he asked the waiter if he knew an actress called Tamar.

The big guy with a moustache smiled. "Sure. Everybody knows Tamar."

"I was supposed to meet her here at seven," Martin said.

"So don't worry. Seven, eight, nine for Tamar is the same thing. But she did not say she is coming back today."

"You mean she was here?" Martin exclaimed.

"Sure, one, two o'clock, she is here."

"Two o'clock!" Martin was dumbfounded. He checked her note. Her handwriting was childlike but could he possibly have mistaken a 7 for a 1?

"Did she leave a message?"

The waiter shrugged. "She had a coffee and left. Maybe she is looking for someone. Don't worry if she is not back today, maybe tomorrow, one day she will be back. *Beseder*?"

He hung around for another half-hour then wrote the words *Kibbutz Kfar Hanassi* on a card and signed it *Martin*, leaving it with the waiter to give to Tamar when she eventually turned up again.

The following morning he left for the kibbutz that was near Rosh Pinna, just south of the Golan Heights. There he laid up irrigation pipes in the orange groves, vaccinated baby chicks against coccidiosis, and learnt how to tell the difference between the Syrian Migs and Israeli Mirages in a skirmish over the kibbutz. He never heard from Tamar or Arik again and he wondered if the waiter had given her his note, and if Arik had kept his job. It was like a short story that'd ended halfway through the chapter. But at least it was an unforgettable half.

He met Esther working in the orchard. She had a first-class degree in law and was due to start a training contract at Linklaters in the autumn. He watched her as she threw a ladder against a tree, climbed up, twisted the grapefruit off its branch, and dropped it into a basket. She was dead cute; with her short dark hair and elfin looks she could've been Mia Farrow's twin. It was the look on her face when she caught him staring at her legs that kicked off a conversation.

"They go all the way up," she said.

"I can imagine," he smiled, admiring her figure.

"Then you'd better make the most of it, 'cause when you get to the top it's just dreams; dreams and grapefruit," she chided.

"Sounds great. I love grapefruit," he grinned.

"I prefer oranges," she said

"As a matter of fact, so do I. How do you feel about peeling an orange together after lunch?"

"Why would I want to do that? Peeling an orange with you really doesn't do a lot for my enzymes."

"What are they?"

"Proteins that cause a chemical reaction in the body that keeps you alive. You know, gives you a buzz."

"Funny, mine are really buzzing," he smiled.

"How nice for you."

"It would be nicer still if you felt the same. Look, I hope you're not totally revolted by the idea."

"Not at all. I haven't got anywhere near as far as that. I'm just at the positively completely disinterested stage."

"That's great. I like to see the obstacles."

"I'm glad you can see them."

"I can. Only I think, in the spirit of the kibbutz, you're not giving your enzymes a fair chance. I mean, that's what kibbutz life is all about, isn't it? Sharing for the greater good. The strong have the same as the weak, the hard worker the same as the shirker, the greedy the same as the generous, and the indifferent the same as the passionate. They all bring out the best in each other. Why not give it a try?"

"Well, I would, except I'm not that kind of kibbutznik. I only share what I want to when I want to and with whom I want," she said firmly, twisting off another grapefruit.

"Now, I am very sad," he said dolefully.

"Moping won't work," she said without sympathy.

"But I need you."

"For what?"

"Because I'm in love with a German girl I can't forget."

She held a grapefruit up in her hand and made as if to throw it at him then she laughed.

Later, he told her the whole sad story, and she agreed to

take the case saying, "I like a difficult case. They're the most interesting."

She had the right formula: smart, pretty, combative, ambitious and Jewish. Her family was in the coat business. She liked to argue about politics, fairness, equal rights for women and oranges over grapefruits, but they were attracted to each other. He was growing fond of her and who knows if when a smart Jewish hat meets up with a smart Jewish coat you've not got a chance for a great line in a smart Jewish ensemble? Soon they were planning a trip to the Greek islands together. There was only one important stop he had to make. Six weeks later he wrote to Leni telling her he was in a relationship with a Jewish girl called Esther. In her reply she informed him that Karl, the doctor, was a good, honest person and they planned to marry at the end of the year. She hoped everything would work out well for him and Esther.

Two days before he and Esther were due to leave for Greece Martin was on duty in the dining hall handing out bowls of soup for the hungry kibbutzniks. Esther was one of five girls serving. A few minutes after dishing up twenty bowls of the delicious looking soup several cries went out. *Ma Zeh!* What's this! It turned out Martin had dished up twenty plates of gravy from the huge saucepan next to the one for soup. Esther did not think it was funny. Nobody did. But when she said later: 'What is the matter with you?' there was something irritable in her tone that worried him. Leni had often spoken the same words to him but from her mouth the words were a sonnet. Suddenly he wondered if he were doing the right thing in going to the Greek islands or if he should be taking the next flight to Germany. He scratched his head and thought of Martin Buber. First thing in the morning he took the bus to Talbieh in Jerusalem. He stood outside the old man's house, thinking; *Of course I should've made an appointment. This isn't just anybody I'm going to see. This is Martin Buber. This man has people*

169

from all over the world seeking his counsel. He started to walk away. The thing was, he knew he might not get another chance. He started to walk back to the house, rehearsing his apologies for disturbing him without an appointment. Yossi, the taxi driver, had said lots of people called on Buber, seeking advice, but surely not at such short notice. Then again, from what he'd heard about the great man, he was more interested in an individual's problem than either his own fame or importance. Martin stood there, on the opposite side of the road, in his customary state of catatonic indecision.

Later that evening back at the kibbutz Esther asked him if Buber had given him the answer he was looking for.

CHAPTER 14

In a genuine meeting one does not look to score points. There are no individual goals, no winning strategy. There is only a genuine desire to meet and have a dialogue – a dialogue where differences lead two people to climb ever higher in order to see both sides in their striving for a good outcome. These were Buber's words to Martin. They were not spoken to him from the great man's mouth but from his words in a book bought in a shop after Martin had finally walked away. Now, several weeks later, back in London, and after a four-week stay on the Greek island with Esther, he finished his story about three strangers who meet on a ship, one of whom can't pay his passage. He entered it into a national competititon and wrote to Leni.

3rd August 1961

Dear Leni,

In a few months I too will be married. If we must say farewell, please let it not be in a letter, or on a phone, but in a street, or across a table, or even across a room, for then it will always be a memorable street, or a memorable room. It is too hard to deny each other at least that. I must know that we are doing the right thing. Only you can convince me of this. We are facing a lifetime in different worlds, with different partners, and I will face it boldly, as you will, if you will only meet me and tell me to my face that you are truly happy. Then all I ask, as your dearest friend, is a few last hours in which to wish you all the good luck I could not bring you.

Love Martin

Leni's wedding was to be in eight weeks' time and his to Esther not long afterwards. Much to his surprise Leni agreed to a meeting. What was he playing at? Was he really flying to Strasbourg for the day just to hear she was happy? Was that really all he would ask of her? Was he honestly prepared to just wish her good luck and walk away like a brother? Hadn't he learnt anything in the past year? Didn't Esther have the coat that fitted? Didn't Doctor Karl have the right medicine? He wasn't a falling apple, he was a man with a free will. He could change his mind and not go. But the laws of gravity aren't just physical, they're mythical; they deal with men's hearts and souls, and they, he and Leni, were soulmates. That was why he was on the plane to Strasbourg.

He walked through the Petite France Quarter in Strasbourg with its medieval half-timbered houses, past the old tannery by the river with its wooden galleries, till he came to Strasbourg Cathedral. He waited for her outside. At eleven o'clock a series of metal figures appeared on the clock tower, ringing bells. Then a cock crowed three times, angels rang more bells and the figure of Death struck a bell with a bone. It was hot. He thought it must be at least eighty degrees and he was perspiring, so he took off his jacket and slung it over his shoulder. He looked at his watch. She was five minutes late.

He thought of Tamar and the misunderstanding over the time of their lunch date, and he began to think perhaps Leni might not turn up. Then he saw a girl walking towards him, wearing a yellow summer dress, in white high heels, and he knew it was the girl with the raised eyebrows and the searchlight-blue eyes. She smiled at him in the sun but she didn't look like Bardot, she didn't look like any other, and when she spoke she didn't sound like Dietrich nor did she sound like any other, only the smell of Chanel was the same, for now she was the one who was like no other.

"Hello, Martin."

They embraced warmly.

"You look great," he said. "I'm so glad you came."

"Are you all right? You look worried."

"I'm all right now. I need a drink, that's all."

"I know a very good bistro. It is not far," she said, "and after I shall show you Strasbourg. It is a beautiful town. I want you to remember it."

"You are here less than a minute and it's already an unforgettable day."

They walked through the Old Town, through narrow cobbled streets, into the church of St Thomas where she showed him the organ on which Mozart had once played. Then they walked down to the River Ill and stopped at a bistro and sat down outside at a table for two. Next door in the background a jukebox played Elvis Presley singing 'Wooden Heart'. It was a year since they'd last met. They searched each other's faces for signs of change. It was Leni who spoke first.

"Every time I ate grapefruit I used to think of you up a big tree in the kibbutz orchard."

"We had one every day."

"How about your fiancée, Esther?" she asked.

"She prefers oranges."

She shrugged. "It is good you like different things."

"More to fight over," he said, only half joking.

"Perhaps you should make her a hat," she teased.

"I have not been lucky with the hats I make."

"I hope you will be lucky this time," she smiled.

"We spend a lot of time arguing."

"Like us." Her eyebrows arched.

"Different things."

"But you are getting married."

"If we don't fall out over who does the housework before the wedding. She believes men and women should be equal in everything."

"I like this idea."

"I like ideas too, so long as you can discuss them. But for her this one is not an idea. For her it's a religion. That's an idea with a wall around it."

"I don't like walls," she said firmly. "We have a new one in Berlin. It is not very nice. I hope your wall is not so high like this."

"No, it is not so high," he said, truthfully. "And if it were she would help me climb it. She has a ladder for everyone. She worries about the homeless and dengue fever in Asia. She'll help anyone in trouble if she can. She's a good person and we get along great, except she doesn't recognise Beethoven on the radio. I miss that."

"You must be patient. If she loves you this is not so important. I hope you are not scouting any more for au pairs at the Moulin Rouge," she smiled.

"I won't be doing that again. The best don't go there any more. They're getting married."

"Naughty one." And her eyes sparkled.

"You shouldn't wear such a pretty dress. It makes me dizzy."

"Vruuuum!"

Martin and Leni's attention was drawn across to the table next to them where a well-dressed English woman was sitting with her two sons. The younger one, probably about six years old, sat next to her, while the older, a precocious-looking nine-year-old, sat opposite running a pale blue Dinky car up and down the table, around a plate of unfinished lasagne, making exaggerated racing noises. "Vrruuuum!" he cried again.

"Can I have my car back now, Andrew?" whined the younger boy. "Motherrrrrr!" he appealed, as his older brother appeared totally unaware of his existence and continued with his imaginary race.

"Have you decided to live alone in the world, Andrew? I

don't recommend it at your age," the smartly dressed lady said.

"Sorry, Mother, just coming into a pit stop." The boy grinned, slowing down the blue racer.

"Return the car to Peter," said the mother, commandingly.

"I thought it was my car," Andrew complained.

"It is, dear, but I've told you before, each day we have to give something up."

"Why?" The boy whined.

"Because it's good for one's character and because you decided to give up your car for the day to Peter. It was your decision."

"Well, actually I only meant the morning."

"That is not what you said."

"I think at nine years old, Mother, you should be allowed to change your mind."

"Not when you're smart, Andrew, and you are very smart, smart enough to know that it is not acceptable, because it is not how life works. It doesn't let you take things back, as you know very well. Once a thing is done, it's done. You can't undo it. Now please, it's far too hot to argue today, so do try to act your age."

"Please, Mother, just a few minutes while I put some petrol in."

"You can put in all the petrol you want tomorrow."

"But he won't be able to use it without petrol and I don't see why I've got to do it just this minute," said the precocious boy.

"The reason you are going to give it up this minute, Andrew, is so that when you are a grown-up and find you have to give up something you particularly want, you will be able to do so beautifully and be able to help others who may not have learnt to do it as well as you will have done. Learning to give things up and share generously is the best way to avoid wars."

Martin and Leni were both still smiling as the waiter returned and asked, in French, if they wanted some wine. He ordered two glasses of Riesling and then they both decided on a Greek salad.

"I had it on the island nearly every day – they call it *horiatiki*."

"You went to Greece?"

Martin had forgotten he'd not mentioned that he and Esther had been to one of the Greek islands but she didn't seem phased.

"Which island?" she continued.

"Tinos. It has windmills and mountains just like the Alps. You wouldn't believe how many poor kids came running to meet us off the boat, tugging at our sleeves, begging us to stay with their families. It wasn't easy to choose."

"How long were you there?"

"A month."

"A month," she repeated.

They no longer belonged to each other so why should he feel inhibited? But he did. In the past she'd always been able to absorb a bitter truth because she'd a starring part in a big picture. Now they both were playing supporting roles.

"How is Karl?"

"He is looking to buy a small house for us in Freiburg near the hospital. It is a very pretty town, in the heart of the Black Forest."

"You should be very happy there."

It sounded banal even as he said it, and he felt his stomach churn. House, family, children, music and a cat because she loved cats. Wasn't that what everyone wanted? Wasn't that what he wanted for her?

"What about you? Where will you live?" she asked.

"We'll find a place," he shrugged.

The waiter brought over their wine, and then returned

with their salads and asked if there was anything else that they wanted. Leni translated and Martin said everything he wanted was at the table.

Leni smiled. "You haven't changed so much, darling."

He raised his glass. "To Goethe and Beethoven, who brought you to me, and to you, who brought me to Goethe and Beethoven!"

"To you, darling. To you and Esther."

"And to you and Karl."

It was only a moment, but she seemed to study the glass held in her hand intently, before she looked up smiling at him enigmatically. Then they clinked glasses and drank.

"Karl didn't mind you coming here today, did he?"

"He doesn't like sharing."

"Doesn't he trust you?"

Then, defiantly: "I am here, aren't I?"

She was too honest to have said nothing. He guessed she'd got round Karl somehow and that he'd trusted her. It was all perfectly clear. She'd accepted her second prize. He suddenly completely lost his appetite.

"You are happy, aren't you?" he said.

"I am not as sad as I have been with you." She thrust her fork into the salad and ate.

"Good, I hope you never will be. I'd hate to think of you being as sad as we were in Engelberg," he said, knowing it also to have been the happiest time of their lives.

"I will not go back," she said.

"Nor I. We'll keep it locked in our minds free from change. We'll both find new places to be happy."

"I think you already have found some new places, darling."

"Have I?"

"In Israel and in Tinos of course," she said, flicking Tinos up like a shuttlecock and smacking it lightly.

"Yes, I suppose I have," he said.

177

He was surprised just how relaxed and composed she was. The little family at the next table had left and the restaurant was now full of polite, boring, well-behaved families.

"Soon we will be part of this scene, winners of agreeable second-prize marriages, with second-prize children, and grandchildren. Do you believe in agreeable marriages?"

"I believe in an agreeable life, darling, even if sometimes you must make a very disagreeable decision."

She was a statue of calm, in the centre of a boring sea of compromise, and he wanted to throw in a large pebble and create some ripples. Somebody played Elvis, again, on the jukebox while he told her all about his trip on the ship with the refugees, and his two Israeli friends, and how he'd got stuck in the shower in Haifa, and she laughed. He told her about the Eichmann trial and Yossi the cab driver. He told her he'd written a story and entered it in a competition and promised to send her a copy when he was back in London.

The waiter served them two coffees. It was two o'clock. The great bells of Notre Dame Cathedral rang out. The clock was ticking. Time was slowly opening the goodbye-door. He had a return flight booked for London via Paris at ten that evening. She wiped coffee from her lips with the serviette and he wondered if she ever called Karl *darling* or *naughty one*.

"You are a good storyteller," she said.

If I were that good, he thought, *I'd tell her that, even now, we could still turn ours into one with a big wow ending.* But he couldn't tell her that because he knew what Karl was offering was the real deal and that he was still daydreaming.

"But you did not tell me about Tinos," she continued her eyebrows raised. "Maybe because you are too happy."

"You might not like it if I told you about my happiest time."

The conversation, now, seemed to be taking her further

178

away from him. He thought of young Andrew who didn't want to give up his Dinky car. Well, he would have his precious car back tomorrow. Martin wouldn't have Leni back tomorrow. He didn't want to mess with her, but he was about to lose her forever. That was a long time. His heart began to race as he threw the first pebble into the mix.

"Do you think that second prizes can ever grow into first prizes?"

"I do not know this, darling. You must ask me when I am an old lady."

"I should like to," he said.

"If you do not forget me." She turned away. "Isn't the river beautiful?"

Yes, he thought, *the river is beautiful, Strasbourg is beautiful, you are beautiful and tomorrow I will see none of this*. Nothing makes you catch your breath quicker than the fear of an imminent loss. Martin threw a second pebble as hard as he could.

"I want to be alone with you," he said, reaching across the table and taking her hand.

"Really I am right – you have not changed so much," she said, withdrawing her hand.

"Did you want me to?"

"Why didn't you answer my letter when I told you I had a job offer from Volkswagen?"

He gulped. Her challenge was harsh. "You're disappointed in me."

She looked at him sadly.

"It is not your fault, darling. But now you have Esther, you must try to make it work. I do not want to be a problem between you."

"Do you love Karl?"

"It is different."

"How?"

"He is a decisive man."

179

"And I am indecisive."

"You are indecisive with Volkswagens," she smiled.

"You think I didn't think about Volkswagen?"

"Darling, you are always thinking."

She was right. He was always thinking, and he was thinking now. A decisive man knows the price of a day and he only gets charged once, whereas an indecisive man pays the same bill again and again, and he's always in debt. Each day he runs the same old figures over in his mind borrowing time from the new day, hoping to gain something, but all he gains is more time lost. You can't lose what you have, only what you might've had, someone once said. They still had some more to have.

"You're right," he said, "but I have loved you as much as this indecisive man can, and maybe that isn't as much as your decisive man, but it's all that I could offer. I know it wasn't enough, and maybe I'll be asking myself the same questions about this for the rest of my life. Look, maybe the truth is second prize isn't such a bad thing. Maybe most people would gladly settle for that. Maybe they do. Maybe everybody in this restaurant has. Maybe that's how life works. Maybe that's what you're doing. Maybe it's what I'm doing. Maybe that is what's best for everyone. But I have a plane at ten and we're not *making do* now."

"You are crazy," she said.

"Yes, I'm crazy. And we still have a few crazy hours left."

Martin leant forward in his chair and took her hand again as he joined in 'Wooden Heart', singing it in an emphatically reasonable way.

"Can't you see?
I love you.
Please don't break my heart in two.
That's not hard to do,

180

'Cause I don't have a wooden heart.
'Cause if you say goodbye,
I know that I would cry.
I would definitely die
'Cause I don't have a wooden heart."

"Stop it, everyone is looking at you! And you are not Elvis!" she said, pouting at him crossly. A number of people had indeed turned round and were staring at Martin, who never afraid of making a fool of himself was undeterred and was now making heartfelt gestures with his hands and kneeling at her feet. She looked away even more crossly, but when she looked back her searchlight-blue eyes were laughing.

"There's no strings upon this love of mine.
It was always yours from the start
Treat me nice,
Treat me good,
Treat me like you really should,
'Cause I'm not made of wood
And I don't have a wooden heart."

When he finished a young girl clapped and Leni said she would never be able to go back to that restaurant again. Martin stood up, bowed to the girl and gestured to the waiter for the bill.

"Do you want to know the best thing that ever happened to me in Tinos? I'll tell you."

"It is not necessary, darling."

"But I want to tell you. I want to tell you about the time I was so happy I cried. Two days before we left the island I dropped a bag of tomatoes in the street. While I was running around picking them up I must've dropped my wallet. There wasn't a lot of money in it, about fifty drachmas, but I didn't want to lose it. I went back to the stall in case I'd left it there,

181

but the woman told me, in Greek sign language, that she never saw the wallet, that I'd paid with cash out of my pocket. Then I went back to the house thinking maybe I'd never had it with me. Well, it wasn't in the house either. We walked along the beach in the afternoon looking for it. I even went to the church of Our Lady, which has this miraculous icon, and I made a Jewish wish. Of course, I never found it. Then the morning we were leaving, this young Greek boy came running up to me as we are about to embark for Piraeus and he had my wallet. I don't know who he was – it certainly wasn't Paulos, the boy whose family we'd been living with. I was amazed to find everything still there. I gave him all the money. He grinned and ran off quickly as if he was worried I'd change my mind."

"That was generous, darling," she said. "It is not like you. Maybe you have changed."

"Esther thought I was crazy, but she didn't know everything that I had in my wallet."

"So you have a secret," she said.

"One secret for two people," he replied.

Martin opened his plain black wallet, took out a carefully folded piece of tissue paper and opened it tenderly on the table. Inside was the ginkgo leaf.

"It goes with me everywhere. Do you remember?" he asked.

"I remember," she said softly.

"All I'm asking is a couple of hours together for a lifetime apart."

"I cannot, darling."

"Why?" he protested.

"Because my second prize will not like this."

"Mine too. But they have us for a long time."

The sun blazed down on them, casting the shadow of the bridge across the river. He didn't want to take anything from

182

Karl or Esther, but these hours belonged to him and Leni. They'd paid for them with hours and years of heartache.

"We will never ask anything from each other again," he insisted.

"Never?" she asked him.

"I shall do whatever you ask of me."

She frowned. "Does your father like her very much?"

"Esther, yes, he likes her," he said honestly.

"I always wanted to make your father happy," she said.

She was clearly thinking this over very seriously before her face broke into a wonderful golden smile and she seemed to embrace the idea.

"Every day we must give something up. It is good for the character, don't you agree, darling?"

He didn't know what had caused her mood to switch quite so joyously but he took her spirit of abandon as a positive sign. They were going to make the most of it. There'd be no what-ifs or buts. They were living for the moment. They walked around the Orangery and spoke of happy days. He promised to send her a copy of his short story then they waltzed goodbye for two hours in a hotel room in Strasbourg. At the station she told him quickly that she had to leave, kissed him warmly on the cheek and with a finality he hadn't heard before, she said the familiar "Take care of you, darling." Then, without looking back, without a wave, she melted gracefully into the crowd, as if she were on a mission.

On the flight back to London he thought what a very special day it had been… yet she'd been so detached at the station that he began to wonder if she'd had regrets about their last waltz and would tell Karl. If she did, in a way he felt Karl ought to understand. As Martin had said to Leni, Karl would have her for a lifetime, wouldn't he?

A couple of months later he was sitting next to his father in the synagogue on *Yom Kippur*, the Day of Atonement.

183

The cantor led the chanting and the congregation droned on hypnotically, all except Martin whose attention was back in Strasbourg. Since the day Leni had kissed him *auf wiedersehen* she hadn't replied to a single call or to any of his letters, not even when he'd written that his short story had won second prize in a national competition. She and Karl had probably had the most terrible argument and now she was holding Martin to that flippant remark: two hours for a lifetime. What a disastrous ending to their relationship. That was not how he'd wanted to say goodbye. He felt an extra organ had been added to his body – an organ of pain and guilt. He was snapped out of this spasm of self-inflicted grief by a nudge on his shoulder. Everyone stood as the Arc was opened revealing the holy scrolls and Martin rose too.

Outside, the rain beat relentlessly against the stained-glass windows that depicted the twelve tribes of Israel. Inside, a man trapped in the age-old snare of Jewish persecution, pain and *pilpul* turned the page in his prayer book and chanted the litany of sins, beating his chest in the annual act of contrition. But the only thing Martin was contrite about was that he was at an Orthodox service he didn't believe in and had given up first prize in love for second prize.

Some time later, having taken yet another break outside, Martin returned to his seat just in time for the concluding prayers. His father hadn't moved from his place since early morning. It was a stomach-rumbling charge to the finish. At the end of the service the ram's horn was sounded. Martin folded his *tallit*.

"Another year gone," his father said, putting his *tallit* into a blue velvet bag. Then he smiled and shook his hand with that familiar strong grip that never boasted strength, but gave strength and said *"Yom Tov"*, as his eyes staring hard but full of love said, "I know all that is in your heart and I am with you, my blood, my soul, all that I am, all that I have." Martin looked up at the balcony where the women sat and saw Esther smiling down at him looking so positive, and attractive in her brown suit and wearing her beautiful new beige turban he'd made for her. What was he thinking about? He'd struck the best deal for everyone. From now on he'd spare Leni the heartache of any more letters from him. He was going to marry Esther, throw himself into the family business and make a fresh start and there was only one way to do that. When you genuinely want to please people you don't offer them half of anything, you smile and offer up the whole shebang. And you stop looking back, asking yourself why, because it's mean and ungracious and bad for everybody's digestion, including your own. Ten minutes later walking home with his father he made up his mind one day to join a community where you didn't have to accept blindly how much *lockshen* you had in your chicken soup. The only question a rabbi asked was when you sing 'Hatikvah' do you sing from the heart?

CHAPTER 15

There are many categories of thief. There are those who break into your house to steal your watch, or whatever you've left in your piggy bank; so when you wake up you call the police and phone your insurance company. Then there are those like Tricky Dicky, the US president, who, because he couldn't bear saying goodbye to his fellow Americans at the next election, tried to fix things at the Watergate Hotel so he wouldn't have to. Finally, there are those you know and trust who don't break in. They don't have to because you've invited them in. They don't do anything to break the law, yet sometimes what they take can leave your peace-of-mind-account in the red for years.

The 28th of August 1974 was a sunny day. Martin had left an apparently untroubled Esther at home with their six-month baby son, Ben, to spend a few hours with an *old friend* in Paris and told her he'd be back home late that night.

Twelve years had passed since he and Leni had parted in Strasbourg. Then two months ago, out of the blue, she'd called.

"Hello – Martin?"

The familiar low, velvety accent shot through him like a live current.

"Leni!"

"How are you?" A quiver in her voice gave away her nervousness.

"I'm fine – I think, and you, are you okay?" An image of

her flashed in front of him like a trailer from an old movie. After twelve years of silent pictures talkies were back and his favourite film, *You and Me,* was showing again.

"Is it all right to call? Are you alone?"

"Yes. Yes. No problem. How did you find my number?"

"The London Directory."

"Of course."

"Are we still friends?" she asked tentatively.

"Is that a joke? You're the best friend I've ever had."

"You are still married – to Esther?"

"Yes, and you to Karl?"

"We have two boys."

"And I have a six-month-old baby son." Then he took the nimble thief's first tiptoe step. "How is Karl? Is he still the kind doctor?"

"He is always busy, first at his surgery and then at the weekends he is building an aeroplane with a friend. Sometimes we hardly see him." Immediately his pulse quickened. When she told him she'd just heard Sinatra's 'All The Way' on the radio he knew this was his cue.

"Of course. I remember." It was from a film they'd seen together, *The Joker is Wild.* "We must write," he said.

She readily agreed. They excitedly exchanged addresses. He told her it would be no problem for Esther writing to him at home and she told him she'd make sure she picked up the post before Karl. A brief correspondence began.

3rd Aug 1974

Dear Leni,

It is not easy to express my feelings about the years I thought I might've lost you. Now without my looking you appear and the words trip off my tongue.

Like Marco Polo and Columbus
In dreams I explore the world.

187

I search for land that is no more
Till I awake and all is here
In you who wake inside me.
Love Martin

A week later Leni agreed to meet him for the day at a friend's flat in Paris.

Martin had never considered himself a thief because the truth was Leni would always see through his darkest thought and still offer him all she had, peace of mind included. Now, as the cab made its way to the 6th Arrondissement, he wondered how much she might've changed since their tryst in Strasbourg. He started to plan what he'd say when he saw her again. How it would be between them.

How do you like Paris? She'd ask.

I'm not sure, he'd say. *It's too soon to tell. You said you wanted to see me, and for a long time I've wanted to see you. When we parted in Strasbourg, for months I waited for news, but there was none, not even a note. I was afraid you'd closed the book. I guess I'd hurt you. I hadn't intended to. I was desperate to know what had happened, but I'm not going to ask that now,* he determined, *because I know you must've had a darned good reason.*

Then she'd stop him and kiss him on the lips, they'd drink wine and make love all day, and tell each other how glad they were they'd found each other again. This fantasy conversation played until the cab finally arrived outside her friend Michelle's apartment. It was in an old nineteenth-century building. He climbed up the three flights of stone stairs two at a time, a little too quickly, holding onto the iron railing, then knocked on the tall panelled door, panting. As Leni opened the door they fell into each other's arms, not like lovers, rather like old school friends at a reunion.

"Hello Martin. You are early. Are you all right?"

188

"There are a lot of stairs and it's hot," he said catching his breath.

"You did not have to run."

"I wanted to."

"I was running too, back and forward to the window," she laughed, embarrassed. "I saw you arrive." She beckoned him to come in. "How do you like Paris? Isn't it beautiful?"

"You look lovely."

"I'm so glad to see you."

"When I left you in Strasbourg, I was afraid you'd closed the book. I'm glad you opened it," he said smiling like a schoolboy who'd got all the quotes right in a test paper.

Just then the phone rang.

"Excuse me a moment, Martin," she said guardedly as she turned sharply and moved to answer the phone.

As soon as she spoke in German he knew instantly it must be Karl. Probably checking to see if she was okay or else with a question about the children. He watched her. She certainly no longer looked like the Bardot of the late fifties. Her short-sleeved shirt was buttoned up to the neck, and tucked into a grey cotton skirt, falling well below the knee. A black belt accentuated a slightly fuller waist and stilettos were replaced with low-heeled sandals. Her hair was swept back off her face into a smart French pleat. She looked like a very respectable doctor's wife, and he found her attractive in a new way. He felt he was eavesdropping in spite of not understanding a word. He looked away and studied the room. It was typically French, with a high ceiling and two tall casement windows opening out onto a small balcony over the street. A picture of Jacques Brel smoking a cigarette hung on the wall. Leni put the receiver down.

"Is everything all right?" he asked.

"Yes, he is taking the boys to see their grandfather in Tübingen."

189

"So he doesn't mind you having the day off in Paris?"

"No, why should he? For the past six years, when he is not with his patients, he is so busy making his aeroplane. He always liked planes even when he was a student. Now, it is my turn. I told him I need a holiday from my children."

"Are they a handful?"

"No, not really. They are well behaved, like their father. I am the naughty one. I told him I am coming to Paris to go shopping for them," she laughed.

"We can do that if you want," he said.

"No, darling, I have already bought two very smart shirts for them. The rest of the day is for you. Michelle is staying with her boyfriend. She said he is having a party this evening. If we like to go she will see us there. It is not far, in Montparnasse."

"We will go wherever you want," he said, thinking he wanted to stay right where they were. He hadn't envisaged a party in his scenario. "I'm so glad you phoned," he said as he took her hand and pressed it.

"We must go for a walk, darling," she said. "It is such a beautiful day, and I want to show you the Luxembourg Gardens and hear all about your little family."

They took the short walk to the gardens and stood near the statue of a stern Marshal Ney wielding a sword. He borrowed her camera and took a photo of her with her index finger pressed to her lips, pouting flirtatiously at the Marshal, indicating to the great man not to tell her secret to anyone. Then they sat down on a bench watching some boys throw a ball for a Doberman.

"Nick sends you his love."

"He knows you are here?"

"He dropped me at the airport. He's got forty shops now."

"He always wanted many shops. And Esther, she knows?"

"Yes, she knows."

"And she doesn't mind this."

"Why should she when we have not seen each other for so many years? Perhaps I shall not see you again. What is wrong? We are sitting in these beautiful gardens looking at flowers, a statue of an old general, watching some boys play with their dog, and talking about our families and old times. Must we be ashamed of this?"

"No, but not everybody sees life like you, darling."

"You mean Karl?"

"He is like an old clock. Tick tock! Tick tock! He likes everyone's temperature to be normal and he does not like so many surprises. So I told him I am seeing an *old friend* too but he does not know it is you. He would not be so relaxed about this as Esther. He is a marvellous doctor, an amazing engineer and a wonderful father. I am very lucky," she said, but she did not sound lucky. "I would like to be honest with him," she sighed.

"What happened at Strasbourg?"

She shrugged. "We said goodbye."

"For twelve years? And not even a farewell wave!"

"You wanted me for two hours, remember, and I wanted you for much *longer*," she said with her characteristic uptick on the last word. "I was still waiting for Walter." After an awkward pause she asked: "How is your father?"

"He's good. He's talking to my mother again."

"No! What about your stepmother?"

"She died some years ago. My mother came round with my grandparents when Ben was born. My father was there. She passed him the baby and they've been corresponding ever since."

"My God. After all that happened? That is amazing."

"You know what else, fifty per cent of our trade is export now. Kaufhof is one of our largest customers."

Suddenly, the boys playing with the dog threw a ball that landed at Leni's feet. The dog came bounding over and stood

191

watching expectantly as Leni picked it up and threw it back. The dog leapt away.

"*Merci, Madame,*" shouted one of the boys.

"My boys would like a dog, but Karl says they are not hygienic."

Two minutes later a fight broke out and two of the boys were rolling on the lawn, and one took a punch in the face and ran off crying with the dog running after him.

"I've heard girls are easier," Martin said. It wasn't easy making love to a married woman when there were kids around reminding one of one's responsibilities, even in Paris.

"Karl does not want more children."

"He may change his mind."

"I don't think so. He likes to keep to his plans."

"You told him, didn't you – about Strasbourg?"

"Yes, I told him," she said boldly.

"I thought you had. That must've gone down well."

"He said he would forgive me. I told him I did not want forgiveness for this, because I was not sorry for one minute. It did not matter what he thought of me. I did not care. You were getting married and I had promised myself not to see you again. I really was not very nice to him, but he was very kind and patient. He said that I have, how do you say it in English, a *chronic illness*, and I must stay with him because he is sure he can help me; and in a few years I will be better. This is why I did not reply to your letters. So, now we are married and I have a beautiful life with two wonderful boys and a lovely home. I teach some children French and English and when I have time I am learning Spanish."

"So now you are completely better!"

"Not completely," she smiled with charming gravity.

"I'm glad… not completely."

"Naughty one!"

"You don't regret coming, do you?"

"Why should I? You are right. We will be two old friends who share everything they can see and that is all. You agree, darling? It is a wonderful idea. We will be like Goethe and Marianne von Willemer."

It was not exactly what Martin had in mind but he kissed the back of her hand like a nineteenth-century gentleman.

"If Goethe could do it, so can Solomon."

They had nine hours left to share together and spent the afternoon wandering around the gardens. He affectionately called her Madame Marianne and she called him Monsieur Goethe, in an *amitié amoureuse*, as she called it. They admired the chess players, and stood together by the famous fountain of the Medicis. Nearby, a violinist played Debussy's *Girl with the Flaxen Hair* in an area shaded by trees.

"That's a lovely piece," he said, but he didn't tell her that ironically it had immediately reminded him of a girl with short brown hair playing that piece on the piano. He wasn't going to tell her that just as Beethoven always made him think of her, Debussy always reminded him of Esther.

Leni was looking at him intently.

"If Marianne had looked at Goethe like that, they'd have nipped behind a tree *tout de suite*. Why do we have to behave like them, anyway? Why can't we pretend we're David and Bathsheba instead? That would be much more fun."

She laughed. They took some tourist photos with her camera, but none of them included him. Then they left the violinist who was now playing some pieces from *Carmen*, and made their way out of the park. They walked along the Left Bank to Notre Dame. Behind the cathedral, a small gate led to the Memorial to the Unknown World War II Deported, commemorating the 200 thousand French people of all faiths who'd been murdered in the camps. Above the door were the words *pardonnez mais n'oubliez pas*.

"Yes, I think that's right," Martin said. "Don't you?"

"Since I met you I can never forget," she replied.

He squeezed her hand. Soon they were strolling down the crowded Rue de Buci, with its tempting food stalls, and glorious wafts of cheese and fresh fruit.

"When I am with you everything looks and smells tastier," he said. Then he sang: *"When somebody loves you, it's no good unless they love you all the way."*

They made their way down the Rue Bonaparte, past Le Pré aux Clercs, where Hemingway and Fitzgerald had often shared a drink, and finally sat down at the corner of Boulevard St Germain at the Café de Flore where Sartre, Simone de Beauvoir and Albert Camus used to meet. They ordered coffee and croissants. Most of the tables were occupied and there was a buzz of conversation and the tinkle of clinking glasses.

Seated at the next table were an attractive middle-aged woman and a dignified grey-haired gentleman drinking wine. He had a professorial air and eyed Leni like an artist considering her for a portrait, while his companion was engrossed, reading a book. Martin asked Leni what he thought the couple's story was. She said she thought she and the professor had been married for many years, they probably slept in separate beds, and she was a little bored with him which was why they had nothing to say to each other and she was reading a book.

He had a feeling this answer was born out of personal experience, and he was upset in one moment that her marriage might be so dull, and then in the next, he was glad of it.

"I liked your short story. Have you written anything else?"

He told her that winning the short story prize had initially spurred him on, but he'd found prose heavy going and had switched to drama, joining a playwriting group to improve his technique. It was there a group of writers, some published, others not, met once a week to hear their latest scene read out by members of the group before it was cut to pieces in a post-mortem.

"I spent months writing my own scene before this genius stood up."

Martin now in the self-mocking style of a great classical actor his voice a vibrant baratone proceeded to bombard his listener with a patronising critique. "'Frankly, Martin, the amount of time you've spent munching over each word to construct this little scene may be worthy of a Proust; but compared to Proust, who has an excellent feel for language and is a literary giant who has achieved a ten-out-of-ten result for his literary efforts, you are a mere minnow, with a minnow's feel for language, and at best a two-out-of-ten literary talent with a two-out-of-ten hope of ever achieving any serious worthwhile literary results.' Then as if that wasn't enough he carried on: 'When I was at Oxford one wet Sunday afternoon I wrote a three-act play between lunch and tea that won the Radio 3 Play of the Year Award. Might I respectfully suggest you stick to making hats?' That little criticism held me up for a bit."

"What on earth is the matter with you?" she exclaimed. "Why do you let him talk to you like this? He is so arrogant." With that she opened her handbag and pulled out a carefully folded piece of paper, which she opened and thrust into Martin's hand. "Is this a two-out-of-ten feeling?"

Martin recognised the poem he'd sent her only a few months earlier about Marco Polo and Columbus exploring the world.

"Well, it may have feeling but it's hardly Rilke."

"I am not asking you about Rilke's feelings. I am asking why must you listen to this stupid man. He has no feeling at all even if he can write *three* plays in an afternoon."

"I think he only criticised me to that extent because I'd made a punchy criticism of his work the previous week."

"I am not interested in him."

"He's a clever fellow – he could give a lecture on Kant in German, Italian and French."

"I don't care if he can lecture about sausages in Russian. I did not come to Paris to see my milliner – I want to see my poet."

"You're a dreamer."

"I have your story and I have your letters. I know what you are."

"I'm no Dostoevsky."

"And I did not come here to see Dostoevsky," she said.

"I want to go to bed with you."

"Now you are a very bad Goethe," she scolded.

Their croissants and *café au lait* arrived. As he was watching the passers-by, a young woman caught his attention. She was in her early twenties, striding purposefully towards the cafe, her high heels hammering the ground, her expression fixed and dark. She entered the cafe, marched stridently over to the professor, picked up his glass of wine and threw the contents straight into his face. The professor's wife just looked up from her book without raising an eyebrow.

Everybody else within earshot stopped mid-sentence, flabbergasted, and waited to see what would happen next. "*Merci beaucoup pour le grand illusion, Monsieur le Professeur. Enfin adieu!*"

Then the young woman strode off. The professor stood and bowed to everybody, mopped his face with his serviette, put it down, shrugged and smiled at Leni.

"*Un grand au revoir peut-être une comédie ou une tragédie, mais jamais de routine,*" he announced with aplomb, then sat down as if nothing at all had happened.

The customers gradually resumed where they'd left off their conversations and the man's companion, returned to her book.

"Well, we never do routine goodbyes, do we?"

"No, darling, it is never routine for us, only comedy or tragedy."

196

They both laughed and tucked into their croissants.

"What did you think of the professor? Martin asked.

"I did not like the way he bowed to everybody. He is a show-off."

Leni caught Martin studying the woman with the book. "Perhaps if you will sit with her she will put her book down."

He remembered when they were younger how jealous she'd been over Jeanne and how jealous he'd been over any boy she ever smiled at. If she was going to risk everything for one last night of passion she needed to know that they were both archaeologists digging deep and that he'd not turned into an early bird, who'd stopped by to snap up a worm. She needed to know just how much she meant to him. He leant forward across the table. "I'm not interested in her. I am only interested in you and if you were made of marble, and your dress was marble, and my plane was leaving in ten hours instead of five, I should stay here with you and hold your marble hand until the plane took off."

"You are a naughty one," she smiled and her face flushed.

She waved away the flies hovering over her croissant. "I think these flies followed me from my kitchen in Freiburg."

Her mind seemed suddenly elsewhere. She'd travelled back home to be with her husband who loved her and her two children who depended on her. He knew the three flies pestering her most; he knew their names: Boring, Predictable and Decent. They were buzzing around her plate right now driving her crazy. She was the lady who was bored. Hers was the life that was too predictable, and she was the one in the separate bed! She was tempted but Decent was making her feel guilty. Meanwhile, he had a couple of flies buzzing around his plate too called Noble and Gallant. He swept his arm aggressively over his plate. She looked reflective and he knew she was still lingering in a world in which he played no part.

"Come back," he pleaded, and she looked as sad as he felt.

And he loved her for the beauty of their troubled young love, and for the beauty of their troubled new love, and most of all for the terrifying beauty of love that must be lost. *Beauty is nothing if not the beginning of terror we must all endure,* Rilke had said. Well, they would endure.

She smiled. "I am here."

"We must come here again," he said.

"I would like that, but I don't know if it will be possible."

"Why not? Do you know how much I wanted to see you today? Didn't you want to see me?"

"Of course."

"I hate these separations, especially when they last twelve years."

"So do I, darling, but we have no choice."

"Why not? I should like to do this every year."

"You are crazy."

"It's not so crazy. For Christ's sake, we're not in Germany now, we're in Paris, the city for lovers."

"I think you have too much sun."

"Maybe you haven't had enough."

"If I have too much I may go home with a bad headache. Karl does not like patients who make themselves sick."

"Karl won't know."

"But I will know, selfish one."

"I want you to know," he said.

She was being more sensible than he wanted her to be, but her eyes shone as he tried to sell her an old suit. She liked the cut, and he was still her favourite tailor, but like all sensible and mature women she was weighing up what she could afford and what she could not.

"Michelle said Jacques Brel's daughter might be at the party."

The restaurant was noisy enough, and he didn't want to spend his last few hours with her at a crowded party in Paris with Brel's daughter or anybody else, and he had a feeling she didn't really want that either. Time was running out.

"Can I ask you something?" he said. "Do you really want to go to this party? Because, if you do, I'll go and hate every minute of it."

"That is not very kind."

"To who? A crowd of people I've never met?" He placed both his hands on the table and leaned forward. "Are you afraid to be alone with me?"

"No, why should I be afraid?"

"That's right, you shouldn't be. You are perfectly safe. You're the good Marianne, aren't you?"

She put her right hand over his left and squeezed it. "Yes, I am still Marianne, but I think my Goethe wants to resign. You must be good, darling."

The old cheeky uptick at the end of resign and the small squeeze of his hand drove him wild. Good was the last thing he wanted to be.

"Good! Look, we've only a few hours left and you want us to be in a place that's safe with a crowd of strangers and what I want is for us to be alone in a room full of hippos. Once you thought this too, remember?" She withdrew her hand. "Now I am losing you," he said, as he slumped back in his chair.

The sharp withdrawal of her hand was like a wound and left him feeling sad and defeated. It was not the response he'd hoped for. Then to his astonishment her demeanour suddenly changed; all trace of caution disappeared. Her eyes were utterly fearless.

"No, darling, you are not losing me." Once more she placed her hand on his, only this time it was firm and full of confidence. "And I will not lose you."

The sexual chemistry always smouldering beneath the surface flared up crackling like a log fire. Martin paid the bill and they walked back to the apartment in silence. The moment they entered the door he pulled her to him and kissed her violently on the mouth until she pulled away breathless.

She placed two fingers on his jawline just below his right ear and slowly traced them lightly round to below his left ear then with little finger steps she marched lightly back and forth across his lips. He wanted to cry "Stop", but she always knew where and when, and how much to press. Any direction from him would've broken the spell of unendurable pleasure. "It's all right," she whispered as she kissed him.

At one o'clock in the morning they were both naked as she lay half asleep, her head in the hollow of his arm. He'd failed the Goethe test just as he'd wanted to.

"Marshal Ney," he said dreamily.

"Rue Buci," she responded, in her sleepy, sexy voice.

"Café Flore."

"Pont des Arts."

"Goethe."

"Marianne."

"David… and Bathsheba for now we are like them. We must remember these names."

"Oh, darling, if we do not meet again, perhaps one day we will meet in another world."

"You believe in this."

"I wish it."

"I wish it too. I wish I shall have eyes and ears and that we shall both be twenty again and we shall be together longer."

"You are so sweet, like I remember."

"But what if we return as goldfish? Some people believe this. How will I know you?"

"Then I shall blow you lots of bubbles." Suddenly she sat up. "What about Esther? She'll be worried you missed your plane."

"I'll call her in the morning before I leave," he reassured her.

"She will be furious."

"She'll work it out."

"I hope so. I only wished for one day and we have taken more. I do not want to hurt her. We have been greedy."

She sounded worried and he kissed her as she laid her head back down.

"You are not sorry, are you?"

"No, I cannot be sorry. I wished for you to come to me and you did."

"You must be careful what you wish for because I will always hear it."

"Always?"

"Always."

She turned and looked up at him face to face her blue eyes sparkling in the moonlight. "I am wishing now," she said testing his powers of telepathy.

"Shall I tell you?"

"Tell me."

"A few hours ago you were a married woman with two children and a husband who trusted you. Now you have made love with me and have a secret day and you wish that *you* will not be sorry. Am I right?"

She smiled, "This is my secret." Then she pressed her fingers to his lips, so he wouldn't press her further. Slowly he turned and raised himself on top of her. Once more he found her mouth again. His fingers reached down over her warm belly and he cared as much for Karl as the Judean king had once cared for Uriah the Hittite.

"I love you," she whispered. "I always have."

He awoke early in the morning to the sound of Bach's *Cello Suite No.1* wafting down from the apartment above. He reached over to where Leni had been sleeping beside him but the space was empty. He sat up abruptly to find her fully dressed, sitting on the side of the bed smiling at him.

"It's nearly six o'clock in the morning!" he exclaimed looking at his watch and slipping out of bed. "Isn't it a bit early for practice?"

"Michelle told me she is very good but if you don't like it you can knock on the ceiling if you want and she will stop."

He shook his head and slipped on his trousers. "Michelle is right. She's too good and we mustn't upset the angels. If I knock they might make us sorry."

She got up and walked over to the window. "How beautiful Paris is early in the morning. I love this silence when the city wakes and life just begins." A Vespa buzzed down the street and as Leni turned to face him all sign of alarm had vanished. Her smile licked his face like a cat's tongue. "This is the best time," she purred.

He joined her at the window, wondering if she really believed it, but she seemed happy and that was good. "The best," he agreed. "Perhaps we are growing into our answers."

Half an hour later he hailed a cab and with the Sunday bells of Notre Dame ringing out across Paris he kissed her and took her in his arms for the last time. She seemed far away as if they'd already parted and were on their separate journeys.

"I wasn't a very good Goethe."

"And I am not a very good Marianne."

"You must go!" she ordered him.

"Don't forget…" he said sharply, pulling her to him. "This is not a tragedy, or a comedy, and it's not going to have a dull routine ending. Today we have a future! One day each year in Paris."

"Take care of you," she said as he got into the cab.

This time he knew she'd reply to his letters. Life felt good. But the most important thing to remember was not to be greedy. Didn't they have the most wonderful arrangement? Climbing the metal steps to board the aircraft he thought of the forlorn Nixon turning to give his big-brave-final-wave-goodbye for the cameras. That wasn't for him. This time Martin was coming back. He phoned Esther from the airport but there was no answer. He left a message on the answerphone.

When Martin arrived home at lunchtime he walked into the kitchen to help himself to a Coca Cola from the fridge and discovered that Esther had worked her pain out from a paint pot and painted the white back door a garish green that was still glistening wet.

"What's behind the green door?" he said, rocking it sweetly like Frankie Vaughan.

"You tell me," Esther replied, not amused as she put away some dishes from the dishwasher.

Martin dabbed the door with his fingers. "It's still tacky. And you've got some paint on the glass. You didn't mask up. That's not like you. And there are bristles in the paint. You should've waited 'til I got back. I could've helped you."

"Yes, you could. That's why I did wait. I waited and waited. I was so worried about how it would turn out. I waited all night!"

"All night?"

"Stupid of me, wasn't it?"

"No, that was stupid of me. I'm sorry. I should've phoned earlier."

"Well, that makes everything better, doesn't it?"

"You knew where I was. I never hid anything from you."

"No, you didn't and I never thanked you for being so blatantly blunt. You made it perfectly clear from the start where you stood. You were going to Paris to see your old friend whatever I thought or felt about it. Well, now you're back; only it wasn't just a case of your seeing her was it? 'Trust me', you said. 'We'll go out for lunch, take a walk in a park'. Tell me is that all it was: a walk in the park? Tell me!"

His silence only goaded her on. "You're still in bed with her, aren't you? For God's sake, Martin, I wasn't born yesterday. You want to put two homes at risk? Have you no sense? What is the matter with you? We're not living an on-off romance! We've been married ten years. We have a young baby. We're a family now. Well, I don't know about you but that's what I've been working for and now I've got it you're not going to spoil it. You're as wilful as your mother. If you've got a problem, running away for a night isn't going to solve it."

Martin wasn't running anywhere. Why should he? He didn't feel bad about this; he felt good. He felt alive. This wasn't any woman and it wasn't just a fling. It was Leni, his soulmate, someone who knew him better than he knew himself, a wonderful person for whom he still had strong feelings. He didn't think of it as infidelity. It was shared fidelity. The crazy love he'd given away had never belonged to Esther. The familiar, sober, measured love that tossed and turned so evenly in their daily lives hadn't been lost; he'd brought it all back with him safe and sound.

"I'm sorry if this hurts but it wasn't a fling. I've just spent a few wonderful hours with somebody who still means a great deal to me and stupidly I hoped you might understand."

"You screwed her."

"It doesn't mean I don't love you."

"Then what does it mean?" she snapped impatiently. "I'm a loyal wife, Martin, and I'm trying desperately hard to keep to a broad canvas because I believe that's what loyalty's about. But when you daub all over it with your strong feeling for your wonderful friend and tell me it's not just a fling, it hurts. Don't you understand? It doesn't help – it hurts! You've had your time together years ago! Get over it. Why can't you move on? You just can't say goodbye to her, can you? Well, how's all this supposed to end? Or should I ask her?"

"I don't think you've got the right tone," he said quietly.

204

"And what is the right tone, Martin? I book a holiday? We all go away together like one big happy family? I look after the children with her husband while you two go off and have a romantic candlit dinner? Or perhaps we all eat together and pretend there's nothing else going on as you sneak an eyeful of mournful messages to your old soulmate while I drool over your grateful glances at me for my empathy! Perhaps you'll get a book out of it. How liberating. How Bohemian. Well, I can't do this, Martin. I can't. You think love is taking a free dip into whatever life experience you want. You think that's how love works? Well, it's not how it works for me. When it comes to my family I'm selfish and old-fashioned enough to believe that love is one dip with one person and sticking with it." Her lower lip quivered as she steeled herself. "And when that doesn't happen it's feeling betrayed, jealous and resentful, and upset, and very sorry. I want the crazy hours too! Last night wasn't just about the waiting. I missed you. Whenever you're not here I miss you. When I'm completely pissed off I miss you and when I feel as separated from you as I do right now, I miss you!"

She'd stopped suddenly, breathing heavily, and her vulnerability pricked him. She looked on the verge of tears and sad as a little girl who'd lost her best doll. How could he now tell her all he asked was to spend just twenty-four hours of his life each year with Leni? For her Leni posed a threat to all she held dear. He didn't want to lose Esther and he didn't want to lose Leni again. He knew what it felt like as a child to have a parent walk away. He wasn't about to do that. It was the age-old problem: he was being asked to plump for one or the other oranges or grapefruit. Esther would never know him like Leni did, but he knew she loved him and he loved her for the crazy green door and because in spite of her predictable bourgois prejudice *The Girl With The Flaxen Hair* still played in his head because however irritable the pitch of her voice, he'd become used to it as a pair of cherished shoes that pinch. When the baby cried he was ready for it.

"I'll see to him," he said, placing his hand on her shoulder. Then he walked out of the kitchen. He knew what she needed. He'd tell her a nice doll story every day for three weeks. Three months later Leni put a stop to any further communication between them.

CHAPTER 16

Kehl. 5th Dec 1974

Hello Martin,

> *'Tears, tears, idle tears I don't know what they mean.*
> *Tears from the depth of some divine despair*
> *Rise in the heart, and gather to the eyes,*
> *In looking at the happy autumn fields,*
> *And thinking of days that are no more.'*

Oh God! Why did I always like tragedy? Perhaps it would be better if we had not met in Paris after we both are married. Then I think of our last amazing hours together and I know I will never change this. But these last months have been difficult for me. Karl knows everything and he is so possessive! We have said the most terrible things to each other. I do not want to break up my family, nor your little family. I am sure Esther is not really so contented with all this as you think.

I know you do not see it, but Karl is right: only when you and I no longer reach for each other can we heal our lives together. I have promised I will not see you again. I have two young sons to look after – and you have a young son too, and a wife who loves you. Please understand you cannot write or telephone me again.

You must promise!

I will always remember us.

Love leni

This was the last letter that Leni wrote to Martin and the last that he read that morning. He slipped it back into its funereal black envelope and dropped it on top of all the others strewn about on the floor. He'd reached the end of his journey. It was a good story! He should've applauded, gone downstairs, and got on with his life. But he couldn't – not yet. It was an unsatisfactory ending. *What had made her confess to Karl about their secret tryst in Paris? Could Karl have found one of his letters? Was it her friend Michelle? Had she dropped her in it? She'd been right. Their love was doomed.* From the day they'd met they'd been prisoners of other peoples' rules and prejudice. Mechanically he slowly started to put their story back to bed when a heart-shaped piece of litter floated down. He picked it up. It was the old gingko leaf, now brown and brittle with age. *Two as one*, she'd said. He wrapped the leaf carefully in paper and put it in his wallet next to the photo. Was she all right? Was she still on this planet? Then he climbed down the loft ladder, Goethe's book in hand. As he neared the landing he found himself gripping the side rail so tightly his white knuckles were ready to break through the skin. His feet walked him downstairs into the study. He was about to put the book away where it belonged between German literature and Jewish history when he turned to the other side of the room his eyes fixed on the telephone that sat expectantly on his desk. All these years he'd kept his end of the bargain. Not once had he questioned Leni's promise – not until now – not until the last mystifying twenty-four hours. Now the question was burning him up. Surely, after so many years, even the most dangerous prisoners were entitled to parole. He walked over to the desk and put the book down. He searched all the drawers for an old address book – he found her number. *But what were the chances of her still living in the same house?* He thought of her family, his family, black holes colliding – a spaghetti outcome. Common sense told him to go for a walk, take a cold shower. His hand stretched out to pick up the receiver but for a second he froze. Then like a man on a high diving board he took a deep breath.

If a man answered he'd hang up. He dialled the international number.

"*Hallo, Leni Koffler am apparat.*" *Joy oh joy!* The voice was as deep and seductive as ever. "*Bitte?*" she prompted.

"Hello," he said, feeling nowhere near as calm as he was trying to sound.

"Who is this?"

"It's me, Martin."

"Martin?" she gasped.

"Hello, Leni."

"My God. I can't believe it!"

He heard her breathing heavily and could hardly breathe himself.

"I was afraid you might've moved."

"It is a long time. How are you?"

"Can you speak?"

"Yes, it is okay." She hesitated, then reassuring him: "It is good to hear your voice."

He sighed with relief she was on her own. "You're not upset I've called?"

"No, I am glad," she affirmed as if she were more than just glad, as if maybe it was the best news she'd had in a long time and he sensed there might be something wrong.

"Are you all right?" he asked.

There was a pause like maybe she wasn't then she told him more restrainedly Karl had had a stroke and given up his general practice and that she would shortly have to collect him from the physiotherapist. It had been a difficult few years. "But you are all right?" she asked with some urgency.

"Never better." He didn't mention his near-death experience a year ago or his recent heart attack. He didn't want to say anything to alarm her.

There was another awkward pause like she was picking her words carefully.

"How are your parents?" she asked.

"My mother is frail and my father has Alzheimer's and is in a home."

"I am so sorry," she said and he knew she was.

"I've sold the factory. I've been thinking of writing a book – about Walter."

What had made him say that? He'd talked to Esther about writing a book ever since the day he'd made up his mind to sell the factory, but he'd been completely undecided about what to write. Something to do with Germans and Jews maybe, but he couldn't think what. The idea of Walter as a subject was as fresh an idea to him as it was bound to be to Leni. He held his breath wondering how she'd respond to once more hearing Walter's name.

"I always liked Walter," she said.

He felt her relax and imagined her smiling, and her faith in the ever-elusive Walter thrilled him. "I know you did. That's why I thought you might help."

She didn't pick up the hint and he thought perhaps he'd made an error of judgement presuming upon her.

"How is your little boy?"

"My little boy is getting married to a Hindu girl in a synagogue this Sunday."

"Big changes since our days."

"I've been thinking about that. This morning I went up into the loft and I came across this photo of a girl I used to know, taken in Heidelberg. I've been reading her letters all morning. She wrote a lot of letters."

"All addressed to Nick Gutmann," she said, a teasing rise in her voice on Nick's surname.

"Yes." He still felt shame in the pit of his stomach for all the years she'd had to write to Nick to avoid his father finding out about his German girlfriend.

"How is Nick? Is he still keeping secrets for you?"

"Now I have none to keep!" It was then he plunged in

head first. "What happened to you after Paris?" The silence that followed was painful. "I'm sorry if I made life difficult for you. I was never much good at putting you first. But what great sin did we commit? All we had was a few hours together." He'd done his best to sound calm and reasonable but even so he had the feeling she was wrenching herself away. Still she said nothing and he wondered if mentioning Paris had been a mistake. "Hello! Leni?"

When she finally spoke her tone was decisive.

"It is not your fault, Martin. I was to blame."

He felt like a squirrel that had foolishly thrown all its nuts away and suddenly discovered the one person he'd wanted to find them had gathered them up. "Are you crazy? There is no blame."

"I was not very clever. I told Karl that I had always loved you, that I would always love you."

"But we all say things on the spur of…"

"I said we are like David and Bathsheba, Martin," she interrupted. "Do you remember you said that to me once?"

"Why should we feel guilty? We didn't kill anybody. It was a beautiful day."

There was a pause. "You do not know all that was said."

Something was bothering her. All the anguish and sorrow he'd not shared with her and could only imagine welled up inside him.

"I'm sorry," he said. "I wasn't a great Walter."

"Esther – she is out?" Leni asked.

"She's in court. She's a solicitor."

"Yes, I remember."

They were touching their past together and he felt her closer.

"Yesterday I thought I saw you walking down Oxford Street. Of course I knew it couldn't be you, but I almost got hit by a car running across the road. And, well, remember you

211

had a dream once running across a graveyard? Well last night I had the same dream, except you grabbed my hand. Strange, isn't it? I just had to know you were all right. Look, I know you must think I am crazy phoning you up like this but ever since yesterday I couldn't get you out of my mind. This morning I was wondering if you still read Rilke. And what were you doing when the Berlin wall came down. I've been walking up and down with Goethe's book in my…"

"I have been thinking of you also." Her voice was warm, deep and embracing, like a big hug.

"Have you?"

They were dancing now, dancing apart, but dancing in time.

"I was in Berlin."

"When?"

"After the wall came down. The next day."

"No, I'd like to hear more about that. But I mustn't be greedy."

"You are not greedy, darling."

They were going around and around, he slowly leading her to a place they might dance together. When she called him *darling* he sensed an opportunity.

"Aren't I? What if I tell you I'd like to see you?"

Once more she was silent and he knew instantly it had been too soon to propose this and immediately regretted it. He'd pressed too hard. The anguished words had sprung from his tongue because he couldn't withhold them but he felt like he'd groped her.

Then, it was as if she'd been waiting for this – expecting it.

"Do you remember Heidelbeg?" she said wistfully.

"Yes," he said and he knew instantly she understood everything. "They have great hats there."

He imagined her smiling at the memory, just as she had long ago when she'd posed in the white cotton hat with the wide brim in Kaufhof's millinery department. But he restrained himself from chasing her further.

"If you can go to Heidelberg I shall see you."

She'd spoken quite casually. She might've been making an appointment with her hairdresser. It had all been so simple he could've wept.

"Yes! Yes! I can be there!" he said, the words now jumping like young lambs in their first spring.

"In six weeks. I will be there then."

"Six weeks?"

"I am visiting my daughter, Nelly, on August 28th."

"You have a daughter!"

"It's been a long time, darling. She is a doctor at the university hospital."

What nachus! He smiled. *A doctor for a daughter!*

"You – and Karl must be so proud."

"Yes. She is very clever and she has a big heart."

"Like her mother!"

"Like her father," she corrected.

He'd never thought of Karl that way but clearly he'd been a wonderful father and Leni was loyal to a fault.

"Where shall we meet?" he burst out, before she might change her mind.

"Do you remember the Marktplatz in the Old Town? If you go to Max's Bar, it is around the corner from the Alte Brucke. I shall be there at twelve o'clock. Can you remember this?"

"I'll remember. I'll write it down."

"You must take the plane to Frankfurt. A train to Heidelberg is one hour."

He scrawled all this on a scrap of paper by the phone:

Max's Bar 12
Alte Brucke
F to H 1 hr.

213

"Are you on email?" she asked.

Martin gave her his email address and assured her there'd be no problem from his side. "You will see me too," he assured her.

"I will be waiting," she said. "Now I must go, I am pleased you remembered Heidelberg."

How could he forget? His mind went back to Walter and the night they'd all first met.

"I'll wear yellow trousers and a bright blue jacket, like the poet, so you'll recognise me."

"I wonder if you will recognise me! Goodbye, darling. Take care of you!"

They both hung up at the same time.

His heart was racing down a dream runway. After twenty-seven years was she really ready to take off once more? What had suddenly made her agree to see him after all this time? He took the photo out of his wallet.

How could he ever fail to recognise Leni?

CHAPTER 17

As the groom, Benjamin Solomon, stood up to make his speech the guests cheered. He was a slim, unassuming young man of medium height. Everything about his presence suggested one comfortable in his own skin and a natural communicator.

"What an unbelievable day! To those of us who are Tamil I say *valakum*. To everyone else I say welcome and *shalom*. To my new mother and father: I am Jewish as you know and I'm used to being well fed. But from the moment I entered your house I've had curry, cakes, biscuits, tea, tea and tea... lavished upon me. I never seem to be able to eat or drink enough. More than that words cannot do justice to the grace with which you have allowed Lara to convert and marry me. To you both from my heart I say *nandre* and *paaraattukkal*. For our Jewish guests: that's Tamil for thanks and *mazeltov*!"

Drawing his speech to a close some minutes later Benjamin concluded with a trip he and Lara had made to Jensen Beach in Florida just a year ago.

"Sitting on the edge of a jetty
Anchored, washed and splintered feet,
Firm through silt and sediment,
Years of fishing-rod stories
Told late into the night after rows,
The river swallows time whole. "

He looked over at Lara, smiling proudly. "My wife wrote those words that night on that jetty on the Intracoastal Waterway in Florida. It was that night I proposed. Lara you are the most astonishing, beautiful girl I know – sincere, compassionate, loyal – a true poet and teacher. Whether we hold each other in silence or we are apart – we are together. I can't wait to spend the rest of my life with you."

There was a sigh of "ahhh" from the guests. When the ensuing applause had died down Benjamin and Lara, left the hall together. Arul Kumeran, Lara's father, a big smile on his chubby face, put his hand on Martin Solomon's arm and delivered his verdict like the circuit judge that he was.

"My God, Martin, that Benjamin of ours knows how to make a speech I must say."

Martin liked Arul. He was always smiling and direct, but this was the first time he'd referred to Benjamin as ours.

"Can I tell you a secret, Arul?"

"Please do," he chuckled. "I hope it is one I could never imagine. I have always liked the exotic, you know."

From the reception room behind a dividing curtain a sitar could be heard playing classical Indian music.

"I had a pretty good clue about this wedding four years ago."

"That sounds like a really good secret. Where did you hear it?"

"It was on the telephone. Benjamin was ill in bed with the flu at the time so when a call came through for him I answered it. That was when I heard this melifluous, gently insistant voice ask me: 'May I speak to Benjamin please?' I thought this doesn't sound like a Jewish girl. After I put the phone down her tone stuck in my head like a piece of music, and I had this strange feeling one day we might be related. That was Lara."

"You know, Martin, I think you must have some Tamil blood. I had a very similar experience. I met Benjamin three years ago, but immediately I saw him, I thought, well, he is definitely not looking like a Hindu boy, but immediately he made a big impression. Lara was so happy and soon I thought perhaps this is meant to be; but I did not think she would become a Jewish Tamil."

"So how do you feel about it now?"

"How do I feel? Terrific. Two great cultures coming together. Better than smashing things up, isn't it?"

"I must admit I don't know if I'd've been so philosophical if Ben had told me he wanted to be a Hindu. Ah, if only there were a few more Jews like you, Arul."

"And more Muslims too, keep the crazy ones out of trouble. And what about the Christians and Buddhists. They have their bad boys too you know. Even we Hindus are not always so kosher I can tell you. The truth is my dear friend if only everybody is a little bit more like me the world will be perfect."

Martin roared with laughter. "Arul, it would be worth a try."

Arul put his arm round his shoulder. "Seriously, Martin, it is how you are as a human being that matters and we Hindus are very charitable. Remember there are more than a billion of us. You poor Jews are only twelve million. You need all the support you can get! If we take one little step to help it is no big deal. Tagore said: *If you cry because the sun has gone out of your life your tears will prevent you from seeing the stars*. I am lucky. It is true, in the beginning I did see the sun slip behind a huge cloud and confess I felt a bit chilly, but now I see it is a beautiful warm evening and our children light up the night sky."

"I see where Lara gets her poetry from."

"Oh, that is not me – that is Sundra," he said and smiled, stroking his wife's arm. "She is the big reader in our family, and she is the first one to blow this big cloud away."

Sundra, wrapped in her magnificent red silk sari who had been listening quietly as she always did, now chipped in.

"Beauty is a coat of many colours. This is in your Good Book, Martin," she smiled, her words rippling softly like a tide on its way out. She was as kind and patient a woman as Martin had ever met.

Nevertheless, he thought, *they must've been very impressed with the way Benjamin drank his tea in order for them to have overcome any nagging doubts or prejudice. Not all fathers would've taken it so well,* Martin reflected.

Just then a young Indian man dressed in a long ivory tunic over loose ivory trousers slipped into the dining room, barefoot, playing a traditional Tamil tune on a clarinet. Gradually, the talking ceased as at every table he passed by he nodded his clarinet in welcome. Then, magically the Tamil tune blended into the haunting Israeli anthem, *Hatikva*. Now the two tunes were part of one whole, timeless and seamless. Then as suddenly as the man had appeared, he vanished behind the curtain separating the reception and dining areas. Martin looked round and was astonished. It was as if everyone present had been lulled into a stupor of beguiled smiles and drunken togetherness.

A few moments later the bride and groom emerged from behind the curtain, now drawn aside. Lara had changed from her white wedding gown into a stunning burgundy sari, edged in gold braid. Arul's sister pasted a thumb mark of sandlewood paste on each of their foreheads, according to ancient Hindu custom. As the young couple took their place for the first dance the band played 'Still The One'. They danced, foreheads touching. When 'Stand By Me' played Esther and Martin joined the young couple. Soon others followed and the dance floor was full. The petite dynamo that was Esther, dressed in her new floral silk chiffon two-piece cosied up to Lara and asked if she knew the clarinettist was going to play 'Hatikva'.

"I had no idea Arun was going to do that."

"It was totally spontaneous," Benjamin added.

218

"Amazing!" Esther enthused.

"He said that when he first heard it he hadn't the vaguest idea of playing it. Then when he was playing the Tamil piece, a phrase of 'Hatikva' just sort of popped out. It felt so right that he kept on playing it."

"Inspirational," Esther said.

"He's a very spiritual person," Lara exclaimed with approval. "It was a call to the heart!"

"I think it was a call to everyone's heart," Esther corrected.

A few moments later Martin's daughter, Rachel, danced next to them.

"How do you feel, Dad?" she asked. "Bet this beats the cranberry juice?"

"What do you think?" Esther asked her daughter.

"I'm asking Dad," Rachel insisted.

He knew she was referring to his trip to Miami just a year earlier where he'd gone with Esther to attend his mother's eightieth birthday. What he'd never expected was to wake up two days later and find himself in intensive care with more tubes running in and out than at Kings Cross Station. Septicaemia, a major heart attack, multi organ failure and hooked up to a ventilator – it was a shock! Lying awake in the dark – alone – vulnerable – playing back moments of his life over and over like a cracked record, sleep repeatedly broken by a delirious bingo-caller in the next cubicle calling out 'fifty f i i ve, fifty f i i ve'. He'd called the five like the winning number and maybe it was. It'd been good for Beethoven and Chanel and good for Leni too. On the other hand, maybe it was the losing number and it was goodbye to all that – goodbye to everything. His two children sitting at his bedside a couple of days later who'd flown in from London certainly must've thought so. *This is not a good sign,* he thought. Worst of all when the nurse finally removed the trachy tube and put an oversized oxygen mask over his face and he was supposed to feel better –

he felt worse. His throat was now dry as a beach of baking hot sand. He'd begged for water but it had been a long wait before he was given his first heavenly sip of cranberry juice.

Martin smiled. "You can't beat cranberry juice," he joked.

"Wow!" Rachel smiled and danced away.

"I don't know how you can joke about it," Esther scolded.

As Martin threw himself ever more enthusiastically into the dancing Esther reminded him of his great smash on the tennis court just a few months ago that had landed him back in hospital after a second heart attack and ordered him to rest.

Now, sitting on his own, he watched her dance by chatting away to a tall, handsome Sikh with a magnificent beard. Ben and Lara stopped at the table and told him they were going to Goa for their honeymoon. Martin was happy for them, happy for everyone. Sitting alone at the table from inside his dinner jacket pocket he took out the email Leni had sent him that morning.

Hello, darling,

 'Perhaps all the dragons in our lives are princesses who are only waiting to see us act just once with beauty and courage. Perhaps everything that frightens us is in its essence, something helpless that wants our love.'

 Yes, I still read Rilke and I think he writes these words for us. Is it really true I am soon going to see you?

 Good luck with the wedding.

Love

Leni.

It was a strange message. He was glad she wanted to see him and there was a sense of urgency that excited him. She sounded so liberated. Could this reunion be that one beautiful act that Rilke had written about? But what was the helpless thing that wanted their love? He was puzzled why now after all these years had she suddenly felt free to break out? Could it be there was some deeper meaning in Rilke's words. Well, he'd find that out soon enough. Meanwhile, she'd seemed to need assurance he would be there so he had immediately emailed back.

Yes, I will be there. And I ask myself the same question: is it really true you will be there too?

Martin felt a tap on the shoulder. It was Nick. With his paunchy stomach, leary grin and droopy eyes – he was a dead ringer for an ageing Walter Matthau.

"What's up, Solomon?" Nick asked, sitting down beside him. "The deal gone through? You certainly look thoughtful."

Martin quickly folded the email and pushed it back into his inside jacket pocket. "We completed on Friday."

"Congratulations. A lot of stress in selling a business. Esther pleased?"

"It was her idea. Thinks I'm lucky to be alive. Suggested now that I'm banned from tennis I take up bowls and write a book."

"Lucky you. Any ideas – for the book, I mean?"

"Perhaps something about repercussions of the Holocaust."

Nick's mournful look gave him the thumbs down. "Ten plays that wouldn't buy you an icecream and now you want to write a book! And about the Holocaust *noch*! Been done to death, hasn't it?"

"That depends how you see it."

"And how do you see it?"

"There are a lot of repercussions we don't hear about."

"Oh yes?"

"I've been giving it a lot of thought recently. How's your new villa coming along? Must be beautiful down there this time of the year."

Nick's black eyebrows raised. "Got a chapter in Antibes have you?"

"All the stress of the past year I could do with a break. Just for the day you understand. Next time you go I could keep you company."

Nick played along. "I'll treat you to lunch. Any particular day in mind?"

"As a matter of fact – August 28th."

"We're opening our 150th store on the 28th. I'm supposed to be having lunch in Birmingham."

"Perfect. I'll be having mine in Heidelberg."

"Heidelberg?" Nick repeated. "You're joking... Not Leni?"

Martin smiled as Nick's mouth remained open like a worried gargoyle. "I'm meeting her for lunch."

"Ahhhh, *those* repercussions."

"It's just a lunch, Nick."

"Is it? What happened? You phoned her?"

"All you've got to do is drop me off early at the aiport. I'll get a taxi on the way back."

"After all these years you want to start this up all over again?"

"You know I never liked the way the story ended."

Just then Nick's eyes flashed a warning and Martin felt two familiar hands on his shoulders.

"What are you two up to?" Esther was now standing directly behind Martin and looking over at Nick.

"You're accusing two babes in the wood," Nick pleaded, his eyes two pools of innocence.

"Am I?" she asked, one eyebrow raised, doubting.

"I was just saying to Martin what a wonderful wedding it is. Wasn't I, Martin? The speeches were great. Lara looks absolutely gorgeous and that Hindu boy on the clarinet – amazing! I said to Martin that was one of the most moving moments I've ever experienced at a wedding. And your outfit is dazzling, Esther."

"Thanks, Nick." Esther smiled. "I'm glad you're enjoying yourself. By the way, have you heard the one about the white man and the red man?" Nick looked puzzled. "It's a good one to remember." Then bearing down deeper onto Martin's shoulders, she continued drawing imaginary circles with the finger of one hand on the table. "The white man took a stick and drew a small circle in the sand and told the red man, 'This is what the Indian knows'. Then he drew a big circle around the small one and said, 'This is what the white man knows'."

"Is that it?"

"Not quite. You see, then the Indian took the stick and drew a huge circle around the two inner ones and said, 'This is where the white man and the red man know nothing!' Isn't it odd how cowboys always imagine they know so much more than the Indians?"

"Not this cowboy," Martin assured her.

"Just as well." Esther squeezed Martin's shoulders gently before she promptly left to have a word with Rachel who was busy chatting away to the clarinettist.

"Always best to agree with the Indians," Martin said. "Or at least say that you do."

Nick leant forward in his chair, confidential-style. "She knows something."

Martin laughed. "Don't worry. There's no way she's on to this."

"Isn't she? Why don't you just tell her? She wouldn't stop you going, would she?"

"Probably not. If I told her my idea for a book she'd probably encourage me but at the back of her mind an alarm bell would go off. She might not say anything but it would be ringing away. She's got a big case she's preparing. Scratching her head right now wouldn't help anyone. Believe me, it's the best way."

"You may be right. That last time you saw her in Paris Esther wasn't exactly singing 'J'attendrai' when you came back, was she? Splashed her warpaint on the kitchen door, didn't she? Green, if I remember."

"Exactly," Martin grinned.

"Better make sure you don't leave any fingermarks on the fridge." Then waving his arm at the array of swishing saris on the dance hall he said, "I wonder what your father would say to all this!"

"*Paaraatukkal,* Nick. *Paaraatukkal.*"

Later that night, back home, Martin was standing in the bedroom by the open window in his pyjamas staring out into the starlit sky.

"What a fabulous wedding! Sundra and Arul are such a charming couple," Esther said, glowing as she put on her night cream at the dressing table.

"I'm thinking of going to Antibes for the day with Nick to check out his villa."

"So that's what you two were plotting. When is this little excursion supposed to take place?"

Her antennae were twitching. Nick was right. He needed to be careful.

"End of next month. I could do with a break. You could come with if you want?" he suggested, turning to face her.

"Now that wouldn't be very clever of me, would it? You know very well I have a difficult court case coming up next month. No, you go with Nick. It might do you good to get away. You might even find an idea for a book."

"You're so sensible," he grinned.

"At least you won't have to carry any heavy luggage, will you? Not for a day trip."

She'd weighted the words luggage and day like Columbo,

and he wondered, just for a moment, if she'd read his mind. But that was impossible for she never knew what he was really thinking and lugging about. It was one of the things that frustrated him about her. She relied entirely upon material evidence. Yes, she was sensible and clever and he liked her Red Indian story but the truth was she'd always lacked intuition. Their marriage was a jigsaw they worked at every day, sharing habits that irritated and endeared as they fitted the little pieces of pleasure and sorrow together. But it was the fitting that got him down. He'd never caught Leni fitting the pieces together.

"No, no luggage," he smiled still gazing out of the window.

"What on earth do you keep looking out there for – or are you thinking of jumping?" She removed her dressing gown and prepared to climb into bed. "Well, when you've decided which it is please turn the lights out and perhaps we can get some sleep. I've a client meeting at ten tomorrow." With that she rolled over, covering her head with the duvet.

Martin paid her no heed. All he could hear and see as he gazed out of the window was the continental band at the Moulin Rouge playing 'La Paloma' as a beautiful girl with the Bardot-looks and searchlight, blue eyes danced by.

CHAPTER 18

The rolling lawns surrounding the majestic Victorian nursing home were a lush green. It could've been Eden even for those who no longer knew what Eden was. Martin parked the car and watched as Rachel walked ahead of him to the veranda that skirted the front of the building. Her hair bleached by the sun swished across her shoulders. She reached to pick some honeysuckle growing up one of the wooden supports.

"Come on, Dad. Get a move on!"

Martin followed her as she stepped forward to ring the front doorbell. Moments later they were greeted by the new assistant matron.

"Good morning, Emma. How's my father?" Martin asked, impatient for news.

"Albert's well," she said. "But I'm afraid he doesn't talk much and does need a nurse to walk with him. But he does sit up very straight in the chair and he still likes to have his moustache trimmed like Douglas Fairbanks."

They walked into the shiny lino-floored hall. Smells of polish and leaking bodies wafted towards them as they progressed down a long corridor. It was only eighteen months since he'd first heard about his father's problem.

Ellen had divorced her GI husband in the early seventies and married for a third time to tall, handsome, retired coat manufacturer from New York, Benny. A few years later, on a visit to London to visit her elderly parents, Ellen flashed her dark eyes at Albert telling him Benny was losing it and that he'd lost all his money on the stock market. Albert had always carried a torch for her and it wasn't long before she'd divorced husband number three and remarried him. Albert now sold his house and moved to Miami. When Ellen insisted that Benny was a good man and she couldn't very well kick him out as he had nowhere to go, Albert agreed; so they all lived together as a *ménage à trois*. It raised a few eyebrows in the condominium but she wasn't fazed. She had her own rules that you challenged at your peril. As for Albert – so long as he could lie in the sun, go to Temple every Shabbat, return home every summer to see the family and make a new hat for Ellen – cobra spit was just par for the course. When Benny died they had a few good years together alone. Then the ominous day came when Ellen wrote to Martin that his father had become impossible to manage and put him on a plane back to London. Esther prepared a room for him in their house and Albert seemed content, but at work Martin discovered not only had he forgotten all the old hat numbers he'd forgotten how to make them.

The doctor told him it was Alzheimer's, but nothing could prepare Martin for the downward spiral. One day he found him lying flat on his back in the driveway, legs akimbo, kicking the air like a beetle trying to right itself. Checking and re-checking the time on every clock in the house, his social life collapsed – playing Bridge – impossible, then banned from the day centre for threatening behaviour. He'd always been a mild-mannered man, but now helping him dress in the morning was like putting pants on Stalin and getting a zets for your trouble. How do you tell Stalin he's got the wrong door to the bathroom? Esther soldiered on, but Martin felt bereft. The one ameliorating note in all this was Albert humming a few bars of Schubert's *Serenade* over and over whenever he sensed something had gone wrong. When the doctor told Martin the cure was inevitable he finally caved in and dumped his father in a nursing home. A few days later he came across an unfinished letter to his mother in his room. 'Everybody seems to be leaving the world. I feel so alone. I miss your loving,' it read. Martin was frozen to the spot, remembering. He knew he'd always loved her but his father's need was gut-wrenching.

"Come on, Mr Solomon. You did all you could. It's our turn now," Emma said, ushering them into a large lounge with French windows looking out onto the garden.

"How's he getting on with the nurses?" Rachel asked.

"Oh, he still says 'Hello, doll' from time to time."

Martin smiled but somehow every observation contributed to a further sadness, and a longing for one more real encounter.

"I understand you're going to play the piano for us," Emma said to Rachel, "and I hear you've won a number of prizes."

Rachel glared at her father. She could blow her own trumpet.

"I'll just go and fetch Albert," Emma said and left.

Rachel opened the lid of the Chappell upright and warmed up her fingers with some scales.

Martin was pensive. Was it only a year ago he'd caught his father at the front door – coat and hat on, car keys in hand, dressed to go out on a Saturday night?

"Dad, where do you think you're going? It's late and you know you're not allowed to drive."

"Who said?" Albert snapped waspishly.

"The doctor. You're a danger on the road."

"I'd like to hear that from the doctor."

"You did. It's your memory, Dad. I've told you before umpteen times."

"A lot of people my age have memory problems."

"You drove through red lights."

"Nobody told me that."

"For Christ's sake, I was with you! I told you!"

"You need to see a doctor!"

"Dad, you don't know what you're doing."

"I know what I'm doing."

"You don't know where the toilet is. You've been pissing in the cupboard under the stairs. Now it's ten o'clock at night. I need to know where you think you're going."

Martin had tried to be reasonable but he'd ended up berating his father and cursing life for dropping him into a pit of snakes.

"I'm going to Ruth," Albert said as he turned the front door knob.

Martin's heart sank. "I've told you before, Dad, Ruth's dead. She died a year ago!"

He watched the blood drain from his father's face as once again the news of his younger sister's death sunk in as if he was hearing it for the first time. His hand dropped slowly to his side.

"Please, give me the keys," Martin pleaded. "Don't you understand? You're not well. The truth is you've got Alzheimer's! You can't remember what's been said to you from one minute to another. Chances are it's going to get worse and I'm trying to help but I never know what's coming next. I don't want to let you down but this could end up one day, with me taking you to a home, because it's the only place they can give you the full-time care you need."

Martin's voice had reached a pitch. He was trembling and overwhelmed with a sense of betrayal, grief and filial failure. Then Albert's eyes suddenly flickered into recognition. The stranger disappeared and he felt his father's presence of old. The voice was steady.

"I'm glad you told me that, Martin. Now I know where I stand. That's how it should be in a family. Whatever happens here, from now on I want you to do whatever you feel you have to do. Family comes first. I don't want you to worry about me. Nobody is going to let anybody down here!"

Albert surrendered the keys and they hugged each other, but nothing could stem Martin's tears, for he knew, in minutes, he could revert.

Emma appeared at the doorway pushing Albert in a wheelchair. "Look who's come to see you, dear."

He looked all right and he was sitting up straight as an arrow just like Emma had described but his eyes were distant. For a second Rachel seemed immobilised. Then a broad smile lit up her face. She went over to meet her grandfather, planted a kiss on his forehead and presented him with the honeysuckle. He held it gently, looking at it in bemused wonder.

"Hi, Gramps! You've put on weight," she teased rubbing his tummy.

In a familiar gesture Albert cocked his head back with a half laugh. Then he noticed the flower in his hand and studied it. He brought it slowly to his nose.

"Isn't it beautiful?" said Emma to her passenger as she wheeled him over to the French windows and parked him next to Martin in the front row near the piano.

"I understand your father used to make ladies' hats."

"For fifty years."

He didn't tell her he'd had a memory like a computer; that not only could he remember each sample since the Second World War he could make them, every one. When he picked up a piece of cloth it had prospects.

"Enjoy the concert," Emma said.

As the nurse went out Rachel bobbed down to her grandfather's level.

"You know you've got the most beautiful green eyes, Gramps."

He looked up at her and smiled a warm hello as though she'd just that minute arrived. But he said nothing and Martin wasn't sure if he was afraid of talking gibberish or just could no longer put words together.

It was not long before the residents trouped in, those who could still walk unaided, those with sticks and those in wheelchairs with nurses to steer. Last to arrive was a short ,stocky woman in her eighties, her silver grey hair was swept back severely into a tight bun. Gert had been a concert pianist in the fifties and had a reputation for being a bully. She made a beeline for her chair next to Martin.

The audience seemed preoccupied and with as much enthusiasm for the concert as a lesson on the Gomorrah. Then Emma announced that Rachel was going to play. There was silence before she began Sondheim's 'Bring on the Clowns', one of Albert's favourites. Immediately, there was a deafening roar.

"Get that bloody girl off the bloody piano! She can't play a bloody note!"

It was Gert. There was a stunned silence. Then, before anyone could say a word, Rachel spun round and quick as a flash she beamed and said, "Give us a chance, love, I've only been learning a week."

There was another hush. Then one of the residents cried out "Give her a chance!"

Then another, "Yes, give her a chance! She's only been learning a week!"

Several others then joined in the cockamamy chorus. "She's only been learning a week! She's only been learning a week!"

At this point Rachel spontaneously launched into the arresting first chord of Chopin's *Fantaisie Impromptu*. Albert sat bolt upright. He turned to face Martin. His eyes were fierce and desperate as he grabbed his forearm. He'd arrived! He was there! Yesterday was back in print. He began to weep uncontrollably not with a bowed head but with his head held high. Martin felt the full impact of his anguish. He knew this naked show of emotion was not what his father would ever have wanted him to see. As Rachel reached the famous cantabile Gert suddenly started to sing. Slowly, the iron grip on his forearm relaxed. Rachel raced to the final rip-roaring run of notes to the end of the piece. The moment she finished Gert jumped up and announced:

"She's got a nice touch that girl. I can tell you know."

Martin gulped for air. A few of the residents applauded but the real Albert had departed. Rachel took her bow and then came straight over to her grandfather and kissed him on his forehead: "What did you think, Gramps? I played that for you. Don't pretend to me you weren't listening."

Once more Albert cocked his head back in that familiar way and studied her. Then he stretched his arm and put his hand up to her face and touched her cheek.

Minutes later Martin left Rachel talking to Gert, who now seemed to regard her as a long-lost daughter and he wheeled his father out into the magnificent gardens.

"I have news, Dad. Last Sunday Benjamin married Lara, the Hindu girl I told you about. She converted. Remember? The wedding was amazing! Lara's father was so magnanimous. He said about his daughter's conversion 'you Jews need all the support you can get.' What do you think of that?"

Martin stopped the wheelchair, crouched down on his knees and searched his father's face for signs of approval or disapproval, but Albert was neither alarmed nor joyful – just silent and far away. It was easy to be honest now.

"Do you know you're a Jew, Dad? Do you know that Schubert and Hitler were both Austrian? Do you remember Leni, my German girlfriend? What would you say if I told you I was going to visit her next week? What would you say if I told you I was thinking of writing a book about her? Race! Religion! Nationality! None of these is a problem for you today, are they, Dad?" Albert looked up at him and just for a moment Martin thought he'd understood everything and was going to pass an opinion, but he started to hum Schubert's *Serenade*.

Martin smiled. "Do you know what I think? If the world had a touch of Alzheimer's we might all be better off!"

A few minutes later Rachel came running up and took her grandfather's hand. Then Martin noticed some saliva oozing from the corner of his mouth. He carefully wiped it away with his handkerchief. Slowly his father cocked his head back and looked up at at his son. Then he extended his right arm, opening his hand, a gesture he'd often use when rehearsing a conversation, but he said nothing.

On their way home in the car Martin asked Rachel what she thought Albert had meant by his vague gesture.

"It's obvious, Dad. He was telling you not to make a fuss."

CHAPTER 19

Three weeks before Martin was due to go to Heidelberg he received an email from Leni.

Hello, darling.

I am sorry I did not reply to you sooner; it has been Karl's birthday two weeks ago and we have had friends from Berlin staying with us. A lot of cooking and Karl needs much help. I have been very tired. You do not need to email me again. Do not worry, whatever happens soon we will be together in Heidelberg!

This you must believe!

Love

Leni.

His email to her on the day of the wedding hadn't requested a reply but when one didn't come he was alarmed. The past few days he'd had an uncanny feeling something had gone wrong. She'd had an accident. Guilt had got the better of her. He'd become convinced she was going to cancel. Now he knew it for certain once more they would be together in Heidelberg. He was elated. *This you must believe* she'd written. It was she who was afraid he might not turn up! How could she ever have doubted him? Surely she knew nothing on earth could've stopped him. The very next day he took the tube into town to buy a new summer jacket. Rushing up the escalator, two steps at a time, at Oxford Street Station, he experienced a sudden tightening in his chest. It was the same feeling he'd had on the tennis court a few months before the wedding when he'd suffered his second heart attack. He'd been lucky and managed to avoid a bypass with a couple of stents. He stood still and let the escalator take the strain for the rest of the upward journey. He slowed his breathing and took small, safe steps to complete his shopping mission. Soon the pain disappeared. Just as well, he thought, he hadn't bought the bright azure blue jacket and yellow trousers to hang up in a cupboard. It was indigestion and it was going to stay that way until after August 28th. After that he wouldn't mind being checkmated.

As the last days flew by he became increasingly cheerful and optimistic. On the morning of the twenty-eighth, reunion day, he was in excellent spirits. He still feared Leni might phone or write to cancel but he'd heard nothing. He'd mislaid the scrap of paper on which he'd written the directions to Max's Bar, but he knew how to get there. He walked triumphantly downstairs into the lounge, wearing his new outfit. There he was met by Esther dressed in her smart black trouser suit and crisp white shirt about to leave for a client meeting.

"Do you have a part in a film?" she asked. "You look very specific."

"You like it?" he said, showing off his jacket in a grand gesture.

"It's different. You've thought about it and that's rather nice, but I thought Cannes was over."

"You never know who you'll run into," he smiled.

"Very arty. You could pass for a poet."

If only she knew how close she was but he knew she hadn't read Goethe's story and he'd never told her how it connected him to Leni.

"I don't think so. My hair's not long enough."

"You're right. I wonder if you should take a hat. I'm sure it'll be hot in Antibes." Then as an afterthought, "Don't forget to drink plenty of water."

He knew she was worried about him becoming dehydrated as had happened the first time he'd had an episode back in Miami.

"Don't worry. I'll be fine."

"Good… Well, while you're slumming it on the Riviera I'll be in court fighting for my client, a very successful fruit importer, who's probably going to win his case and lose a daughter."

"How did he get to be so smart?"

"My client retired to Spain and left his trusted son-in-law to run the business. The young man thought he wasn't being sufficiently rewarded for his new responsibilities, and neither did his daughter. In one year he created enough phoney invoices to buy himself a Ferrari. He'd promised to take care of things. But it wasn't entirely his fault. It wasn't the first time a few pears had gone missing. Dad should've known better. He wasn't listening. He only heard what he wanted to hear. Leave a rabbit in charge of your lettuce patch you get what you asked for. Nobody leaves you more clues to their true nature than your own."

He ignored the innuendo and wondered why the family couldn't've reached a peaceful settlement instead of the two factions shooting it out in an unholy war. It was a hopeless case but he knew that lawyers earned a good living out of bad listeners.

"No chance of a settlement then?" Martin asked blithely.

"My client calls them terrorists."

"Well, perhaps one day far into the future, if we ever get there, some inspired Isaiah will come along and blow the whistle on all the nonsense we have to live with. Then everybody will be forced to consign their disagreements to history and start afresh with new supersensory listening powers!"

"Yes, well, I suppose all families screw up one time or

another. The important thing is, when we do, to make sure we do everything we can to straighten things out, even if sometimes that requires a little sacrifice."

"You are so sensible."

"Even the supersensory have to start somewhere."

Her mood was light and bouncy, but he wasn't sure whom the little sacrifice was for. He wasn't sure if she was talking about a bomb on a bus, the fruit importer, or themselves.

At that moment Martin heard a car drive up the gravel driveway. He looked out of the window. It was the blue Bentley. The driver jumped out and made his way up to the front door.

"Nick's here," he said.

"Passport?"

He patted his inside jacket pocket. "Check."

"Ticket?"

"Check."

"Did you want to read this on the plane?" she asked, picking up from the coffee table a slim paperback with a picture of Goethe wearing an eighteenth-century dashing blue jacket on the front cover.

"I nearly forgot." He nestled the thin paperback into his inside jacket pocket. It was a long time since he'd read Goethe's tragic short story and he was looking forward to reading it again. "You're so *good* to me," he said like Roger O. Thornhill.

"That's because you're careless, thoughtless and as blind as a bat."

"I'd be lost without you. I don't know how you do it."

"If you don't know your own who do you know?" she said as the doorbell rang. "Make sure you get on the right plane, won't you?" Then she leant forward and hugged and kissed him as if he was going off to war. "Come back safe."

"I have to," he said, struck by her momentary display of emotion. "You know how I hate to be independent."

237

"I'm counting on it."

In the car on the way to the airport Nick nattered on about England losing the last Test at the Oval to the Australians, a pop star opening of his new store in Birmingham, and his son's place at Cambridge. Realising Martin wasn't listening to a single word he congratulated him on not being found out by Esther.

"It wasn't that difficult," Martin grinned.

CHAPTER 20

As the Boeing levelled off at 30,000 feet, Martin gazed out of the oval window at the clouds below. Goethe's short novel rested in his inside jacket pocket unopened. All he could think about was Leni. He reminisced about a twenty-year-old girl in Engelberg wearing a thick blue jumper and black ski pants. That was the time when their love had deepened and shone brightest in the white light of the snow; when she was fearless on the slopes and prepared to risk all and he'd been afraid to live off-piste.

The air hostess asked if he'd like a drink but he wasn't there. He was sitting opposite Leni, at Max's Bar. Her beautiful face was unlined, and the same searchlight-blue eyes of old were looking across at him. Her lips trembled as she spoke of the hundreds of times she'd thought of picking up the phone, or writing to him. How, in all the years that had passed, she couldn't bear, even once, to return to Engelberg.

He revelled in the verbal foreplay. He'd sympathise as she told him of her struggle to conceal her true feelings from Karl. She'd confess that, though she'd tried to be a good wife, deep in her heart Martin still was her one and only true love. Then he'd reassure her and say he was sure that she was a wonderful wife.

He knew, in her own way, she loved Karl, and the fact that she'd kept silent for a quarter of a century was proof of that. After this he'd tell her that he couldn't count the number of times he, too, had picked up the phone and put it down again. He'd tell her how he'd been afraid of upsetting her, and she'd smile and say teasingly: *Now you are a considerate one.* Then he'd take her hand and ask her forgiveness for all the moments he'd tried and failed to be Walter. He'd give her the leaf he carried in his wallet, and her eyes would fill, she'd smile, and in her deep husky voice, say:

I am glad you still like me a little?

Just a little, he'd say.

He'd tell her he didn't know if they'd been *meant* to fall in love when she was eighteen and he was nineteen, and he didn't know if he was *meant* to lose her when he was twenty-two, or lose her again when he was thirty-four. But of one thing he was sure, this day was meant to be for them. Then he'd explain his new idea for a story in which Heine, Rilke, Goethe, Beethoven and Sholem Aleichem would bind them together forever in a book. Then she'd fill his memory with all he'd forgotten. He imagined placing one hand on each of her shoulders, his fingers not squeezing but touching her oh, so lightly, their eyes would lock. In an instant they'd do all they couldn't do, and say all they couldn't say – with just a look as he'd transfer his entire life force into hers in a vortex of unconsummated love. And he'd say: *eyes only.*

Martin was so absorbed with this glorious reunion that was about to take place in the wonderful world of the *soon-to-be* that he hardly noticed he'd left the plane and was now travelling on in a railway carriage full of chattering holiday makers. The train jolted to a stop at Heidelberg Station and he'd arrived. The station buzzed with passengers rushing to their platforms and to the exits. A porter directed him to Bismarckplatz, and he set off by tram for the Old Town.

From the moment he arrived, around every street corner, he expected to bump into her; from every shop he expected her to wave. The Old Town was busy and there were hundreds of legs walking towards him and walking away, but none of them had the right face, and he thought how fantastic it was the number of people walking around with arms and legs all with the wrong face, yet he knew somewhere in the streets of Heidelberg she was on her way, and he felt her near.

He passed by the Church of the Holy Spirit where she'd told him all about the Rabbi of Heidelberg. He was forty-five minutes early but perhaps she'd be early too, already seated at Max's, waiting, but she wasn't, so to kill time, he walked down to the Old Bridge over the Neckar where he'd walked with her forty years ago. There he saw a statue of a large brass monkey crouching, with what appeared to be a brass mirror in its hands. He didn't remember it being there last time. A young couple stood reading the inscription on the mirror and he asked if they could translate it for him. In excellent English the young man said, "If you look into this mirror you might see something as funny as me." Then he told Martin there had been another monkey there, but it had disappeared years ago in a war. The new one came in 1979.

"According to legend, the statue is a reminder to the citizens of Heidelberg that neither city dwellers nor those who come from outside the town are better than anyone else, and they should look back over their shoulder whenever they cross the bridge so they will always remember this." The young man continued enthusiastically, "If you rub the monkey's hand you will have good luck."

Martin thanked the young couple, gave the monkey's hand a good rub and strode off to his rendezvous.

He sat down at a table outside Max's Bar to wait. At first he didn't see anybody who looked remotely like Leni. He smiled benignly at four elderly women with drooping breasts and faces like the Rock of Gibraltar sitting nearby sipping their coffee. *Leni could never look like that!* He was glancing around, watching life pass by in the square when he had the growing feeling that he was being watched. He looked over his shoulder and as the sun disappeared behind a cloud he saw a young woman with long blonde hair sitting by a window inside the bar. They looked at each other for a moment then he turned away. When he spun round to take another look she'd vanished.

He settled back again searching for Leni. As the sun reappeared he shielded his eyes with his hand, able to see a young woman in a pretty floral sundress weaving her way between the tables towards him. It was the girl with blonde hair. He watched her, eyes glued as she approached.

She stopped at his table and asked in a voice that sounded familiar. "Excuse me. You are Walter, no?"

He was stunned by the resemblance. "How...?"

She smiled shyly. "Perhaps your jacket?" she suggested. Then you must be..."

"Nelly."

He rose and they shook hands. "What a surprise! For just a moment I thought... I was expecting to see your mother."

"I am sorry to disappoint you."

"No, no, not all," he smiled. "Is she...?"

"She asked me to meet you," she interrupted. "Are you all right? It is very *hot* today."

"I'm fine. Can I get you something to drink?"

"Well, I only live fifteen minutes away. We thought you might like to come back for some English tea."

"That sounds a great idea," he said, thinking what a charming, composed young doctor she was. Considering the rather unusual circumstances, she wasn't embarrassed at all.

What an extraordinary day it was turning out. From the moment Martin had arrived in Heidelberg he'd felt as if he were experiencing life so much clearer and sharper than usual but then Leni had always had that effect on him. *How would it be when they finally meet?* he rhapsodised.

"You work at the hospital here, don't you?"

"But today I have the day off. How long are you staying in Heidelberg?"

"I'm flying back this evening," he said, as they walked down the bustling Hauptstrasse towards the river.

He wondered how much Nelly actually knew about Walter and how much more she knew about his relationship with her mother. *Mother and daughter must be pretty close,* he thought, *for Leni to send her daughter to bring me back to join them for tea. What else could this be? Unless Karl's health had suddenly deteriorated, and she'd had to stay behind to look after him.*

"Is your father all right?"

"He is okay," she said kindly but firmly.

Considering they'd only met a few minutes ago, Martin was beginning to feel remarkably at ease. He was surprised at the way she took his arm when a cyclist nearly mowed them down as they crossed a busy street. He was being taken care of and he liked it.

"There are a lot of bicycles here in Heidelberg," she smiled.

"That was close!"

"If we do not arrive together I will let my mother down."

She had the same lovely smile as Leni but her expression was sphinx-like, withholding. A few minutes later they were sitting on a bus on the way to her apartment.

"Did you always want to be a doctor?" he probed, wondering how much she knew that he knew.

"When I was twelve I wanted to be a trapezist in the circus."

"But you gave up that idea."

"I heard about a student who gave up engineering for medicine. He had been a very good student, first in his year."

"He preferred to fix people more than machines."

"He did not prefer it, he *had* to do it. One day, when he is studying for his final engineer examination, a friend came to him with a problem. The student told his friend to come back the next evening. That same night this friend jumped off a bridge and was killed. The student blamed himself for not seeing his friend's terrible problem because his eyes are closed. After this he wanted to do something where his eyes will be always open. That is when he made up his mind to be a doctor." Her words now took on a bold, distinctive rhythm. "But he did not want to be a doctor who waited for a call. He wanted to be a doctor who responded to a need, or at least one who tried to. I wanted to be someone like this."

"A rare breed," Martin said, moved by her seriousness and the man's conversion.

"This is my father," she said, proudly.

Martin was pulled up short by this revelation. This did not describe the Karl he'd come to know through Leni.

"It was a big choice. It is not so usual for him to change his mind. Now it is his turn to be cared for. He has had a bad stroke. Now he cannot fly his aeroplane, he cannot ski and he cannot climb."

Martin thought how young and pretty she looked, her eyes shining with pride.

"I'm sorry. It must be difficult for a man like this stuck in a chair."

She shrugged. "His mind is free."

He couldn't help wondering if, by colluding in this clandestine meeting with him, Nelly felt she was betraying the father she clearly so admired or if she were harbouring any negative feelings about Walter; but she gave no sign of either. *Maybe, this was her way of responding to the family's needs,* he thought. She was quite a girl!

"Still it must be difficult for him – and your mother – for all of you."

"They have good friends."

Good, he thought. *One of their friends is probably with him for the day.* He wondered how Karl would feel if he knew he was sitting on a bus, talking about him with his daughter and about to have tea with both her and his wife.

Away from the bustle of the Old Town, by the river,

they stepped off the bus and approached a row of charming art nouveau buildings. His eyes flitted from house to house, as he anticipated a door being opened by an ageless princess from Shangri-La. When they entered a silent, small one-bedroom garden flat and Leni was not there to greet them he was disappointed. Nelly told him to make himself comfortable while she put the kettle on. The apartment was simply decorated with white walls, and a dark wooden floor. A Monet print hung on the wall above an old linen sofa made good by a rustic coloured throw. There were rows of books on a shelving unit, a hi-fi system, and a glass desk that had a corkboard fixed above it on which was pinned a collage of photos of Leni and the family. From the front window he could see out across the Neckar. As he turned and sat down on one of the chairs around a wooden table he noticed next to a large bowl of fruit a book of poems translated into English. It had been left open apparently at random. He started to read:

'Show us the sun slowly
Lead us step by step from star to star
Gently let us learn how to live again
Or else a bird's song
Or the filling of a bucket at the well
Could break open our pain so lightly sealed
And wash us away.'

Nelly called from the kitchen: "Milk and sugar?"

"Just milk please."

She returned with two mugs of tea, and some fruitcake and sat down opposite him passing one of the mugs. "Is that all right?"

"Perfect," he said, disappointed they weren't waiting for Leni before having tea.

"It was a birthday present from my mother many years ago," she said, glancing at the book he was now closing. "The poet was a survivor of the Holocaust. When her lover was tortured to death by the Gestapo she lost her voice and could not speak for weeks."

"She found her voice here all right," he said tapping the book with his fingers. There followed an awkward silence. For the first time since they'd met, Nelly's relaxed demeanour turned as brittle as a figurine on a white porcelain vase. "Your mother *isn't* coming, is she?"

She didn't reply immediately. The seconds seemed to pass like minutes.

"No, Walter, she will not be here."

Time stopped. Immediately Martin felt something ominous in her tone. Her stricken eyes were the only outward sign of distress.

"She died two weeks ago."

"Died. Two weeks… " he stammered. He leant forward clasping the arms of the chair. "Leni?" he gasped. "It's not possible."

"She was ill for some time."

"I spoke with her on the phone only…"

"With myeloid leukaemia there is not much hope," she interrupted.

"But two weeks ago she sent me an email!"

"I know."

"Leukaemia. Leukaemia," he repeated under his breath, like a dirge. "Two weeks."

When the news is really bad by repeating the dead words you try to stall it. Reality is often a few steps behind the news that brings it. He felt the blood drain from him. An hour ago every street in Heidelberg had been a Yellow Brick Road leading to her, every shop a gingerbread house from which she might magically appear. He'd been sniffing the air for the smell of Chanel. He'd stroked the legendary monkey's hand for good luck. That was one sick monkey and this was one sick joke. While she was dying of leukeamia he'd been in Oxford Street buying his blue jacket and yellow trousers.

"Did she know... how sick she was?"

"She knew."

Then why had she said they'd be together in Heidelberg? *You must believe this,* she'd said. He'd much rather have known the truth six weeks ago. He'd've been prepared. What would he have come for? This was a charade! He'd missed her suffering and missed the funeral but he hadn't missed Death. Death had been waiting for him all along here in this room, waiting for him to catch up. She was going to help him with his book. She was the other half of a story. The half of his life he'd left behind and hoped to find. She'd let him believe all that would happen. Now she was gone and he was half of nothing. He felt cheated – angry. To hell with the book! He didn't want to say goodbye like this. He wanted to put his head in the big hippo's mouth that had taken her and scream *I love you! I love you with your cancer! I love your rotting corpse! I'll love you forever!* He suddenly felt cold – eviscerated. He wondered if she'd sat on the chair he was sitting on talking to Nelly across the table. He wondered when she'd first told Nelly about him, but most of all he wondered if she knew she was quite so sick when they'd spoken on the phone, why had she let him fly over?

"She didn't want you to hear it in a letter. Are you all right?"

He'd been aware she hadn't taken her eyes off him for a moment. Now she was looking concerned. Had his skin turned grey? Were his lips blue?

"I'm fine, but what about you? Not only have you just lost your mother, you've had the job of telling me!"

"It is what she wanted."

Acceptance was what he read in Nelly's eyes whilst with every fibre of his own being he was still willing Leni back into existence. He knew the only way for her to materialise now was

247

by remembering. Not just any remembering, for he could not bear to trust her portrayal to the casual eye or an approximate view. If he wanted her lungs to fill with air, if he wanted her to breathe he had to see her through the eyes of somebody who knew her well – somebody who could reveal with insight the minutest detail of her life. He wanted somebody who could recapture all the colours of her soul like a great artist.

"Do you think Rembrandt could paint from memory?"

She told him she had no idea, but for the next couple of hours he learnt about school concerts, poetry readings, climbing holidays, tears at Nelly's graduation from medical school, how her brother Joseph had had nightmares for years and how Leni kept telling him he was strong until he was strong. How strict she was when Nelly was naughty but could never hide a smile for long. She told him about their trip to Checkpoint Charlie the day before the wall came down. The grand reunion the next day that had people crying for joy in the rubble and dancing in the streets as Trabi cars from the East hooted greetings to the Volkswagens, Mercedes, and BMWs in the West. How Leni took three small pieces of concrete from the rubble and drew a white dove with a flower in its beak for each of her three children. She said she'd never seen Leni quite so excited which was surprising because she was a person who liked to knock walls down without anybody noticing. It was then she told him that two weeks before Leni had died she'd asked her to meet an old friend from London called Walter who was writing a book. She'd said he was her first love and that she might've married him but he was Jewish and his father was a difficult one.

He was expecting difficult questions to follow for she seemed pensive as though weighing up something terribly important, but all she said was: "Would you like some cake?"

After tea he added to the picture she had painted. He told her where he'd met Leni and how she'd been reading Goethe's story about Werther and how he'd wanted to change the tragic ending to a happy one – how he'd kept calling Werther – Walter.

"I told her, I wouldn't've killed myself and I wouldn't've let anyone stand in my way... I'd've done whatever needed to be done to keep her – sacrificed everything. She liked my ending. I'm afraid I never was as committed a person as Walter. I think perhaps you should call me Martin now."

Her head tilted back slightly as though she were considering her next move on a chessboard then she stepped forward and shook his hand warmly. "I am glad to meet you, Martin," she smiled. "I have read much about the Jewish people and their troubles in our country."

"Germany did not always make it easy to be a Jew," he said sadly.

"Germans did not always make it easy to be a German. First the war and after the guilt – but people can change, now it is very different from those days. Today in front of the university, where they burnt Heine's books, there is a memorial by a Jewish sculptor. Five years ago I studied medicine in Heinrich Heine University. Today we have streets all over Germany called Heinrich Heine Strasse. Here in Heidelberg we have a beautiful synagogue and a University for Jewish Studies. In Berlin there is the Holocaust Museum. After the wall came down there is a new law in our country. Now every Jew who wants has the right to come and live in Germany."

Martin was still reeling at this remarkable revellation when she took two steps over to the table and held up the book he'd been reading earlier.

"Do you know the first German writer to win the Nobel Prize since the war is a Jewish poet? You have been reading one of her poems. Her name is Nelly Sachs." She laid the book back on the table. "And my name is Nelly!"

She'd spoken softly but her voice rang in his ears like an

iron tongue sounding a cathedral bell. This was dead men breathing. This was how they came back. This was how they survived. Being remembered. She'd actually named her child after a Jewish poet. And Karl had gone along with it.

"Your mother was a very unusual woman."

"On the last day she asked me if she had been a good mother. I said I was a very lucky daughter as this was not a question I ever asked myself, because in our house I had known no other. She asked me again so I repeated my answer. Then she said, *I am not always so good.*"

He guessed Leni had been referring to their brief affair in Paris but he wasn't going to tell her that.

"Does your father know that you are meeting me today?"

"My father knows nothing. I have never heard him speak your name. She said he did not like you because once you made her quite ill."

Was it the abortion she was talking about when she'd first met Karl? Strangely, she didn't seem curious to ask him directly what Leni might've been referring to and he wondered if there was something she was withholding.

"Would you mind if I played some music?"

"Good idea."

He watched her as she took out a CD from its box and placed it on the tray of the player. The sublime notes of Bach's *Cello Suite No.1* filled the room.

He was completely taken aback. The last time he'd heard that was with Leni when they'd been awoken early in the morning in Paris by a student's cello practice. The angels had been good to them that day. He couldn't swallow the lump in his throat.

"She wanted this played at her funeral. It was her favourite piece."

"Was it?" He turned away and walked casually over to the array of photos on the corkboard so as not to betray his feelings. There was Karl in his pilot's gear with Leni and the

250

three young children, standing by a small two-seater plane. He was a handsome, forceful, decisive-looking man, his mouth set firm. She was smiling into the camera and looked as contented as a mother hen. Then there was another of her nestling against Karl outside a hotel he recognised at once as being in Engelberg. Hadn't she said she'd never go back there, or had he imagined it? He wondered if she ever said *Take care of you, darling* to Karl the way she used to say it to him.

"Everyone looks so happy."

"Next month would be their fortieth anniversary," Nelly said, now standing beside him.

He was just about to sit down when he noticed a small photo of Leni in the top right-hand corner of the collage that stopped his breath. It was the photo he, himself, had taken of her standing next to the statue of Marshal Ney in Paris. She unpinned it so he could look closer.

"It is a great picture, no?"

"It certainly is," he replied cagily.

"She was very beautiful," Nelly said, passing him the photo.

"Yes, yes she was." He looked at the back of the photo; there in familiar handwriting in green ink; *Luxembourg Gardens 1974.*

"My father took this picture when they are on holiday in Paris."

"Your father?"

"And I am there too," she smiled.

"You?" he exclaimed.

"Yes, you cannot see me yet. I am just a little idea in here," she said tapping the side of Leni's head in the photo. Then pointing to Leni's abdomen in the photo she smiled and said, "The next morning she told me I am here."

Martin gulped for air. "She told you that?"

"She said I was a miracle because my father did not want…

any… more… children." Her voice tailed off to a whisper then picked up again, "but *she* did and if you wish something strong enough you can get it. And she wished for me."

"That really is extraordinary!" he said reeling from the realisation that the little idea might just have grown up to be his own daughter.

"They were staying at my Aunt Michelle's apartment near the Luxembourg Gardens, she said, watching him as she took the photo back. "I think my father does not like this picture because she is flirting with the marshal. That is why I brought it back here. Pehaps my father is a little jealous," she said in mock sadness, "but I like it because it is cheeky. I would like to know what she is saying to the marshal," she said seeming to search his face for a reaction.

"She was probably saying: *Don't tell anybody.*" Then suddenly afraid of having said too much he quickly added, " – about the wish!"

"That is a good guess."

If she were suspicious of his answer she gave no sign of it as she casually pinned the photo back on the corkboard. "I have something for you. I am back in a minute." With that she left the room.

Martin's head was spinning. He looked up again at the collection of photos. It was just so amazing. But how could he be absolutely sure if she really was his daughter? There'd never been any mention of her being pregnant. Even in her last, very final letter there'd been nothing about a third child. So why? Unless… Unless… What if Leni hadn't kept their secret because she couldn't? What if, after three months, Karl had noticed she was pregnant? That night, he'd thought it was all right, but what if it hadn't been? Karl didn't want more children, and Karl wasn't a man to change his mind without good reason. Even Nelly had said that. And Leni had confessed on the phone six weeks ago she'd told Karl they were like David and Bathsheba. What *more* had she said that she couldn't tell him? What *more*? My God, it was obvious, wasn't it! It was in the Bible!... *And David and Bathsheba had a child, and they called it Solomon.* He didn't need a DNA test to know who Nelly was. He was there when Leni made the wish. They were lying side by side. Nelly was his blood. Why hadn't they told her? After all these years a child had a right to know who their biological parents were. Karl should know that. All that wonderful talk about responding to *a need!* What about Nelly's need and her mother's need? Hadn't Leni sacrificed enough? Must she atone beyond death? Now he understood her doubts about being a *good mother.* He wondered what Nelly would make of it when he explained what Leni had meant. When he told her she was a Solomon! How would she feel about this secret Karl had forced her mother to live with all these years? This man who'd doted on his daughter her whole life and lied to her from the day she was born? Now he, Martin, was being asked to do the same. Leni must've guessed this might happen and left it to him to decide. Well, he'd decided it was time to pierce this suppurating boil and for this father and daughter to have an honest introduction. He turned to take one more look at the photo. Every muscle in his body was taut. He'd been so absorbed in his momentous thoughts he hadn't noticed Nelly now standing next to him holding a cardboard box.

"Bach is not supposed to do that," she said, as he turned to face her.

His heart was full to bursting but it was not physical pain just an ache that comes from the bittersweet pill of love lost, and a love that couldn't be named. At least not until now!

"Do what?" he exclaimed.

"You look as if you are going to jump off a bridge."

"Do I?"

"You are my mother's good friend. She would not want you to come to a bad end, and neither do I."

Didn't Leni want him to tell Nelly the truth? Did she just want him to know it – feel the terrible ache she'd hid in her heart all these years and do nothing? He needed to clean things up. There was only one way forward now: the honest way.

"Maybe jumping from this bridge won't be so bad."

With that, Nelly put down the box on the table stepped, forward and kissed him warmly on the cheek.

"Is that to save me?" he said, both touched and astonished by her spontaneous reaction.

"Perhaps. My mother asked me to give you this," she said putting her hand on the box on the table. "Many of your letters are in here. When you go you must take them with you. Now you will have Leni's story and your story too. Maybe it will be better if one day you will put this bridge in your book." With that she smiled at him so gloriously that all the drama and tension he'd felt in the past few minutes evaporated. He didn't know what had made her kiss him at that moment. Was she protecting Karl, herself, him, Leni's memory? Suddenly something new happened, something so fresh and unexpected it overwhelmed him. Every vital urge to clean things up was gone. Tears filled his eyes as all thoughts of to whom Nelly belonged and of who owed what to who vanished. This summer parting was never meant to be a day of sorrow or recrimination. It was meant as a gift. This was how Leni wanted to say goodbye… here in this room with their daughter, surrounded by pictures of her and her family, and memories that she wanted them to share together… a beautiful gift that had fallen from the sky, unwrapped and offered up in all its wondrous colours. Now he was filled only with feelings of gratitude and an urge to be gracious. Whatever he thought about Karl, he'd been a great father and was much loved and respected by his daughter.

"Your father is a very lucky man."

"I think we are all lucky that your father is a difficult one!"

He knew what she meant. Neither his children in London nor her or her brothers would've been here today if it weren't for his father. Oh, how he now yearned to tell her more about her grandfather, and about a father she'd never known. Again he felt an impulse to explain what Leni had meant about not always being the *good mother*. The drum in his chest was banging furiously. He had to be careful. If she saw he was under stress she might kiss him again and he might weaken.

"Your mother was as good as it gets." He glanced at his watch. "I must go soon."

She looked at him once more like she was on the verge of saying something quite important but she only replied: "I'll walk with you to the bus stop." Then she disappeared into the bedroom.

A warm breeze wafted in through the open window, and though he saw no one else present in those last few minutes he sensed an old friend had joined them. His heart was full as once more he turned to look at the family picture of Leni and Karl and the children standing by the plane. She was still smiling, only this time it wasn't the camera she was smiling at – she was smiling at him. It was as if she'd been waiting for him. That she knew one day he'd be standing here on this very spot looking at a photo that told him this was where she was needed –with Karl, the boys and their love child Nelly. Then he heard her whisper:

Isn't it funny, darling, I told you I will see you, and now you know it!

For the past six weeks he'd lived for this day, the day they'd be reunited and now they were.

When Nelly returned, Martin picked up the box of letters and said, "Thanks for these." And they left her home in silence. He was deep in thought and guessed she was too. What an extraordinary afternoon it had been! He wondered if Nelly too had sensed that this day had been no chance meeting and that somehow it had been preordained. He'd called out to Leni across the years and almost with her last gasps she had grasped him to her. Then with a clever mother's instinct she'd miraculously initiated this wonderfully healing encounter with his daughter. Nelly unexpectedly broke the silence telling him about the boyfriend she'd been dating for four years who was a member of the Green Party and believed in renewable energy.

"Fifteen years from now solar energy and wind farms will produce eighty per cent of Germany's energy needs. What you take from the earth you cannot put back, but what you take from the sun and the wind is always there."

Martin was a little disappointed she wasn't hanging out with a brain surgeon, rather than a saving-the-planet-protestor, but it was only when she told him her friend didn't believe in marriage he became alarmed. He thought he recognised a drifter.

"So long as he doesn't run away when the weather's bad."

"Don't worry, he is a *committed* person," she smiled. Her slight emphasis on *committed* hurt and he sensed an edge. Suddenly changing her tone she said, "I'm sorry, that is not nice of me."

They walked as they talked. It was easier talking so candidly while walking. He shrugged sheepishly, he was certain at the back of her mind she was thinking her mother had deserved someone who'd put up a greater fight for her than he had.

"Why not? I was the master excuse-maker. I had wonderful intentions. Then I told myself the circumstances were impossible, so I settled for building dreams with fantasy solutions. And when none of them worked out I told myself I'd done my best. I was never really brave enough."

Abruptly she stopped walking and upbraided him.

"What is the matter with you? Why do you want me to think so little of you? Your intentions are great and you do not need excuses for them. For you this love is not possible. You had a great battle with your father and you lost and this is sad, but there is honour in this struggle and that too is great. And if it is my father who is so upset I think I too shall struggle." She hadn't indicated which side she'd plump for but she was clearly genuinely concerned. She was still trying passionately to save him. She'd sensed his shame and taken *rachmonous* on him like a true Jewish daughter! *If only she knew.* "I hope you are not ashamed for this," she said challenging him.

She was right about one thing; he had given his all in this struggle and if it was never enough it was all he had. "No, I am not ashamed, not now. It could've been a very different story but I'm glad it isn't," he smiled. "Very glad."

"Good," she said, and they continued walking.

In an afternoon wrought with emotion, for the first time he felt a blanket of calm descend. In one swift move this young daughter he'd never know had erased any doubts he may have had about his worthiness. She'd made him feel sad and proud – like the slow movement in a Beethoven piano concerto. He was privileged to be with her and relieved that the tension between them had been so quickly resolved. Then just as they arrived at the bus stop, with the bus approaching thinking that was the end of it Nelly put him on the spot.

"It was you, Martin, wasn't it? It was you who took this photo in the Luxembourg Gardens?"

He was completely taken aback. She'd spoken with such conviction she had to have proof. Well, he was glad if she had. He wanted to be found out and was relieved the game was over. Hide and seek with him hiding behind a curtain from his own daughter was not a game he'd wanted to play. He'd had enough of that game with her mother. All he had to do now was jump out from his hiding place and say: *Yes, here I am! I'm the one with the camera!* What a relief! If cleaning up the story was a fall from grace he welcomed it. What a way for all to be revealed – at a bus stop in their last few moments shared together. What duty did he owe Karl anyway, this wasn't his father, this wasn't even a friend – this was the blind, stubborn, frightened man who'd sentenced them all to a life of silence. He was about to open his heart to her – when the poet's words rang in his mind *perhaps all that frightens us is something helpless that wants our love.*

"I wish it had've been," he said firmly.

He waited on tenterhooks for her response, more than half-hoping she'd pop her head over the wall and cry: *Got you!* But when it came it was not the response he'd expected.

"I just wanted to be sure. Forgive me – I am not very tactful," she smiled mischievously like a naughty child and he still wasn't sure if he'd been spotted or not. "My father would not be very pleased with me talking to you like that."

"I don't suppose he'd be too happy you talking to me anyway!"

"No, you are right. He has lost a lot, Martin. *I must show him the sun slowly.*"

Once again he caught a wisp of a smile and he wondered if that meant one day she would actually talk to Karl about him, or maybe one day Karl would tell her the truth. Maybe he'd unwittingly given something away. Perhaps a surprised look when she'd told him about the photo. Had she guessed about Paris? Maybe one day in the future she would come to him again. Whatever happened he made up his mind he, Martin, would never be the first to speak of it. All need to tell her who she was and call her *daughter* had once more disappeared. She was Nelly, a daughter of the world. Tears brimmed his eyes – not for what he'd lost or for what he'd found, but for the years Leni had held her silence. The bus pulled up and the doors opened. He embraced her once more, holding her tight to him then he turned quickly away stepping onto the platform before he turned to face her for the last time.

"I loved the Bach."

"Good luck with your book."

"It's just an idea," he said.

"So is *The Sorrows of Young Werther* at one time."

He found a seat and waved goodbye through the window to his Good Samaritan. After all, had she not saved him from jumping off a bridge? He sat down, the parcel on his lap thinking of Leni waiting, waiting for a moment that she would never see. Then he took out his notebook and wrote down three words: *Waiting for Walter. Not a bad title for a book*, he thought!

After fifteen minutes he left the bus and a warm glow seemed to carry him like an updraught all the way to the Alte Brucke. He stepped lightly past the brass monkey and walked across the bridge, stopping halfway. Then he took the ginkgo leaf from his wallet.

Beneath the bridge the river flowed ever onward. He held the leaf gently.

Then he let it go. It floated down into the river below; that leaf that was one and also two. He wished Leni back to the world of measurable time, calling her back from infinity, assuring her he would keep the secret. He watched and listened. Did he see bubbles on the surface of the water as the current carried the leaf away? But, no, there was nothing, not even a last whoosh of *take care of you, darling.*

She had risked everything for their child, lived through anguish and uncertainty and kept her promise to Karl right until her last breath. Through it all she had trusted in her intuition and led him to Nelly and he had almost without noticing, become the Walter she'd wanted him to be. Her last goodbye was neither comic, nor tragic, but for him it would always be an extraordinary act of beauty and courage. The sound of children laughing running toward him snapped him back into the wider world. He turned and walked back across the bridge towards the Old Town. As he passed the wise monkey he turned and looked back over his shoulder.

Flying home from Frankfurt he took out Goethe's short novel from his pocket. As he opened it to read Leni's inscription on the inside cover, a piece of scrap paper fell out. It had the appearance of having been screwed up and then straightened out. *How sensible of her* he thought as he smiled at the material evidence and reread his own handwritten instructions that he thought had been left behnd:

Max's Bar 12
Alte Brucke
F to H 1 hour